Also by Hannah March

The Complaint of the Dove
The Devil's Highway

A Distinction of Blood

A MYSTERY OF GEORGIAN ENGLAND

Hannah March

A SIGNET BOOK

SIGNET
Published by New American Library, a division of
Penguin Group (USA) Inc., 375 Hudson Street,
New York, New York 10014, U.S.A.
Penguin Books Ltd, 80 Strand,
London WC2R 0RL, England
Penguin Books Australia Ltd, 250 Camberwell Road,
Camberwell, Victoria 3124, Australia
Penguin Books Canada Ltd, 10 Alcorn Avenue,
Toronto, Ontario, Canada M4V 3B2
Penguin Books (N.Z.) Ltd, Cnr Rosedale and Airborne Roads,
Albany, Auckland 1310, New Zealand

Penguin Books Ltd, Registered Offices:
80 Strand, London WC2R 0RL, England

Published by Signet, an imprint of New American Library, a division of Penguin
Group (USA) Inc. Originally published in England by Headline Book Publishing.

First Signet Printing, May 2004
10 9 8 7 6 5 4 3 2 1

PUBLISHER'S NOTE
This is a work of fiction. Names, characters, places, and incidents either are the
product of the author's imagination or are used fictitiously, and any resemblance to
actual persons, living or dead, business establishments, events, or locales is entirely
coincidental.

For Eileen Beeke

Chapter One

"I don't know who that fellow is with Lord Mortlock," said a voice in a drawled whisper, "but 'pon my soul, he can no more play whist than I can whistle 'God Save the King' out of my . . ."

The rest of the remark was lost in laughter. Robert Fairfax looked back at the gaming room, but he couldn't tell which of the fops gathered about the green tables had spoken of him thus; and Lord Mortlock was already heading downstairs.

"That was my fault, I fear." Fairfax glanced uneasily at his companion as they came out of White's, the coffeehouse and gambling club in St. James. "The revoke—"

"Aye, that finished us. You played like something of a donkey, Fairfax, but then whist is something of a donkey's game, to my mind. All right as an appetizer to the evening, but the money don't move fast enough for my liking."

The money had certainly moved fast enough for Fairfax, who was still sweating a little at the thought of it. Thirty guineas had disappeared across the green baize in as many minutes. Of course, to the man he had partnered, Lord Mortlock, this was a trifling sum; hundreds and even thousands of pounds were routinely lost by the aristocratic gamblers at White's. Moreover, the money with which Fairfax had played had not been his own. But it still made him shudder to see it go so quickly.

Well, at least that part of his deception called for no pretending. Or perhaps he ought to show more nonchalance. The role that Mr. Appleton had asked him to play tonight was that of a gentleman of ample means with a taste for gaming. If he had a fit of the vapors every time he lost, his companion might suspect he was not all he claimed to be.

But it was a damnably difficult role to carry off. Years ago, before the disgrace of his father and the wreck of his fortune, Fairfax had had a brief taste of being the young man about town: he had diced and drank and swapped unlikely tales of conquests with other gauche would-be bucks. It was more shadow than substance, however, and even then, when he had been comfortably off and with a gentleman's expectations, Fairfax had known the world in which Lord Mortlock moved only from a wondering distance. Then had come years of impoverishment, ended by the very modest competence he now earned as a private tutor. Hardly a preparation for the high life.

And Hugh Mortlock, the fifth Baron Mortlock, lived very high. He had a name for it, although his reputation was not quite as notorious as that of his late father, the fourth baron, known as "Black Peter" because of his vices and his temper. Back in the age of Walpole, Black Peter had cut a scandalous swath through society, one of the original Mohocks who had carried aristocratic ruffianism to new heights, or depths. Rumor had it that Black Peter and his cronies had even killed a tavern waiter for spilling their wine—run him through with swords, thrown his body on a dunghill, and bragged of it afterwards. Society prided itself on the growth of "politeness" since those crude times, but a new generation of rakes had arisen, and it was small wonder that Black Peter's only son and heir was one of them. Young Lord Mortlock's gambling, wenching, and fighting had kept the town tattlemongers busy for some years past.

But high living took its toll. Not only on the flesh—and the gaunt gray-eyed man crossing Pall Mall beside Fairfax looked older than his thirty years—but on the purse. The town tattle said that Lord Mortlock was hock deep in debt when, five months ago, he finally took a bride: the daughter of a wealthy merchant who brought to the marriage a pretty face and a settlement of thirty thousand pounds.

A plain enough story of the rake reformed. Or was it?

That was where Fairfax came in. Picking his way across frosted cobbles spattered with refuse, feeling awkward in the unaccustomed finery of gold-laced hat and embroidered coat and red heels, he groaned inwardly at the task his employer had set him. He had never wanted to be an actor or a spy, and here he was a combination of both.

"No, if it's deep play you want, my dear fellow, I'll show you the very place," Lord Mortlock said. He whistled over a linkboy to light their way with his torch; the old London streets east of the squares were dark as tunnels in the March night. "There's not much to be said for the company, and you'll get half a bottle of bad wine if you're lucky, but the play is deep. I've seen men drive up to where we're going in a carriage-and-four, and go away paupers. One fellow memorably gambled away his whole property and ended by asking if anyone would take the value of his children's shoes for a wager." He gave a bleak chuckle. "Gaming must be the only occupation in which one can gain fame by utterly losing."

"Well, there is no thrill like risk," Fairfax said. He sounded unconvincing even to himself.

"You've heard of Lady Harriet Froome and her King Street faro bank, I daresay," Lord Mortlock said, striding purposefully after the bare glimmering heels of the linkboy.

"I believe so. Didn't the magistrates take steps to close it down?"

"They tried. First she protested to the bench about her privileges as a peeress. When that wouldn't wash she advertized her gaming nights as 'private assemblies,' if you please. And she's put the house in the name of a manager to shield herself. I fancy the law still looks with a jaundiced eye on her establishment—but what's the law? The magistrates meet but seldom; when they do, she'll make sure to have an informer let her know. As for constables, they're easily bought off, of course."

"Of course," Fairfax said. "You go often to Lady Harriet Froome's, sir?"

"About as often as I please." Lord Mortlock accompanied the words with a quick doglike exposure of his teeth. Fairfax wondered if that was the closest he ever came to a smile. He wondered also whether his own question had been too obviously inquisitive. Suppose Lord Mortlock guessed that his companion had been sent to spy on him? The man was known to have a short temper—had twice fought duels in his youth, they said. Really, this was a tricky position to be in.

But Fairfax had seen no way out of it. Two days ago he had presented himself as arranged at the London home of Mr. Samuel Appleton, who had engaged him to tutor his two young sons on the recommendation of former employers. The boys, Fairfax had been told, were aged twelve and fourteen, bright and biddable; Mr. Appleton was a man who had risen to wealth, offered a generous salary for a term of at least a year, and had a commodious town house in Leicester Fields as well as a villa in Surrey. All in all a reasonably pleasant prospect for Fairfax, whose life had been fraught with insecurity. But when he arrived, there was no sign of his pupils. They were with an aunt by the sea at Weymouth, Mr. Appleton explained. They had both been rather low with a fever caught at the public school he had sent them to—part of his reason for deciding on a tutor instead—and he preferred to keep them there a further couple of weeks until their health was restored.

So, his presence was not yet required, Fairfax thought with perplexity—and dismay, for his funds were low. But Mr. Appleton, a stocky, soft-spoken, deliberate man in a beautifully curled white wig, did not say that. Mr. Fairfax's room was all prepared, and Mr. Appleton was happy for him to join the household at once. And that first evening at dinner, and after a lot of sober careful talk—measuring him up, Fairfax now realized—Mr. Appleton broached the subject of what he wanted his new employee to do in the interim before his pupils returned. Mr. Appleton put it courteously, considerately, but there was never any question of Fairfax having a choice in the matter, not if he wanted that year's employment and salary.

And now here he was approaching the unsavory purlieus of Covent Garden with Lord Mortlock, whom the gossip sheets had once delighted in calling "one of the wickedest men in England," and about to make a rakish night of it. It was fortunate, in this respect at least, that Robert Fairfax was a congenital insomniac, as Lord Mortlock seldom went home before dawn.

Which was one of the things Mr. Appleton had talked to him about . . .

"Stand away, sir!" Lord Mortlock growled suddenly. Fairfax saw that a wand-thin young man, with a rouged face, had stepped with a tentative simper from a darkened alleyway. Realizing he was not wanted, he took to his stacked heels. "I wonder those wretches dare to be so bold," Lord Mortlock mused. "I saw one of their sort clapped in Hart Street pillory last week. By the time the mob had finished with him his face looked like a haunch of mutton." A sharp reaction to such an approach was, indeed, a matter of self-preservation. The legal and social penalties for the vice of sodomy were so fierce that even the faintest imputation was ruinous. But in these seamy streets the taste was still catered for, as were most. Behind and above the chocolate houses and taverns, and even respectable dressmakers' shops, you could buy all sorts of carnal pleasure: you could watch or participate, you could flog or be flogged. The dank night mist rolling up from the Thames covered a multitude of sinners.

"So, you've a mind to try my father-in-law's line of trade, eh, Fairfax?" Lord Mortlock said. He showed his teeth again. "It pays, at any rate; damn me, it pays. As long as your conscience ain't overtender."

"I . . . That I have yet to determine."

"Pah, all money's marked with sweat and blood," Lord Mortlock said, more than usually harsh. Handsome in a bony, hawkish way, wholly elegant in dress and deportment, he had a curiously dry and grating voice. "As for conscience, what is it but a sort of puling cowardice? If conscience *made* us behave better, it might be worth something, but it don't. Mine never did, at any rate. All it did was make me feel temporarily uncomfortable after the deed was done. So I strangled my conscience like an unwanted pup, and do very well without it."

Bravado? Lord Mortlock playing up to his own reputation? Perhaps, though there was no melodrama in his tone. It was just coolly informative. He had touched a sore spot, anyhow. Even before joining Mr. Appleton's household Fairfax had known that his employer's fortune came from West Indies sugar plantations, worked by Negro slaves . . . but what could he do? He needed the position. Every grain of the sugar that was stirred into the tea and chocolate and coffee which the English consumed so devotedly came from slave labor. It was just one of those facts that one knew and ignored, just as after a while one saw but did not see the beggars, the rickety waif-children, the pox-ridden prostitutes that abounded in the streets of the capital. Well, at least being in

Mr. Appleton's employ as a tutor he was at one remove from the grim trade. Thankfully he was not really about to enter it, though that was the fiction Mr. Appleton had cooked up to explain his presence to Lord Mortlock.

"The notion I have in mind," Mr. Appleton had said, over port on Monday evening, "is to introduce you to Lord Mortlock as an acquaintance of mine, staying with me while you look into possible openings in the West India trade. And that you enjoy gaming and . . . the entertainments of the town. Yes, that will suffice. From there it should not be difficult to secure an invitation to join Lord Mortlock on one of his . . . nocturnal jaunts."

"And—pardon me, Mr. Appleton—but where am I supposed to have come from?" Fairfax had said, not quite believing what he was hearing.

"Let us say Scotland. Or rather, the north of England."

Well, that was something: at least he was not going to have to prowl the gambling dens of London talking in a broad Scots brogue.

"The deception is but little," Mr. Appleton had gone on. "All you are required to be is a gentleman known to me, who wishes to be acquainted with my son-in-law."

Yes: Mr. Samuel Appleton, with his square hands, soft Bristol speech, and plain snuff-brown broadcloth suit, was father-in-law to Lord Mortlock. His pride in the fact was plain. Five months ago his eldest daughter, Charlotte, had stepped up to the altar and united herself—and her family— to the ancient and noble house of Mortlock. She was now mistress of a large estate, Minchin Park, in Gloucestershire, and a West End mansion. Her future children—Mr. Appleton's grandchildren—would bear titles; she herself was Lady Mortlock. Mr. Appleton had pronounced all this with dainty relish, though he seemed to savor the words "Lady Mortlock" most of all.

"You perhaps do not know of my own family history, Mr.

Fairfax. It is of little beyond local renown," Mr. Appleton had gone on. "My father, Isaac Appleton, was a country attorney near Bristol. He also acted, in a humble capacity, as steward to the estate of the current Lord Mortlock's father. Later in life he made shrewd investments in the Bristol trade, and amassed a considerable fortune for one of small beginnings. He settled fifteen thousand on my daughter, who was a tiny girl when he died, for her marriage, which I later doubled. I was active throughout my younger years in carrying on my late father's business, and then in extending it. I sailed twice to the West Indies to oversee the purchase of sugar plantations, and now hold some two thousand acres in Jamaica. They are managed by capable agents, and return a large profit. It is this success which has lifted me and my family to a very fair degree of eminence and comfort—very fair indeed. But you can imagine how gratifying it was when, at Bath last summer, Lord Mortlock first took notice of Charlotte. The past association between the families served as an introduction, of course. But when cordiality quickened to admiration, and then a proposal, well, even the most hopeful of fathers could hardly have expected an end so very gratifying."

Considering that Charlotte's grandfather had been a lowly steward to the Mortlock estate, Fairfax silently added. He saw the picture pretty plainly now. After years of extravagant living, Lord Mortlock needed money. Blood without groats was nothing, as the saying went. Charlotte Appleton had money, and her father would jump at the chance of an alliance with nobility. It was not uncommon for old families to refresh their withered stems in this way. An old story, then.

Whether it was a love match was a different matter. It didn't sound like one, but few people would trouble about that. As long as the couple rubbed along reasonably well together, produced an heir in due time, cut the appropriate social figures, and made no open scandal . . .

Ah. There was the problem.

Pouring more port, folding his clean square hands, and fixing Fairfax with a candid gaze, Mr. Appleton had gone on to explain. All was not well with the marriage which, Fairfax guessed, had been the greatest satisfaction of Samuel Appleton's life.

Of course Mr. Appleton had been aware of his prospective son-in-law's reputation. A rake who mixed with rakes, whose name featured in all the gossip of fashion and vice, who was rumored to have been associated some years back with the infamous Hellfire Club of Sir Francis Dashwood . . . Mr. Appleton waved a hand. These were, after all, authentic credentials of aristocracy. Wellborn young blades lived like that, and then they settled down.

The trouble was that Lord Mortlock did not seem to be settling down. He was out every night drinking and gaming. He was scarcely in his new wife's company. He hardly seemed to have altered his conduct at all, except that now there was more money to be spent, and he spent it, with abandon.

So much was hearsay, however. Lord Mortlock never told his young wife what he was about, and she in turn, Mr. Appleton explained, was naturally hesitant to talk to her father of what was going on. But rumor did its work, assisted by the odd piece of concrete evidence. A couple of bills of exchange had come back to Mr. Appleton for redemption — notes signed by Lord Mortlock drawing on Mr. Appleton's credit. They came by way of brokers who dealt in such things, but Mr. Appleton did not doubt they were given by Lord Mortlock as payment for gambling debts. Not content with the disposal of his new wife's fortune, he was apparently spending his father-in-law's money too.

And there was worse. Rumor had it that Lord Mortlock preferred to find his amatory pleasures elsewhere . . . and that the new Lady Mortlock, who had taken to her exalted status very readily, was in turn finding consolation for her neglect with someone else.

Fairfax had begun to feel a reluctant admiration for the man who told him this. It must have been hard for Mr. Appleton, having to broach these unpleasant and intimate subjects with someone who was a mere employee.

Of course, as an employee Fairfax could not make the obvious retort: *But, my dear sir, what did you expect from such a match? Romeo and Juliet?*

All the same, the marriage did seem to have run into trouble rather early and rather mysteriously. Mr. Appleton might well feel that the bargain which had cost him so much was not working out as it should. And might want to know why . . .

"Where the devil are you going?" Lord Mortlock said sharply now.

Jolted from his thoughts, Fairfax glanced round. From his younger years as a Grub Street scribbler he knew this district blindfolded, and he had just turned almost unconsciously into a narrow court that connected with King Street.

"Er—I have a fancy this is the shortest way."

Lord Mortlock raised his eyebrows. "If you say so. You seem to know London pretty well. Where is it you hail from?"

"Yorkshire. But I've been in London on—several occasions. On business, you know."

"I don't know. I know nothing of business, thank God. And what do you do in Yorkshire? Have you an estate there?"

"I have—property there." Fairfax tried to invent an appropriate name. All he could think of was something like Ramsdyke Grange, which he knew he'd not be able to say with a straight face.

"And very sensibly want to get away from. What a blasted

moldering tomb the country is. I haven't been near my place in Gloucestershire for half a year."

"The charming Lady Mortlock has not seen it?"

"How do you know she's charming when you haven't met her? Oh, my precious father-in-law will have said so, of course." Lord Mortlock stepped rangily over a heap of gutter refuse and flashed Fairfax an indecipherable look. "Don't believe everything you hear, Fairfax."

He didn't intend to. But he was going to have to listen carefully, and sift what he heard, if he were to carry out this strange commission from Mr. Appleton.

"It can hardly be my place, of course," Mr. Appleton had said that first evening, "to inquire into my daughter and son-in-law's—affairs. That is why I have need of a confidential agent, who can freely enter their circle, observe, judge, and—"

"Report back?" Fairfax had suggested.

"Precisely." Mr. Appleton offered a tortoiseshell snuffbox, took a pinch and sneezed pleasurably. "I see nothing underhand in this—not really. I am simply concerned that this most auspicious union should fulfill its promise. We live in an age of luxury and temptation, Mr. Fairfax, and one cannot expect old heads on young shoulders. But the wisdom of seniority may perhaps offer the needed guidance and direction, when the time is right."

So. Find out what Lord Mortlock does with his nights. If he gambles, how much, and with whose money. If he's seeing another woman, who. If he is already estranged from his bride, why. Once he had the information Mr. Appleton would presumably do the rest. Sorting out one recalcitrant couple would, Fairfax supposed, be a simple matter for a man who owned a large chunk of Jamaica as well as the hundreds of men who labored on it.

"You are a man of genteel education, Mr. Fairfax, and report speaks of you as a man of delicacy and discretion. I rely on your being so," Mr. Appleton said, and for the first time his forthright gaze wavered. He picked at some crumbs on the tablecloth. "Particularly in the matter of my daughter. If you should learn anything that suggests she has allowed herself to be . . . swayed by the attentions of an unprincipled seducer, then I shall want to know of it, of course. But discretion must be absolute, sir."

He was therefore to find out whether the wife was erring as well as the husband. But why so mealymouthed about it? Fairfax thought maliciously; where was this sensitivity when it came to the slave market? Well, never mind. Lord Mortlock, at any rate, was to be his first quarry.

"My daughter has already made her mark in society, and holds various elegant receptions—tea parties, levees, you know," Mr. Appleton went on, with a new burst of pride. "It should be simple for you to attend some such. In the meantime I shall introduce you to my son-in-law. Let me see, say tomorrow. He is often to be found at Old Slaughter's in the afternoon."

And so the next day, Tuesday, they had gone to Old Slaughter's, a coffeehouse where a mixture of wits, roués, foreigners, and artists gathered, and the introduction had been made. Lord Mortlock hadn't seemed exactly overpowered with respect for his father-in-law, but he responded readily to Mr. Appleton's suggestion that he show the "visitor" something of the town.

"Of course I know it is no longer your habit now, Hugh, to keep late hours, or play too deep at the tables," Mr. Appleton had said pleasantly.

"Aye, aye, I am an old married man now. Don't expect a bacchanal, Mr. Fairfax," Lord Mortlock had said, in his swift metallic way. " 'Twill be curious, indeed, to return to my old bachelor habits. I daresay I shall be yawning by ten. Still, anything to oblige. Shall we say tomorrow night, then? I'll call for you."

All very murky and unpleasant; and now here he was facing the prospect of a long night doing things he didn't like with a man he didn't much care for while pretending to be someone else. (Scarthwaite Hall, he thought suddenly. No, if he got drunk he wouldn't be able to pronounce it.) At least, Hugh Mortlock was the sort of man he'd never imagined himself getting along with, and so far he seemed to have all the repulsive arrogance of his type.

And yet there was a certain fascination in being with this person. The essence of refined carnality and sophisticated vice, apparently, but Fairfax could see no devil's horns or tail. And he had an intuitive impression that Hugh Mortlock, fifth Baron Mortlock, was not a very happy man.

"Sir, will you tell me something?" Fairfax said on impulse as they came into King Street. "You must know your name is associated with the Hellfire Club of Medmenham Abbey. Forgive my curiosity, but—"

"What exactly does go on there? That's what you want to know, is it not? Oh, you are not the first. Well, Fairfax, you may have heard that the motto of the place is '*Fay ce que voudras*,' from Rabelais. 'Do what you like.' I don't know if you're a man of strong imagination, Mr. Fairfax of Yorkshire or wherever, but I ask you to imagine this: imagine 'Do what you like' as a first and only principle of existence. Imagine being told, indeed, that you must *only* do what you like, and nothing else. Could there be a better recipe for dullness, emptiness, trifling folly, tiresome repetition, and general soul-destroying blank stupidity?"

It was not quite what Fairfax expected to hear from a prince of rakes. It was rather interesting.

"I exaggerate—a little. If it were *that* dreadful, then it would at least be noteworthy—which it ain't. And that, I find, is the unutterably disappointing thing about life. Nothing is as dramatic as it's meant to be. The good aren't that good, and the bad aren't that bad. I have a great fear—well,

no, a mild fear—that when I get to the next world, be it
heaven or hell, I shall very soon realize how *ordinary* it is . . .
As for the Club, there is a lot of eating and drinking, and
loose talk, and occasionally some loose women such as you
might find on any street corner around the Garden here. No
Black Mass celebrated on the buttocks of a buxom young vir-
gin, or any of that nonsense. Ha! Where would you find one
in this day and age, anyhow? Here we are."

Lady Harriet Froome's house in King Street, overlooking
the Piazza, was certainly impressive for a gambling den. It
was no less than an old town mansion, with a pilastered
façade and wrought-iron gates opening onto a flight of steps
leading up to a porticoed door; torches burned in sconces and
every window was brightly lit. If it had been further to the
west, among the genteel squares . . . but that was the point: it
was not. It was a survival from the days when "quality" had
resided in this district which was now the haunt of artists,
theatre people, bawds and, of course, bucks on a gambling
spree. Closer inspection revealed cracked windows and peeling plaster, like patches on the face of a raddled courtesan.
And while the pretense of a "private assembly" was kept up
by the appearance of liveried servants to welcome them at
the door, Fairfax had never seen footmen quite like these.
Wall-eyed, muscled like pugilists, they squinted suspiciously
at the arriving guests. One even had a hook for a hand, and
picked his teeth with it as he preceded them up a flight of
stairs carpeted in threadbare crimson. A bleary young man in
the uniform of an ensign of the Guards, coming down, raised
a hand in feeble salute to Lord Mortlock, who said, "Well,
Tom, are you flush tonight?"

The young ensign gave only a broken laugh in reply.
Then, halfway down, he stopped and called up to Lord Mortlock, "I say, did you hear about poor whatsisname—was in
here with you Monday night?"

"Spicer," Lord Mortlock said. "Aye, I heard. A bad business."

"Lost everything, they say," the young man sighed, carrying on down.

"So they say," murmured Lord Mortlock in an odd reflective tone; then to Fairfax, very brusque, "He refers to an acquaintance of mine, name of Richard Spicer. Quite an habitué here. Someone found him in St. James's Park on Tuesday morning with a pistol in his hand and a bullet in his brain. He did love to play deep." An acid chuckle. "Let that be a lesson, eh?"

Social life even of the politest kind tended to be rackety. Routs, balls, ridottoes were noisy affairs of babbling voices, rattling fans, clacking heels; oboes wailed and dancers tramped and fine ladies hallooed at their servants for shawls and chairs. Yet Lady Harriet Froome's gambling house was surprisingly quiet. The large salon with its dusty festoons and cracked gilding and flyblown pier glasses was filled with perhaps forty people, but concentration on the business at hand gave the place a curious hush; more like a church, Fairfax thought wryly.

There were half a dozen small tables, variously occupied by players at whist and piquet and ruff. Though the gamblers were all male, there were some women around: powdered and painted, they leaned on their menfolk's shoulders, yawned, applied themselves to the wine that was circulating on tarnished trays and that was, as Fairfax discovered on taking a glass, rather vile. The waiters were of the same brawny type as the footmen, and there was a little man in a scratch wig, like a decayed clerk, keeping entries in a book by the main table—a large round table with a well in the center. Several players were gathered around it, and they were the most intent of all.

This was the faro table, and the raison d'être of the gambling house. Faro was a banking game, which was what made it profitable for the proprietor. Losing stakes went to the bank, and the stakes here, Fairfax saw at a glance, were set high. He had played faro a couple of times as a young man and knew how addictive it was. Nowadays it was becoming something of a mania with the gambling classes. The players laid stakes on the cards turned up on the table: the banker dealt his pack into two piles, a winning and a losing pile. A game for gamesters, for people with a religious belief in luck.

Without ceremony, Lord Mortlock sat down at the faro table, motioning Fairfax to do likewise.

"Well, how goes it, Griffey? How many poor sheep have you fleeced tonight?"

The remark was not addressed to the dealer, who was another seedy underling, but to a big, pockmarked, fleshy-faced man of around forty in a red waistcoat who hovered watchfully about the table with the cumbrous softness of a dancing bear. The manager of the establishment, Fairfax guessed.

"Good evening, your lordship," the man said in a surprisingly small, high, husky voice, as if through a mouthful of dough. "Pretty quiet tonight, all in all, pretty quiet."

"A sorry business about young Spicer, eh?" Lord Mortlock said, taking out his purse. "You heard, of course."

"Of course. They held an inquest this morning, sir, which I naturally attended, as Mr. Spicer was here on the night before his misfortune."

"Misfortune!" Lord Mortlock said with a snort. "That's a pretty word for it."

"He was a suicide, wasn't he?" said a man across the table. "Shot himself in the head, by God."

"They say the cowkeeper who found him damn near had a fit. Brains all over the grass," said another.

"Yes, a suicide, most regrettably. That was the conclusion of the inquest," Griffey said. "Will you take anything, my lord?"

"Brandy, if you've any that ain't watered. Well, well. Poor Spicer. You'll miss him, I daresay."

"Mr. Spicer was certainly a regular visitor, my lord, since you were good enough to introduce him here," Griffey said, sending a waiter hurrying at a snap of his fingers. "And it is a most regrettable loss, of course: a young man in the prime of life."

"A sad business indeed," came a woman's voice. "But there, people must be left to do what they will, whether it be marrying or blowing their brains out. Our English liberties, most important; I know you'll agree, Hugh. Still, I'm glad to see you have brought a new addition to our circle. Thoughtful of you, upon my honor."

"Anything to oblige," Lord Mortlock said. He did not look up at the lady who had appeared behind him, and he seemed to dislodge the hand she familiarly laid on his shoulder, Fairfax thought, with a certain irritation. "This is Mr. Robert Fairfax, who is something to do with my sainted father-in-law. Lady Harriet Froome."

"I'm happy to see you at my little assembly, Mr. Fairfax," Lady Harriet said, giving him a quick glance from head to toe. "Mondays, Wednesdays, and Fridays I console my widowed state with company, as you can see, and the company divert themselves as they choose, as you can also see."

"Don't fret, Harriet, he's no informer," Lord Mortlock said, laying five guineas on the queen of spades. And then with his doglike grin, "At least, I hope he ain't."

"I've heard a great deal of your assemblies, Lady Harriet," Fairfax said. "The pinnacle of elegance, taste, and fashion was the report, and now I can confirm it." The simpering idiot from Yorkshire. But he couldn't think of anything else to say; and the men here were certainly as fashionable as powder, silk lace, jewels, and a mindless attention to the vogue could make them. Lord Mortlock's dress was sober by comparison, but that wasn't all that was different, Fairfax decided: for all his sourness and lack of warmth, the gaunt, pale-eyed man looked as if he had a brain.

"Aye," Lord Mortlock said, taking his brandy in one gulp, "you can ruin yourself here very elegantly."

"You dear brute," Lady Harriet said, "you know I don't take any notice of you when you're in these humors." She had indeed a kind of perpetual half-smile of indulgence about her, as if at a children's party. Past thirty, Fairfax guessed, thin, sharp-faced, but well dressed and with a definite sensuality about her, and most remarkable violet eyes. "One can't prevent a young man from gaming, of course, any more than one can prevent a dog from barking."

"Or a she-cat from rutting on the roof," Lord Mortlock said, yawning.

"Delightful brute!" Lady Harriet said, smile glinting. "Truly, Hugh, it's the nature of young gentlemen. It's hard to stop them—though mightily easy to get them started."

Fairfax began to have an idea that Lord Mortlock was welcomed here not only for his custom. Such places needed a steady supply of wealthy and naive young men if they were to flourish, and he had a strong suspicion that Lord Mortlock was a supplier. Young dolts fresh to town would be only too happy to be taken under the wing of so glamorous a figure, and introduced to the delights of Lady Harriet Froome's faro bank—and sometimes, if the hints about this Spicer were anything to go by, to their downfall. There must be something in it for Lord Mortlock, if so: a discount on his own gaming debts, perhaps? Or was he recompensed more directly by Lady Harriet? There was surely something between them—it might be hate, but it certainly wasn't indifference. Was she the woman he was seeing instead of his wife?

Lord Mortlock as a kind of paid Pied Piper leading young men to their doom . . . well, it certainly placed him in an unpleasant light, though Fairfax conceded that the young men weren't doing anything they didn't want to do. It gave him an odd feeling to realize that he probably appeared to be the latest victim . . . but then the whole thing felt unreal, not least the guineas he tentatively laid on the table. Mr. Appleton had given him fifty to spend—not, he was glad to learn, redeemable against his tutor's salary. He wondered, if he was lucky, whether he would be allowed to keep his winnings.

"A suicide, did ye say?" said a deaf old roué, who looked like a lacy mummy, from the other side of the table. "Hm. Poor young pup. I suppose he'd dug his grave with debt. Well, I've told you before, Lady Harriet, your stakes are too high."

"Oh, your pardon, sir, I must correct you," Lady Harriet said with smiling firmness. "Any stakes that are laid here are nothing to do with me. That is all the business of my friend Mr. Griffey. It is his house, you know," she said, glancing at Fairfax, "he is the tenant, and responsible for everything. By his favor I maintain a modest apartment upstairs, and do the honors of hostess at these little assemblies. I know nothing of stakes."

It was, as someone grumbled, all my-eye-and-Betty-Martin. But clearly Lady Harriet was careful about this fiction. And though she kept a bright eye on the play, it was Griffey who tirelessly watched every detail, seeming to commit each coin laid and each card dealt to memory, and from time to time rubbing his great hands together in a curious circular motion, as if rolling something between them into a very small ball.

"High stakes all the same," the old man muttered.

"But high winnings," piped up a dandified young man who was watching the play. "I've seen the bank broke many a time—ecod, many's the time I've seen it broke, you know!" He went on to repeat this so emphatically that Fairfax suspected that he was a "puff," paid to do so by the establishment.

"Pah, she does pretty well out of it," Lord Mortlock said

to Fairfax in an undertone, as Lady Harriet moved away to greet someone else, leaving a cloud of pomade behind her. "But then we must all provide for ourselves, eh?"

"A widow, I think she said?"

"Not a grieving one. She is the daughter of the Earl of Pellew, who cut her off without a shilling when she ran off and married one Captain Froome, a charming wastrel who carried on blithely wenching and toping. The latter finished him off a few years since, and she had to make shift to live as best she could. Oh, but she's a rogue herself: she wouldn't live decent even if she was able. As witness the man she's put in as manager here. Luke Griffey comes it very respectable when her ladyship's about, but he's a prize ruffian. And he's got a finger in just about every unsavory pie the Garden has to offer. A renter of properties for various uses, he might call himself. High company, eh, Fairfax? Well, Banker, come on and cut, damn you, what are you waiting for?"

But the banker's eyes were fixed on a commotion at the door. Fairfax turned. A red-faced man was there, loudly expostulating with one of the hulking manservants, who looked in appeal to Griffey. Moving with surprisingly soft swiftness, like an expert wrestler, Griffey was there in a moment.

"I tell you I seek someone here," the red-faced man was saying, "and I want him pointed out to me. A plain enough request—"

"May I serve you in any way, sir?" Griffey said, blandly towering over the man, who was small and stocky, terrier-like.

"You are the owner of this—this thieves' kitchen?"

Griffey coughed delicately. "Your pardon, sir, this is the private assembly of Lady Harriet Froome. Perhaps you're mistook—"

"No, I am not. This is precisely the sinkhole I seek. Leave go my arm, sirrah—aye, wait, I know *your* ugly slab of a face!" The man peered up shortsightedly. "You were at the inquest today, I'll swear it. My poor Richard . . ."

"I may have been, sir; I'm not at liberty to say. All I can say is you're disturbing the ladies and gentlemen——"

The fierce little man shook him off. "I want Lord Mortlock. Is he here? Where is he? Let him show his face."

Griffey seemed about to drag the man bodily away, but Lord Mortlock waved a hand and got to his feet.

"I am Lord Mortlock. Who wants me?"

The little man stalked forwards. He was perhaps fifty, naturally high-colored, though redder with anger; his flared coat and full wig were old-fashioned, as was the fact that he actually wore a sword at his side. Fairfax heard someone give a foppish yelp of amazement at seeing such a thing.

"Sir, you don't know me. But you shall. It is my wish—my ardent wish, sir." The man was so tight and bristling with emotion that he could only jerk the words out of himself in breathless bursts. "I am Sir Anthony Spicer."

Lean, pale, angular, and sardonic, Lord Mortlock could hardly have presented a greater contrast to the small fiery man staring up into his face. "As you say, sir," he said coolly, "I don't know you."

"But I know you—I know *of* you—by repute, very ill repute, sir, and I know what you are."

"I wish I did," said Lord Mortlock with a shrug.

"In short, a villain. A blackguard, a corrupter. Do you deny that you knew my nephew—Richard Spicer—who died a wretched death in the small hours of Tuesday morning? Do you deny it, sir?"

"Certainly not. But I wasn't aware that knowing him made me a villain."

Stamping his feet in agitation, Sir Anthony Spicer cried out, "You insolent young dog—how dare you mock me! But it is no more than I expect from a man like you——"

Suddenly Lady Harriet was at his side. "Sir, forgive me,

but these violent expressions must be painful to the ears of any hostess with a care for the comfort of her guests. Now if I might suggest—"

"Oh, you are the woman who promotes this sordid business, are you? Then more shame to you, ma'am, shame and disgrace. It's no good. I can't moderate myself—"

"Then perhaps," said Lady Harriet smiling airily, and darting a glance at Griffey, "you had better leave."

"I will! I will directly, you need not set your hired bully on me. I stay only to address this man. Lord Mortlock, you do not deny your association with my nephew?"

Lord Mortlock shrugged again.

"You do not deny that you made yourself his mentor when he came young and inexperienced to this city? That you introduced him to this place, most coldly and irresponsibly entangled him in vice and debt—".

"Sir Anthony, you should be on the stage," Lord Mortlock said. "Such high drama! Forgive me, I do not mean to scoff, and young Spicer's end was sad indeed, sad and pitiable. But that I alone brought him to that end, sir, is an absurd suggestion."

"Who else? His letters spoke of you—everyone acknowledges that he followed your lead, poor deluded pup. He was young, and being long orphaned lacked a parent's guidance, perhaps, but he was no fool. He could not have come to such an end without falling prey to a designing nature—yours, sir. My nephew died utterly penniless in his twenty-first year and I hold you accountable—"

"Penniless?" said Lord Mortlock sharply. "I think you exaggerate, sir."

"You mock me—again you mock me. Never mind, I have nearly done, sir, all that remains is this."

Sir Anthony Spicer took a kid glove from his pocket and struck Lord Mortlock across the face with it.

An abrupt silence fell across the room.

"When will it be convenient for you to meet me, sir?" Sir Anthony said, trembling all over.

Lord Mortlock drew a long breath through his hawkish nose, then signaled to one of the waiters for brandy. After taking a deep drink, he said, "You are distracted with grief, sir. There can be no true quarrel between us. Go home, sir."

Glaring, Sir Anthony said: "Are you such a coward?"

Lord Mortlock frowned and spoke with impatient distinctness. "Sir, it is your grief. You are not in your right mind just now. No man can accept such a challenge. I say again, go home."

"In writing then—yes—in writing . . ." Sir Anthony looked about him wildly. "Give me that pen and ink there, I pray you." He took tablets from his pocket and hastily scribbled out a note, then thrust it at Lord Mortlock. "There. That is my cartel. I hold you responsible for my nephew's ruin and I demand satisfaction. Do you refuse it to me, sir, as a gentleman?"

Lord Mortlock glanced at the blotted note, then tore it across and tossed it aside.

"Go home, sir," he said again, and sat down at the faro table.

For a moment Fairfax feared that Sir Anthony's twitching hand would go to his sword. Griffey, moving stealthily closer, seemed to think so too. But instead the little man made a strangled sound like a sob—there were, indeed, tears standing in his eyes; though Fairfax saw them as tears of rage—and then, turning, blundered out of the room.

On impulse, Fairfax picked up the torn note and pocketed it.

Voices rose at once and all eyes were on Lord Mortlock, who calmly drank his wine. Fairfax saw a kind of smirking speculation in some of the glances directed at Lord Mortlock—a man known to have fought duels in his youth, a man reputed for his proud temper . . . What was going on? Had he turned soft?

For his part Fairfax respected Lord Mortlock more for his refusal. However equivocal his involvement in the life and death of this young man might have been, it was surely humane and honorable not to take up a challenge from a man who seemed half-crazed with grief.

"Dear me—extraordinary outburst—what can he have meant by it, I wonder?" Lady Harriet said, fanning herself.

"He is looking for someone to blame," Lord Mortlock said. "A common enough human pursuit."

"Well, you managed him very well, Hugh, and I applaud you," Lady Harriet said—with a note of genuine warmth, Fairfax thought. "Poor gentleman, quite the plucky bantam. But God's life, when can he have been last in town? I never saw such a quaint old creature in my life. That wig . . . Do you recall poor Richard talking of an uncle in the country, Hugh?"

"Hm?" Lord Mortlock was abstracted. "Oh, I believe so—Hertfordshire, I think. I fancy he was the old fellow's heir." He looked sharply up at Griffey, who was returning from seeing the visitor off the premises, rubbing his great hands in circles. "Penniless, eh? Dear, dear. The tale grows sadder. Who would have thought . . . What say you, Griffey? Did Spicer look like a man contemplating suicide when he left here on Monday night?"

Eyes hooded, the big man put his head on one side. "Beg your pardon, my lord? I don't follow."

"Come, simple enough, man. Spicer stayed on here after I left on Monday night. The last to leave, I imagine. I recall he said something about feeling his luck was in that night. How horribly wrong he was, it seems. Well? How did he strike you?"

"I can't say, sir." Griffey turned to trim a smoking candle. "Just about his normal self, I'd reckon."

"Indeed? Curious affair. Next morning, found in the park as dead as a herring. Makes you think, does it not, Fairfax?

We never know what lies around the next corner. A dark alley full of peril, perhaps . . . Well, come, let us play while we can."

They played, though as time went on Fairfax thought "play" a strange word for the relentless, tense, hard-staring, sighing, thoroughly serious business that took place around the faro table. The odd thing was that—perhaps because he wasn't particularly bothered—he kept winning. Others, observing his luck, began to place their stakes on the same cards as he, and the banker had to keep paying out. Lord Mortlock, who followed some intuitive system of his own, smiled wryly, and when Griffey was passing close by his chair, said loudly, "Have a care you don't break the bank, Fairfax. The shock might floor you. As for me, I am losing nicely, so I'm in no danger—eh, Griffey?"

The big man merely inclined his head. Just then someone exclaimed and pointed: a small child, a boy still in skirts, had come toddling into the room, urgently followed by a down-at-heel maid.

Lady Harriet scooped the child up, laughing.

"I'm sorry, ma'am," the maid said. "I was putting him to bed and off he wriggled."

"He wanted to kiss Mama good night, didn't you, my lamb?" Lady Harriet said. She cooed over the little boy, who took hold of her emerald necklace and began examining it.

"He's an eye for a stone, look, Harriet," someone said.

"Ah-ah—you mustn't put it in your mouth, sweeting. It's precious and belongs to Mama."

"Except when it belongs to the pawnbroker," someone else said, and there was a growl of laughter.

"Now, will you say night-night to the gentlemen playing their game?" Lady Harriet said. "Hugh, look, did you ever see a handsomer little fellow?"

"For God's sake, Harriet, do you think it a fit time and a

place for the child?" he snapped in reply, his eyes on the cards.

This echoed Fairfax's own thought: it was close to midnight, and the room was smoky and noisy with drunken voices. But then the child didn't look troubled by it; was he being priggish?

Lady Harriet, studying Lord Mortlock with a coolly speculative look, said: "Never mind him, sweeting. He's turning into a regular dull old bear . . . Well, Hugh, never fear, he shall be put to bed if it pleases you. Though I hardly know *what* pleases you nowadays."

"To be left alone," he said, still not looking round.

Lady Harriet leaned forwards and blew on the back of his neck. "Well that, my dear, is painfully clear," she said as he jerked in irritation. "Hellfire Club, indeed! If the fire can be so thoroughly *damped,* then we none of us have anything to fear."

Lord Mortlock stayed silent, but from the black look on his face it was not a silence Fairfax cared to intrude upon. He applied himself to the game. By now the other tables had broken up, and most people were gathered around the faro bank, including two young bloods who had just come in so blind drunk they could hardly remain upright, and kept leaning their lolling heads together and almost falling off their chairs with dramatic jerks and unlikely recoveries of balance. Fairfax had stopped winning quite so regularly now, but Lord Mortlock had lost steadily and, it seemed to Fairfax, hugely; he had tried to keep track of the amounts his companion splashed around, mindful of the report he would have to give Mr. Appleton, but all he could say was that it was a heartbreaking amount of money.

And now Lord Mortlock was out of coin. Gold was the general currency of the faro table—guineas, half-guineas, some doubloons, and pistoles, Spanish in origin but quite common—though one man produced a banknote and, as Mr.

Appleton had hinted, bills drawn on good credit were also all too readily accepted for gaming debts. It seemed for a moment that Lord Mortlock was going to pay by this means. With a sigh he took a folded bill from his purse, opened it, contemplated it, then looked up at Griffey and Lady Harriet, who had come back to the table, though she seemed to be firmly ignoring him now.

"Well, well. A bill it shall have to be. Forty pounds, drawn on Martin's of Throgmorton Street, hm. Endorsed by—well, the name is clear enough." Lord Mortlock crackled the bill thoughtfully between long fingers, then glanced up at Griffey. The big man had paused in the slow rubbing of his hands; Lady Harriet, ostensibly listening to the clumsy compliments of the drunken bucks, was all narrow-eyed attention.

"What say you, Griffey?" Lord Mortlock went on. "You accept such things here, of course—I've seen 'em taken before, just like this. Eh?"

"Of course, my lord," Griffey said. His hooded eyes glanced momentarily at Lady Harriet.

"And yet, I don't know . . ." Lord Mortlock folded the bill neatly. "I'm a touch sentimental about this bill. I've had it by me a little while now, which is rare enough with me, in all conscience. No, I think I shall keep hold of it. Fairfax, I see you've done pretty well for yourself—will you lend me ten guineas, so that I may carry on with the game? You will greatly oblige me," he said, showing his teeth, "greatly oblige me, my dear fellow."

"Oh, very well," said Fairfax. He wasn't sure what was going on, but whatever it was Lord Mortlock had certainly discomfited Griffey and Lady Harriet, and seemed to be relishing it.

"Thank you, sir. Come, lay your own stake, Fairfax. Let us see if you can go home flush tonight, or this morning rather. Many a slip 'twixt cup and lip, of course. A plaguey perilous city, this: a man can end up penniless, or worse, before he knows it."

They played on, Lord Mortlock absorbed in some dark, bitter amusement of his own. Fairfax had drunk too much bad wine and was a little weary, and patterns of clubs and diamonds seemed to have imprinted themselves on his brain. Lord Mortlock and Lady Harriet—what was their connection? They both seemed to be taunting each other with things he didn't comprehend. There was certainly an intimate familiarity. What was plain above all was that having a wife made no difference to Lord Mortlock. She was not mentioned or, it seemed, thought of. So was he being unfaithful? Possibly. Was he gambling extravagant amounts? Certainly. As for drawing on Mr. Appleton's credit—well, that had been Fairfax's first thought when Mortlock had made that strange parade of producing a bill. But the bill had apparently been drawn on someone else—Martin's of Throgmorton Street—though for all he knew they might be Mr. Appleton's bankers. He'd tried to get a good look at the bill, and had glimpsed the signatures of at least two endorsers, suggesting it had been passed at least twice, but Mortlock had kept it pretty close to his chest.

Not many conclusions so far. The waters were muddied by this business of the dead young man named Richard Spicer. Fairfax wondered what had become of the little fiery uncle: would he continue to haunt and harass Lord Mortlock, daring him to a challenge? Lord Mortlock as the callous corrupter of youth . . . well, it suited his reputation. But Fairfax couldn't make up his mind about the saturnine man beside him. Villains could be complex, of course. But in his experience the worst destroyers of human happiness were single-minded people crippled by lack of imagination, and in Lord Mortlock's pale, unrestful eyes he saw, if anything, too much.

He was tired. When the faro table began to break up at

close to three in the morning, he dared to hope that Mortlock would want to go home. But he knew it was unlikely, and his instructions were to stick with him as long as possible; Mr. Appleton was quite prepared for Fairfax not to return till the morning. He counted out his money: he had twelve guineas left. Not at all bad. The old mummified dandy was leaning his head on his hand and murmuring, "I have lost three hundred and fifty pounds," over and over, as if repeating it would make it less real.

"Well, well, we are losers too," Lord Mortlock said, yawning and scratching under his wig, "which is a pity for us, but perhaps not so. He who loses and goes away lives to play another day — the proverb adapts well, I think, eh, Griffey? Perhaps you could write it up above the door."

Griffey was absorbed in counting up the bank's takings, but he paused and glanced up for an instant in which Fairfax saw a smothered violence under the almost torpid manner. But he only said: "Very clever, my lord."

"I'll not be a moment, Fairfax, we'll go on somewhere rather amusing," Lord Mortlock said, clapping his shoulder. He went over to the fireplace, where — Fairfax saw now — Lady Harriet had drawn herself off and was seated, looking with peevish unhappiness into the embers.

Mortlock spoke to her, sharply it seemed, but Fairfax couldn't hear what was said, and he was more concerned just then with dubiously pondering on what Mortlock meant by "somewhere rather amusing." If he was expected to round off the night's entertainment at a bordello, then he was just going to have to tell Mr. Appleton that this spying business was not for him . . .

Looking round, he saw a man he recognized coming in. The footman, about to bar his way, was stopped by a curt word from Griffey. Fairfax cursed silently.

The young man was Mr. Appleton's eldest son, Lawrence: a very tall, very slender, very foppish stripling of twenty, who lived at the house in Leicester Fields without seeming to spend much time there. Fairfax had met him that first evening, when he came in late, declined any dinner, and swallowed a couple of glasses of port standing up while Mr. Appleton, with no great pleasure, made the introductions.

Or rather, introduced Fairfax in his fictional guise, as a gentleman interested in the sugar trade. Lawrence, smacking his red lips, had looked Fairfax up and down and then said: "Damn me. What a damned curious thing."

"What is a curious thing?" Mr. Appleton had said coolly.

"Why, the coincidence. That tutor you'd engaged for the young whelps—didn't you say his name was Fairfax? Cock's life, I could swear it was." There was mischief in the young man's button eyes as he had looked from one to the other. "Damn me. Perhaps you're related, sir?"

"A curious coincidence, as you say," Mr. Appleton had agreed, with a dismissive look, and after his son had gone smirking off, told Fairfax, "Don't trouble about him. The boy can do no harm: too much of a fool, I fear, for that. Anyhow, we are talking only of a temporary deception." Which did beg the question, Fairfax had thought, of how they were to manage the transition from gentleman-staying-as-guest, to salaried tutor, once his assignment was completed. Presumably he would just be shut away in the schoolroom, and Lord and Lady Mortlock would no longer be any of his business.

Lawrence Appleton, at any rate, had only smiled and raised an ironical eyebrow at Fairfax on the subsequent couple of occasions he had appeared at the house. Dressing fashionably and gadding about town were, Fairfax gathered, the young man's chief interests. Still, he felt a quiver of alarm now as Lawrence came into the gaming room. The young man's narrow face, rouged and patched, was flushed with drink. Suppose he said something to arouse Lord Mortlock's suspicions about Mr. Fairfax, the wealthy gentleman from Yorkshire . . .

But Lawrence looked startled when he laid eyes on Fairfax—startled and, somehow, almost fearful.

"You're here, are you?" he said, gnawing his lip.

"For my sins. I think, though, the gaming is finished—"

"What, is that the young Adonis of Leicester Fields there?" said Lord Mortlock loudly, coming over. "Why, Appleton, it's all broke up. You're taking fashionably late a little too far. Not that you ever stop short at excess, eh, m'dear?" There was an amused but pointed contempt in his voice and in the glance he gave the young man's tightly curled and pigtailed wig and mass of starched ruffles.

"Hugh. How goes it?" Uneasy, the young man made a show of yawning behind his hand. "Vastly tedious, but I have a little score to settle with Mr. Griffey here." He spoke with a slight stutter, avoiding his brother-in-law's eyes.

Lord Mortlock's smile was hard and, Fairfax thought, rather cruel. Whatever had been said between him and Lady Harriet, she did not appear pleased, and had stalked off with a rap of cork heels.

"Vastly tedious, as you say. You should have come earlier, man: Mr. Fairfax here was bidding fair to break the bank, till Dame Luck turned against him. Still, what more fickle than a woman's favor, eh, Appleton? You'd know all about that. Oh, you know Mr. Fairfax, of course? Protégé of your sainted father. How does he do, by the by?"

"P-pretty well, I think."

"Pretty well, eh? Not that you'd mind either way, eh, you young rip?" Lord Mortlock said, laughing and rapping his knuckles on Lawrence's pigeon chest. "Come, Fairfax, we'll leave him to his business. My eyes are pricking. These young blades live too fast for me."

The mockery was not gentle, yet Lawrence's look suggested that he was used to worse. The last Fairfax saw of him he was humbly awaiting the attention of Griffey, who was still busily bent over his piles of guineas. Griffey knew the young man was there though. Fairfax had no doubt of that.

"Lawrence is a frequent visitor here?" Fairfax asked as they went out into the street. He was still surprised that the young man hadn't made more capital out of knowing his identity.

"Well, I've seen him now and then. Not often — but I don't think he's often equal to the stakes. Old Papa Appleton keeps the young fop on short commons, at least for his pretensions. But then, it's all investment with Appleton, ain't it? The old fellow's puffed up with ambition and vanity, and he'll only lay out money to satisfy it. Now what can a lisping popinjay like dear Lawrence do for him? Not much beyond embarrass him with misplaced taste and witless extravagance. Whereas his lovely daughter has hooked him a lord, if you please!

"You may know that old Appleton's family were Bristol traders with no more family than that coachman. Now he has an alliance with the aristocracy. Suddenly he's welcome in a hundred places that would have been closed to him before, for all his money. He has influence and eminence and people clamor for his favor: he's the father of a baroness! Blood, sir: blood will tell. But as for that posturing princox of a son — well, you may have guessed that Master Lawrence makes my gorge rise. Can't help it. I wouldn't so much mind the fellow being a milksop if he weren't so desperate to be taken for a roaring boy. What's more he's forever plaguing his sister for help, and she's too indulgent of him for my liking. Let him keep his dainty paws off her fair thousands, say I. Am I a hypocrite? Not in the least. I have dear Charlotte's wealth at my disposal, sir, because the law says so. In the eyes of the law we are one flesh. The eyes of the law perhaps don't see very well," he added with a grim chuckle, "but there it is . . . Well, whatever it is young Lawrence owes to Griffey, the brute will make sure it's paid. He's mighty careful that Lady

Harriet's faro bank don't lose out . . ." Lord Mortlock cast a narrow, thoughtful look back at the peeling mansion. "Well, now, Fairfax, are you feeling fresh, and will you lend me another few guineas? The town lies all before us."

Groaning inwardly, Fairfax said, "Fresh as an eel, as we say in —" He was about to say Suffolk, his paternal home. "In Yorkshire."

"That's the fellow," Lord Mortlock laughed, and clapped a hand on Fairfax's shoulder. The hand gripped rather tightly. "'Twould be a poor trick in you to desert me now, though I don't fancy you will. Your instructions must surely be to keep an eye on me the *whole* time. Now, now, don't look like that, my dear fellow. I would have to be an entire fool not to spot it, and I'm only half of one. I don't know who you really are and don't much care, for you're reasonable company enough. But I know that old Appleton must have set you to observing me, and noting how far I behave or misbehave myself. Now, isn't it so?"

Fairfax didn't know what to say. He felt obscurely ashamed; annoyed with Mr. Appleton and his ridiculous demands, but also defiant. The rich and powerful — they would grind you small between them, if you let them.

"What would you have me say, my lord? If Mr. Appleton has concerns, he may express them to whomever he chooses. Society is such a nest of spies and gossips that it would be more surprising if I did not share in its general character. If you consider that I have played you false, then I can only beg your indulgence — and add that I did not suppose I would be mixing with the spotlessly pure and truthful tonight anyhow."

Lord Mortlock laughed, and for the first time there was a genuine cheer in the sound. "Well said, sir. Spoken like a lawyer. Is that what you are, secretly? Well, never mind, it don't signify. 'Tis a world of masks, as you suggest, sir, and only a saint or an idiot can get by without one. As for old

Papa Appleton, he may sniff after information all he likes.
His bargain is already struck, and mighty eager he was for it,
by the by: pushed his pretty daughter under my nose like a
peddlar at Bartholomew Fair, and could hardly bear to wait
for the calling of the banns. Well, he's got me now, and it's
no good him wishing his cake dough."

Well, that was fair enough, Fairfax thought, though he
couldn't help wondering what Charlotte herself had felt
about the whole thing. Had she gone willingly to the altar—
or with scarcely more choice about her destiny than the
slaves on her father's plantations?

No use looking to Lord Mortlock for enlightenment. He
talked of everything but his wife as he led Fairfax to a notorious dive in Maiden Lane known as Bob Derry's Cyder Cellar. The town was still noxiously alive at this hour—a couple
of powdered rowdies climbing on each other's shoulders and
trying to smash the lamps with their canes, sedan chairmen
carrying home drowsing old beaux, shabby prostitutes urgently touting for a cully to get the price of a breakfast, the
odd watchman snuffling tipsily into his muffler and hoping
not to see anything troublesome—but the places of resort
still open were fewer, and more unwholesome. The Cyder
Cellar was a long, narrow room, roughly furnished with tables and benches, with a platform at the end where perform-
ers—or anyone drunk enough to step up there—led the
company in bawdy songs and recitations. The air was thick
with smoke, liquorish breath, and the smell of sweaty bodies
mingled with stale perfumes and pomades. It did not surprise
Fairfax to see numerous exquisitely dressed gentlemen
alongside the roughs and drabs. What puzzled him was why
Lord Mortlock, a man of some intelligence and a certain
rasping wit, should choose to spend his time in such places.
Perhaps it was simply the availability of drink—though the
cider was gut-scouring stuff, and while Mortlock continued
toping steadily, it seemed to do nothing for him. He did not

become exhilarated, expansive, aggressive, or sentimental. There was the same hard look of sardonic disdain at the mindlessly smutty songs, at the painted girl with unlaced stays who sat on his knee and presented her almost bare bosom at him, at the two thick-necked bravoes who fell out over a game of dice and began hammering at each other with makeshift cudgels from a smashed chair. It was as if, Fairfax thought, he went through it all as a duty.

Feeling thoroughly sick, but somehow determined as a point of pride to stay the course, Fairfax accompanied Lord Mortlock to his next port of call. It was a coffeehouse in Covent Garden, actually housed in one of the timber shacks fronting the market, and known very appropriately as The Finish. Here, surely, was an end of all sense and dignity. There were streaks of light in the sky, and outside the first market carts were trundling across the square; but inside The Finish a dingy, weary, pointless night went on. Fairfax was not, he hoped, a prig, but rank stupidity offended him. Here, for the price of a pennyworth of sludge pretending to be coffee, you could mingle with such a set of drunkards, thieves, and hopeless lechers as the stews of decadent Rome would have been ashamed to own. Two prostitutes argued over an ancient fop so glassy-eyed with drink that he looked like nothing so much as a well-tailored corpse propped up between them. Another befuddled gentleman was being berated by the proprietress for breaking a tray of crockery, which she thrust under his nose, screeching for payment.

"An old ruse," Mortlock said in Fairfax's ear. "She keeps it behind the counter and tries the trick on anyone who seems so drunk they won't remember whether they did it or not. I'll wager she earns ten pounds a week from it."

Boldly, Fairfax said, "And the amusement of this never palls, Lord Mortlock?"

The peer's icy eyes locked on his for a moment; then came the dour smile. "You mean why do I come to such

places? I'll tell you why, Fairfax, and I make you a present
of this information. I come because here humanity holds itself cheap, and that pleases me. In this little world mankind
is degraded, or degrades itself, to its true essentials. Here I
can see, and hear, and smell, confirmation of what I believe
about our sorry species."

And avoid going home to your wife, Fairfax thought. But
that, of course, was the presiding spirit of such places: not
going home, carrying the debauch to absurd, weary, futile
lengths — anything but go home, and face reality.

His mind was moving along the sharp angular planes of
fatigue. Other revelers were lolling and snoring in their seats,
and there seemed no reason why he should not lean his head
against the back of the bench and doze. Mortlock seemed
content to watch his sordid pageant, and as Fairfax nodded
and started and then dozed again, his ears dimmed to the
sound of the fifth Baron Mortlock coolly having a swearing
match with a shrewish harlot across the stained and scratched
table. Each to his own, of course, but later Fairfax would
think it a pity that Lord Mortlock should spend the last night
of his life in such a way.

Chapter Two

It was remarkable how refreshed Fairfax found himself, after a bare hour's doze in The Finish and a good breakfast at a decent eating house on the Strand. He felt, indeed, rather pleased with himself: soon to be thirty-two, and more accustomed to the library than the tavern, but he could still keep pace with the rakes. Lord Mortlock was visibly wilting. He rubbed a bony hand irritably across the stubble darkening his pale indoor face as they waited for a hackney carriage to struggle its way through the morning traffic of the Strand. Street sellers were crying their wares, drays and wagons lumbering over the flagstones, maids throwing out slops and brushing down steps. The ordinary daylight world had taken possession of the streets.

"You may as well come home with me, Fairfax, if you can keep your eyes open," Lord Mortlock said. "I'm fit for nothing but bed, but my wife will be receiving company now. Aye, she holds her morning levee at her toilette, you know, in the best Frenchified fashion. I fancy you may find it interesting—and you'll want to see, of course, how we live," he added with a dry sniff and a look.

Fairfax didn't refuse. Even if Lord Mortlock had guessed that he was Mr. Appleton's talebearer, he might as well play his role out. And he *was* interested in spite of himself. He was curious to meet Lady Mortlock, the other half of this matrimonial enigma. He could have wished to be a little more presentable and less rumpled, but being fair, his beard didn't show up until later in the day.

"You've seen the tomcat at play," Lord Mortlock said. "Now you shall see what the she-puss is up to. Are you fond of music? All the better. There's sure to be some pet fiddler or piper of hers present."

The Mortlock house was in Hill Street, just to the west of Berkeley Square. Here in comparatively recent years the aristocracy and the wealthy gentry had migrated, to neat and formal and spacious ranks of lofty town houses, away from the smoky huddle of older London east of St. James's. Private carriages and sedans plied the broad streets. The glittering symmetry of the façades was striking at a time when many more modest houses had half their windows bricked up because of the window tax.

The servant who opened the polished street door to Lord Mortlock's rap was a tall, young black man, dressed in full livery—a blue coat with yellow facings, buff breeches, white gloves, and wig. Fairfax remembered Mr. Appleton mentioning that a slave he had brought over from Jamaica had gone to the new household with Charlotte on her marriage. "He was rather attached to the young mistress, so he went as part of her dowry, if you like," he had said. Fairfax, who didn't like, supposed that this must be the man. The garb was that of any white footman—but unlike any white footman, he was not allowed to leave his place.

"Well, Abraham," Lord Mortlock said, thrusting his hat at the servant, "is the mistress up yet?"

"Yes, sir. She's receiving visitors upstairs."

"There we are, Fairfax. All ready for you. Who first invented this business of receiving guests in dressing gown and curl papers I can't conceive. Well—what is it?"

The black servant was coughing apologetically at his elbow. "Sir, if I might speak a word with you?"

"Damn you, can't it wait? I'm fagged to death . . . Oh, very well."

Mortlock curtly gestured the servant over to the other side of the spacious hall, where a door gave on to what Fairfax guessed was the servants' stairs down to the kitchens. Everything of the grandest and newest here, Fairfax noted, except for some obvious family pieces like the great brass-bound linen chest near the foot of the main staircase and the deep-framed portraits that hung up the stairway: Chinese jars, Turkey carpets, silver chandelier, brocade and damask and gilding and carving, with shining mahogany furniture visible through the open door of a stately dining room. Money, real money, was needed to support a style like this. There was the landed estate in Gloucestershire, of course, but estates had to be given a modicum of attention to yield, and Mortlock had made clear what he thought about that. It was plainer than ever why he had married Charlotte Appleton. Why she had married him remained to be seen.

Fairfax approached the foot of the staircase, peering up at the first portrait, wondering if it were of the infamous "Black Peter" and finding with surprise, from the inscription, that it was. The young man there, painted in the early part of the century, did not look so fearsome, though the long-tressed wigs of those days, Fairfax thought, always gave the face a soft look. The man's monstrousness in later life was well attested. Fairfax momentarily wondered what sort of upbringing Hugh Mortlock could have had as the only child of such a father, who apparently had the manners and morals of a crocodile; then his attention was caught by the shouted response of the man himself, who had been listening impatiently to his servant's murmured petition.

"No, damn you. Never! Devil take your insolence, plaguing me with such a notion. And you thought I'd let you do that? I'd see you shipped back to the plantations sooner. Damn me, I've half a mind to do it—"

"Please, sir . . ." The servant's voice rose in supplication. For a moment his dark troubled eyes met Fairfax's. "I meant no harm, truly—"

"Pox on your meaning, you lying rascal. I gave you fair warning about dangling after these trollops, Abraham, strike me if I didn't. I told you I wouldn't have it, and now you come to me with this tale and expect me to help you instead of kicking you out of doors! And don't think I'm not aware of your little pilferings, you rogue—offerings to sweeten the hussy, no doubt. And now you expect me to— Oh, get out of my sight, man, before I knock your head against the wall. Move your shiftless hide and fetch my shaving water. One more word of this and I won't answer for myself."

It was no use Fairfax pretending he had not heard. Lord Mortlock glowered at him as he joined him at the foot of the stairs.

"Damned insolence. The creature's been nothing but trouble since he came. Well, walk up, man, walk up." Stomping up beside him, Mortlock grumbled on, "'Tis not as if he's hard done by here. Why, his fellows on my father-in-law's plantations are driven like horses, and here he has only a footman's duties, clothes all found, the run of his teeth in the kitchen—"

"His status is still that of a slave?" Fairfax asked, quite conversationally.

"Aye, he was brought to England as such and given to us by old Appleton. Why do you ask?"

"Oh, just curiosity. Some Negroes brought here are given their freedom." And others were not. Though one or two jurists had attempted to question the very ownership of slaves on English soil—as opposed to the colonies—as unconstitutional, one still saw advertisements in which the owners of slaves who had run away sought to recover their "property."

"Freedom—hm—what would he do with it?" Lord Mortlock snorted. They passed the door of a grand reception room and mounted a second flight of stairs.

Up to the bedrooms. An odd custom when one thought about it, as Lord Mortlock had said, though well established now among people of fashion. Fairfax remembered, in his youth, attending the levee of a lady who received her visitors lying in bed; when she decided to get up, they turned their heads away as if it were the most natural thing in the world. (He recalled to his shame that he had peeped.) Here, there were two closed doors: one at the top of the stairs and one just along the passage. From behind the first came the hum of voices. Yawning vastly, Lord Mortlock flung it open.

"My lady. A husband's respectful greetings, and apologies for intruding upon the nymph in her bower." Loud and ironical, Lord Mortlock made a deep, sweeping bow to the woman seated at a silk-swathed dressing table. "I bring a gentleman, a lover of music no less, who is ravished at the prospect of attending one of your levees, which are the boast of polite society for their taste and elegance . . ."

He stopped, straightening, as his eyes fell on the gentleman seated loungingly at a short distance from Lady Mortlock. He seemed, Fairfax thought, to flush, though that might have been just the effect of the ridiculous bow.

"Sir," the young woman said, "I—I hope I see you well." She looked ill at ease.

"You see me as you see me." Mortlock's composure, at least, seemed to return as he looked hard at the gentleman. "Sir. We've not, I think, been introduced."

"My lord, Dr. John Nimier, at your service." A well-dressed man of about forty, he spoke with a trace of an accent. "I also had heard so much of Lady Mortlock's charming levees I could not help but present myself. I am doubly honored that you should—"

"Join you? But I ain't going to, my dear sir," Lord Mortlock said with a jaw-cracking yawn. Downstairs there was a knock at the street door. "Too fagged, and besides the morning light has a sickly look, and is much better shut out with curtains. I stay only to introduce Mr. Fairfax here. Someone of your father's, my dear, with an interest in—what was it?—the sugar trade. He kept me company indifferently well last night, and now I deliver him to you."

Fairfax made his bow. *Someone of your father's*—as in creature, lapdog, cat's-paw, pawn, he thought. "Lady Mortlock. I'm greatly honored." Or jackal, minion, hireling . . . Oh, well.

"And so adieu." Lord Mortlock turned and walked out of the room, almost colliding with a small mincing man carrying a tortoiseshell dressing case. "Who the devil— Oh, it's you. Your *friseur* is arrived, my sweeting, with his instruments of torture."

"Come in, Boville," Lady Mortlock said to the little man, a hairdresser, who entered with a crouching scuttle which Fairfax interpreted as a generalized bow to everyone.

He had been shown up by the black servant, Abraham, who now waited on the landing with steaming shaving bowl, brush and towel-wrapped razor dexterously tucked into the crook of his arm. Lord Mortlock gave him a glare.

"What's this?"

"Sir—shaving, sir."

"What the devil? I can't be bothered with that, idiot. I'm dead on my feet." He must know perfectly well that he had asked for it, Fairfax thought. But the servant offered no protest, and his handsome face was expressionless. "Oh, set it down there, man, and get downstairs. I'll ring when I want you."

Abraham set the shaving tackle down on a side table in the passage and bowed. Lord Mortlock, grim and sour, went into the room across the passage—his bedchamber, Fairfax supposed—and slammed the door behind him.

"Oh, Abraham," Lady Mortlock called to the servant, about to go downstairs, "will you have a pot of chocolate prepared and bring it up, if you please?"

"My lady."

She gave Abraham a smile—the first genuine smile, Fairfax thought, that he had seen in the last twelve hours. The look she gave Fairfax himself was polite enough but not so friendly. Saw him as one of her husband's boon companions, no doubt.

"Mr. Fairfax. Please take a chair. You are acquainted with my father?"

"Yes, Lady Mortlock. I have the pleasure of staying with him just now, while I look into the sugar business."

"Indeed? Well, I'm happy to see you, sir."

And that was it; she seemed to accept his presence quite incuriously, with none of the raised-eyebrow skepticism of her husband. His conscience pricked him. Poor woman, he thought, I have been spying on your husband and now I am spying on you; your father suspects that you are both erring and I am to look for the evidence . . .

"A curious vice of the moderns," said Dr. Nimier, in a precise purring voice, "this mania for sugar. Every washerwoman now must have her dish of sugared tea, yet our not so distant ancestors knew no sweetness except occasional honey, and were none the worse for it."

"You think it an injurious habit, sir?" Fairfax said politely. "As a—man of medicine."

"I am a physician." And a fashionable one, Fairfax gathered, looking at the immaculate, dapper, shrewd-featured figure who sat with one long-fingered and ringed hand elegantly extended on his crossed knees. There was another large jewel in the center of his cravat. No effete fop, though: there was a look of latent, almost pantherish vigor about Dr. Nimier. His complexion was very dark, and his accent . . .

"I am a licentiate of several European colleges," he went

on, "and have the honor to count among my patrons the princess Augusta. Though diet has not been my especial study, my experience is not narrow, and I would class sugar as an enfeebling and deleterious substance when over-indulged, in common with coffee and spiritous liquors."

"Not chocolate, I hope, Dr. Nimier?" Lady Mortlock said with a faint smile.

Dr. Nimier dipped his head at her, crisply gallant. "My dear lady, you are an advertisement for its salubrious properties."

"You hail from France, sir?" Fairfax said.

"My parents were of Huguenot stock," Dr. Nimier said, turning his feline gaze on Fairfax. "Though I was born in England, French was spoken about my cradle, and I am known equally as John or Jean. But I am thoroughly Anglicized, sir, and you need not fear contagion."

"It would be strange if I did, Doctor, as I am half-French myself," Fairfax said. It might have established a bond of sympathy, but he knew even as he spoke, even as Dr. Nimier gave him a look of flat assessment, that it would not.

"You have been abroad with my husband last night, I take it, sir?" Lady Mortlock said.

"Yes, ma'am. Your father happened to introduce us at Old Slaughter's the other day, and Lord Mortlock was good enough to invite me to a hand of cards, and—"

"And then another hand of cards," Lady Mortlock said with a smile.

"Just so." Not a bitter or sarcastic smile, though, he thought. But perhaps he was being partial, on account of her beauty. Not that this had struck him greatly at first. Charlotte, Lady Mortlock, did not dazzle the eye with fairness. Yet the eye kept going back to her, and lingering. Somehow there was a changeable quality about her looks: her profile in pensive repose, her full face smiling, were separately fascinating. Perhaps that was her youth: twenty-two at most, he thought, and in the freshness of her complexion a very young-looking bride for the sallow man who had just gone crashing to his bed. She was dressed in a silk peignoir, her chestnut hair loose in preparation for the attentions of Boville, who stood at the dressing table fastidiously unpacking his case of tongs and tweezers and pomades while crooning softly to himself. The bedchamber was in the grandest style: a richly canopied bed, painted screens, a gilt pagoda-like cage of finches, small tables crowded with expensive curios and trinkets, chinaware, discarded novels, fans, and jeweled combs. Did the merchant's daughter, with her youth and prettiness and faint haunting shadow of trouble under her brown eyes, look out of place in the middle of all this?

She did not. Watching her as Abraham brought in the tray of chocolate, as she invited her guests to partake from the tiny thimblelike cups, as she graciously fended off another purring compliment from Dr. Nimier, as she glanced coolly in the dressing table mirror at the first results of the hairdresser's delicate operations, Fairfax saw with surprise that she was every inch the baroness. Her father, Mr. Appleton, was the epitome of the solid merchant, unostentatious in dress and in the comfortable house at Leicester Fields; the portrait there of the late Mrs. Appleton showed a plump woman even more plain and down-to-earth. Young Lawrence for all his finery was rawboned and gauche. But Charlotte might have been born to her high estate. He felt that one question had been answered: if the marriage to Lord Mortlock had not exactly been a love match, it surely offered something she very much wanted.

A love match! he thought, as his ears caught a faint buzzing sound that must have been Lord Mortlock snoring in his adjacent bedchamber. It was hard to see how there could ever have been love. Five months into the marriage and the couple seemed to move in separate worlds, with all the stale indifference of twenty years' disillusioning matrimony.

"Mm—I heard tell you are a music lover, Lady Mortlock," said Dr. Nimier. He seemed to preface nearly all his remarks with a throaty hum, like the purr of a great cat. "Have you heard the latest opera at the Haymarket? Caretti sings, and brilliantly they say, though the piece is a poor trifle."

"Oh, I adore Caretti—I have hopes he may call here someday soon, when he is resting. Saturday, perhaps, I may see the piece."

"Precisely my thought—if it still holds the stage then. I would have gone on Tuesday—the opera house plays on Tuesdays and Saturdays, Mr. Fairfax, if you are not aware—but I was otherwise engaged that evening. As I daresay you were, ma'am?"

"I believe I was," Lady Mortlock said, turning her head to look in the mirror. The hairdresser fussed and clucked, grimacing.

"Mm, indeed. I hope you were more profitably amused than I," Nimier said, his gemstone eyes still fixed on her face. "In freakish mood I attended the masquerade at Ranelagh. A nonsensical business, though I came away not entirely dissatisfied with the evening's entertainment. A man of resource may find interest, even enlightenment, in the most unlikely places."

"I'm sure he may, sir," Lady Mortlock said, uncomfortably, Fairfax thought, and with a conscious flick of her eyes at Dr. Nimier in the mirror. Was Nimier the one . . . ? Quite possible. He hadn't been out of society so long that he couldn't sense an intrigue. If so, it didn't reflect well on the lady's taste, he thought. The jibe about the opera house had galled him. I was at the opera when this upstart charlatan was still grinding powders for an apothecary, he mentally grumbled. But he saw that there was something darkly attractive about the man, and realized he envied Nimier his seamless self-possession.

"You are also an admirer of music, I believe, Mr. Fair-fax?" Lady Mortlock said.

"Devotedly, though I confess my patience for the Italian opera is not unlimited."

"Taste depends on the understanding," Dr. Nimier said.

"Indeed, sir, and I think I understand enough of mechanical ritornelli, expressionless recitative, and endlessly high tessitura to know when I have had enough."

Nimier tapped a silver snuffbox. "You play, sir?"

"The flute and the clavier, neither well — I perhaps shouldn't speak of my devotion to music when I abuse her so shamefully."

"Oh, you must meet Mr. Stephen Pennant — we are sure to see him today," Lady Mortlock said. "He plays admirably on the flute, and he often leads the orchestra at Ranelagh and Vauxhall. He has completed an opera too, though it seems he despairs of getting a theatre to play it."

"I wish him heartily well. An opera by a native English composer is just what we need," Fairfax said.

"Mr. Pennant, I think, is Irish," Dr. Nimier said.

Another knock at the street door; a few moments later Abraham threw open the door to the bedchamber, announcing: "Mr. Pennant, my lady."

A fair, lithe-looking young man, carelessly dressed, came in with a flute case and a bundle of sheet music under his arm. He bowed to Lady Mortlock, dropping half the music in the process.

"Eternal damnation take it, I'm all in a taking today, every finger a thumb . . . Dogged and bedizened by ill luck." He turned to Fairfax, talking as if he'd known him for years. "Last night the second violinist went sick and we had to make do with the most brass-eared tongs-and-bony jack-anapes that ever tortured a poor innocent fiddle into submission. Then there was that infernal baboon who lodges above me doing his wretched single-stick exercises at cockcrow, if you please, and stamping across the floor like the Lord Mayor's procession in hobnails, devil take him. Then the chairmen bringing me here took a tumble in a horse puddle and damn near tipped me on my head, and rot me if it don't turn out that the rear man's blind! Blind as a buzzard, on my oath, and been a chairman these ten years! And yet he managed pretty well, you know: his partner in front called out the directions, left here, bear to your right, and so on. When I quizzed him, he said he got along very happily as a chairman, only he had a yearning to be in front once in a while . . . Ah, I'm obliged to you," he concluded, as Fairfax gave him a hand in sorting out the sheet music.

"I was just talking of you, Mr. Pennant, and your opera," Lady Mortlock said.

Not looking at her, he said, "My opera? I despair of it. 'Twas always a sickly child, and must soon be buried, I fear . . . Not for me, I thank you," he said, waving away Lady Mortlock's offer of chocolate, and sitting down by Fairfax. "Never mind—there is another child of my addlepated muse who promises fair. 'Tis an oratorio called *Ruth*—I have played parts over with the orchestra and they were enthused, or at least they didn't howl for mercy, so *Ruth* now shall be my champion—carry my hopes, stand or fall!"

"Will you play us something from it by and by?" Lady Mortlock asked. "Mr. Fairfax here will be delighted, I am sure—he's an amateur of the flute."

"Is that so? I'm heartily glad to know you, sir," Pennant said very cordially, pumping Fairfax's hand. "You know, my first teacher was disgusted with me for choosing the flute as an instrument, as of all players the flautist has to make the most ridiculous faces. But there, thought I, nature has anticipated me in that regard anyhow . . ."

Not true: Mr. Pennant was a blue-eyed, fresh-colored, good-looking young man, though with something droll about him; he seemed to bring a breeze into the stuffy chamber.

Lady Mortlock was smiling very attentively on him: was *he* the one? Fairfax wondered. Pennant, however, seemed to take very little notice of her. Of course, that could be revealing in itself; the essence of these society affairs was that they were carried on with supersubtlety . . .

"Mr. Pennant, have you met Dr. Nimier?" Lady Mortlock said.

"Don't believe so—heard the name, though, of course," Pennant said. "One of these quacks, ain't you? Beg pardon, but that's the word everyone uses for you grand doctors. Nostrums to soothe the nerves of highbred ladies."

"You jest with me, sir," Dr. Nimier said, very composed.

"Not at all. I have the greatest admiration for anyone who can make a good thing out of nothing. Like the fairground show of a horse with its tail where its head should be—pay your penny and go in, and there's a plain ordinary beast standing with its arse to the manger, eh?" Pennant turned to Fairfax, who could not help joining in his laughter. An amusing young man, though he noticed that Stephen Pennant never fully smiled: his eyes crinkled, his lips covering his teeth.

"A pretty jest, if a little musty," Dr. Nimier said, in his softest and most imperturbable voice. "I fancy you speak, sir, as a young man whose flesh has known no ills, only pleasures. But the time will surely come when the body will betray you."

"Aye, no doubt," Pennant said cheerfully. "I don't fancy myself immortal. But the ills of the quality, sir, whom you treat—can they really be taken seriously by a follower of Galen and Hippocrates? Does a man undertake the noble profession of medicine aiming to deal with the vapors and nerves and gout and whatnot of the pampered few? Surely they're largely the results of vice and indulgence anyhow. 'Tis the poor who break their backs, breathe mine dust and languish in the fever of epidemics."

"Very true, sir. But that is an argument against poverty. It is not a reason for me to refuse to treat a man because he is rich."

"Well, I give ground there, sir," Pennant said. "But what of these cure-alls that fellows like yourself are always touting? They *can't* be cure-alls, else the graveyards would not be so full. Do you refund the money if they don't work?"

"Certainly not. Your music is I'm sure delicious, sir, but if I were to hear a concert of it and found it bored me excessively, I would not think of asking for my ticket money back—though I might with justice say that the music has failed to do what it is advertised to do, that is entertain."

"Well, perhaps Mr. Pennant will play for us now," Charlotte put in.

"To settle the argument?" Pennant said, turning to her for the first time.

"To prevent one," she smiled.

"Oh, never fear, ma'am—the good doctor and I are just fencing, as men will," Pennant said. And then with a hint of a pout, "But as for this music, I am not sure it will please—it is new-minted, and I hesitate to give it currency, pardon me."

Musicians, Fairfax thought. One of the Greek classics had an apt comment on them, he recalled: that when asked to play they wouldn't, and when they did play they wouldn't leave off . . .

"'Twill sound thin besides," Pennant said. "Now at the Haymarket, with a full choir and forty players . . . ah, a consummation devoutly to be wished!"

"Sir, an indecent expression," Lady Mortlock said, to Fairfax's surprise, blushing deep red.

"Nonsense, 'tis from Shakespeare, who is always acceptable," Pennant said with a laugh.

There was another rap at the street door, and soon Abraham was there, announcing, "Miss Vertue."

"Good heavens — Sophie Vertue!" Lady Mortlock cried, as a young woman entered. "Why, it's been an age since I saw you!" She jumped up, to the muttered anguish of Boville who was curling her back hair with the fastidiousness of a sculptor in glass. In her face Fairfax saw a glimpse of the natural girl beneath the fine lady.

"An age — half a year at least. And I find you changed my dear girl, *very* changed indeed! I last saw Charlotte Appleton, and now . . ." The young woman dropped a deep curtsy, "My *lady*."

"Oh, Sophie, you always were full of nonsense," said Lady Mortlock with a deprecating gesture, though she was not displeased, Fairfax thought. After all, where was the girl who would not relish queening it over her fellows? "And so where have you been?"

"Oh! Where have I not been. Hither and thither with my aunt — Bath, and Bristol Hotwell — then she must needs take off to Scarborough on account of the air — forever on the gad — until at last back to town, thank heaven, just on Sunday last, where not only do I hear much of Lady Mortlock's levees, but realize I actually knew the creature in her previous incarnation."

Miss Vertue turned her face to Mr. Pennant as she spoke — an animated heart-shaped face, with large eyes and a generous mouth, framed by soft honey-colored hair. Seeming much struck with it, he said, "Traveling on a Sunday — why, you impious creature, don't you fear for the state of your soul?"

"Well, my aunt Stoddart doesn't, but then she's something of a freethinker," Miss Vertue said. "The 'petticoat infidel,' Johnson called her, which isn't very witty when you think about it."

"Your aunt is Mrs. Louisa Stoddart?" Fairfax put in. "I had the honor to attend one of her receptions some years ago. She flourishes still, I hope." Mrs. Stoddart was one of the

Blue Stocking hostesses, who held receptions for literary circles, where conversation was the rule instead of drinking, gossiping, and playing cards.

"Well, if you know her, sir, you'll know that she fancies herself perpetually ill, and is always robust. I have hardly been able to keep up with her myself—think of that!" Miss Vertue said, turning again to Mr. Pennant, who was hanging on her words like a dog waiting for table scraps.

"I am thinking of it, believe me, Miss Vertue," he breathed.

"Mr. Fairfax, your acquaintance with London life would seem to be extensive," Dr. Nimier said. "You have been often in town? I understood you as a visitor from the country."

Fairfax had had enough of this. He had half a mind to make a clean breast of it: *I am not a visitor from the country, and I have no interest in the sugar trade. My fortune was lost, and so I hire out as a tutor, but I am as wellborn and well educated as any. I know London like the back of my hand, and as for Johnson I know him too and assisted in the making of his great* Dictionary. *And as for what shenanigans you set of overdressed people secretly get up to, I don't care a fart in a bedstead* . . . But he contented himself with saying, "I have been in town often, yes, sir. Often enough to observe that some of the people here are damnably inquisitive."

"A very palpable hit, sir," Pennant said, touching his arm.

"Sophie and I were schoolfellows together, Dr. Nimier," said Lady Mortlock, very much the peacemaking hostess. "Can you picture us peeping from the bow window of the young ladies' academy, the silliest little wretches, trying to see the soldiers going by in their red coats, and giggling excessively?"

"It is an enchanting picture, and altogether untrue, my dear Lady Mortlock. Naive and innocent you may have been, silly never," Dr. Nimier said.

"And as for the soldiers, Charlotte, why even then you reserved your admiration for the *captain*," Miss Vertue said brightly. "But tell me, where is Lord Mortlock himself? Is he not to join us? I absolutely pine to meet him."

"Hugh prefers to spend the morning hours in the arms of Morpheus, my dear," Lady Mortlock said gently. "The god of dreams, Sophie. I may have mooned after passing captains, but I also attended to my lessons."

Much as he disliked agreeing with Dr. Nimier on anything, Fairfax privately concurred that Charlotte, Lady Mortlock, was no fool. He even wondered if she was a person who was too intelligent to be happy. For she was not happy — he was more and more sure of that; for all her ease, her ready sophistication, she was not happy. The dressing table was crowded with all manner of paints and powders, but he doubted there was anything there that could disguise those shadows beneath her eyes.

"Oh! But will the music not wake him?" Sophie turned to Stephen Pennant. "At least, I presume you are going to play, are you not, sir? I think music in the morning most enchanting."

"You have music in your soul, Miss Vertue," Pennant said. "Yes, you do — music, 'tis written all over your face, though not literally of course, as that would look more than a little rum."

"If it were, you could play the notes!" exclaimed Miss Vertue.

"'Twould be an indifferent execution, ma'am — I fear your eyes would distract me so."

"Hugh is a sound sleeper," Lady Mortlock cut in, "but we are not to hear any music, Sophie: Mr. Pennant is in a sulk, and will not play." Downstairs there was another rap at the street door.

"Oh, but I daresay it is not one of those things that one can just do to order," Miss Vertue said. "It is an art, after all, and one must wait for the Muse to descend—yes, I remember *that* from my lessons, Charlotte."

"But it is perhaps a little curious to bring a musical instrument, and then decline to play," Dr. Nimier said. "As if a woman should make a rendezvous with a man, and then say she only wants to talk of the weather."

Abraham opened the bedroom door and announced another caller. To his surprise, Fairfax looked up to see the elongated form of Lawrence Appleton.

"Charlotte." Ignoring everyone, Lawrence drooped over to his sister and kissed her cheek, then folded his storklike limbs into a chair. "You're looking charming. But whatever's the matter with Abraham? The fellow's got a face like a drowned pup this morning."

"Oh, just a mood, I daresay. Hugh's been at odds with him again lately—you know how he is."

Berating the footman, Fairfax thought, was obviously akin to kicking the dog for Lord Mortlock—a convenient vent for his temper. But as he thought back to the altercation in the hall downstairs, he felt there must be more to it than that, on this occasion at least. Whatever Abraham had said to Lord Mortlock, it had provoked the peer to fury—and threats to ship him back to the plantations.

"Hugh took a fancy that Abraham had been pilfering the other day," Lady Mortlock went on. "It was something and nothing—you know there's no harm in Abraham. I'll settle it later. Well, brother, it's rare to see you at this hour."

"If you don't want me, I'll go away," Lawrence said awkwardly.

"You know I don't mean that at all," his sister said with a tolerant smile.

"The blackamoor is fortunate to have so fair an advocate to plead his cause," Dr. Nimier said. "Your sex shames ours, ma'am. If there were only men in the world, I believe we would very soon destroy it."

"Oh, our sex can be fierce too, sir," put in Miss Vertue, "when we are wronged."

"Will you have some chocolate, Lawrence?" Lady Mortlock said.

"Eh? Oh, not for me," her brother said, slumping in his seat and gnawing his lip. "I've never cared for it since I read in Madame de Sevigne's letters about the woman who drank so much of it she gave birth to a baby who was as black as the devil."

Stephen Pennant shouted with laughter, but Lady Mortlock gave her brother a frowning look. Brooding, pale, tapping his feet restlessly, Lawrence looked over at Fairfax and raised one arched eyebrow. "So, Mr. Fairfax, how'd you like your jaunt with my brother-in-law last night?"

"I was very well entertained," Fairfax said, "though, like Christmas, such entertainment would be too much for me every night."

"Ran into 'em, you know, up at King Street," Lawrence said to his sister; but she looked as indifferent as he sounded. Perhaps she was past caring what her husband got up to, Fairfax thought, which did not augur well for Mr. Appleton's hopes of setting all to rights in this strange household.

"Mr. Appleton, won't you join us in pleading for some music?" Miss Vertue said.

"Eh? Oh, I suppose," Lawrence said. "Heyo, you're Sophie Vertue, ain't you? Now, didn't I hear something about you a while since? Damn me, I could swear I did. Oh, beg pardon, no offense—"

"You are as gallant as ever," Miss Vertue said spiritedly. "Don't you know that a woman of fashion *should* be talked about, and is a poor creature if she ain't?"

"Oh, well, it don't signify," Lawrence said, gracelessly slumping into his seat once again, his fiddle-shaped face settling into its usual expression of faintly pettish discontent.

Pennant said, "Well, Miss Vertue, if *you* entreat me—"

"Oh, indeed I do!"

"Then there is no refusing, dear lady." He took up his flute.

A plain enough snub to his hostess, Fairfax thought. If Pennant was the lover, they certainly weren't getting on. Unless this hostility itself were a ruse, designed to deflect suspicion. Masquerades, he thought, this whole society was a masquerade. Offering to turn the music for Pennant, he noticed a spinet half-hidden by a screen; Pennant's eyes fell on it too, and he asked if Fairfax could possibly provide a continuo for him. Fairfax was hesitant—he was no expert at the keyboard—but glancing over the music he saw that the harmonies were hardly adventurous, and agreed. Pennant played a pastorale from his oratorio and then the vocal line of an aria. All very plangent and silvery and conventionally effective, Fairfax thought, jealously. Dr. Nimier took snuff and attended like a sharp lawyer hearing the excuses of a criminal; Lawrence Appleton looked like a bored schoolboy; Miss Vertue was rapt; the hairdresser swayed in time as he teased and crimped. Only Lady Mortlock's eyes were lowered and unreadable.

"Oh, unsurpassably beautiful," Miss Vertue said at the end; there were tears standing in her great eyes. "I never heard anything so heavenly! Charlotte, if it reaches the ears of your husband, he will surely have the most delicious dreams."

"Hugh is not fond of music."

"Oh, my dear, he cannot be such an insensible creature, can he? I know him only by repute, of course, but I cannot conceive that you, my dear, would have married a man who lacked all delicate sensibility. Surely he has a feeling heart?"

"You cannot expect a bride to speak of her husband's qualities without prejudice," Lady Mortlock said.

"Well—Mr. Appleton, you must know your brother-in-

law. You can surely say what manner of man he is?" Miss
Vertue said.

"Eh? What's that?" Lawrence had got restlessly to his feet
and was mooching and pouting about the room, giving no
very strong indication of why he had come here at all. "Oh,
Hugh's all right enough. But I know plenty of smart fellows,
you know, plenty."

"I could listen all day," Miss Vertue said. "It had the most
exquisite melancholy—"

"Ah, so it does, or should!" Pennant said eagerly. "For
you know melancholy is the most beautiful of the emotions."

"It is a curiously English, or I should say British, ten-
dency," put in Dr. Nimier, "this sensual enjoyment of sadness. Like all indulgences, it may lead to great harm, I think.
What do you say, Mr. Fairfax—speaking as 'half a Frenchman'?"

He made it sound, Fairfax thought, as though he had a
wooden leg or something.

"I think that a man who is always cheerful must be a congenital idiot," he said, "just as a man who is always virtuous
must be unbearable."

"Oh, fie, sir, terrible—justify it!" cried Sophie Vertue. An
intensely romantic girl, he thought; indeed something almost
hectic about her.

"Well, do we not groan when, at a play or in a novel, the
good man or woman appears? Am I the only one who finds
Mr. Allworthy in *Tom Jones* the most deplorable egotist, so
wrapped up in his own goodness that he is blind to everyone
else? And as for Mr. Richardson's Clarissa: who could endure to spend an hour in her company?"

Miss Vertue gasped. Fairfax was enjoying this.

"But, sir, it is her sufferings that make her interesting!"

"And Lord, doesn't she know it," Fairfax said.

"In the fictional Clarissa we see, I think, the type of
melancholic temperament," Dr. Nimier said, "which ulti-

mately *embraces* death. Hence the prevalence of suicide in these islands—what they call in France 'the English disease.' I heard of a very shocking case the other day—a young man of twenty-one, found shot to death in one of the parks."

"You are thinking of Richard Spicer, God rest him," said Pennant. "I knew him somewhat—we had been at school together. I had to take a hand in dealing with his effects and so on, as he had no family here in London. Sad business." He darted a look at Lady Mortlock. "Lord Mortlock knew him, surely, ma'am?"

"I daresay," she replied, sounding almost bored. "Hugh knows many young men of the town."

Fairfax thought of the fiery Sir Anthony who had burst into the gambling house last night. Had he shot his bolt with that rash challenge? What if, he thought, as there was another knock at the street door, Sir Anthony were to turn up at Lady Mortlock's levee? That would certainly be a test of her qualities as a hostess. But when no new guest appeared, he supposed it must have been a messenger or street trader.

"Oh, la, 'tis too grim, let us talk of some matter else," said Miss Vertue, shining-eyed, fanning herself vigorously.

"As you command it, Miss Vertue, it shall be," Stephen Pennant said. "What then shall we talk of? How about the King's affairs?"

"Whatever do you mean, you naughty man? Such things you say, dear Lord, you put me quite out of countenance," Miss Vertue said, laughing almost hysterically and drumming her small feet on the floor.

"His Majesty is hardly known, I think, for furnishing gossip of that kind," Dr. Nimier said crisply.

"Why, precisely what I mean, sir," Pennant said. "Was there ever such a dull prince? Five months married to his ugly little German queen and not a whiff of a mistress or a by-blow! What is the world coming to? What say you, Appleton?"

"Eh? About what?" said Lawrence, who had been staring out of the window and gnawing his nails.

"We are after some discreditable tattle, my dear sir. Anything—never mind if it's not true—as long as it's scandalous and disgraceful."

"Why"—Lawrence's stammer became pronounced—"why do you ask me?"

"*Whisht*, man, you're as prickly as a cat in a thunderstorm. Why, you go with a set of smart fellows, surely something must have come to your ears."

"Nothing, I hear absolutely nothing—'tis all monstrously dull," Lawrence said distractedly, then went over and clumsily kissed his sister's cheek. "Delicious to see you and all, Charlotte, but 'pon my honor I must be going—can't stay."

"Lawrence, so soon—?"

"Have to—only meant to stay a trice—honored—enchanted . . ." With some perfunctory bows he left the room.

"What a provoking, odd creature your brother has become, Charlotte!" Miss Vertue said when he had gone. "What does he mean to do with himself?"

"In life? Be a gentleman, I suppose," Lady Mortlock said. "Father had thoughts of the Bar or the Church, but they came to nothing. But a gentleman, I'm afraid, must have means."

"Let us pray he doesn't fall into bad company, which can be the ruin of such young men," Dr. Nimier said.

"Oh, do you think that's really true, sir?" Miss Vertue said with animation. "Is it? Young men, surely, are responsible for their own destinies, aren't they?"

"Up to a point. But I think they can be *undone* by unscrupulous companions, just as surely as an innocent woman by a seducer."

"I thank you—you say very enlightening things!" Miss

Vertue said, her eyes devouring the doctor. Exhausting creature, she must have the heartbeat of a bird, Fairfax thought.
"Do you not find Dr. Nimier a remarkable man, Charlotte?"

"Very," Lady Mortlock said shortly. "Will you play again,
Mr. Pennant, Mr. Fairfax?"

Miss Vertue clapped her hands. "Oh, I would like that
more than anything!"

They played, first the pastorale again and then a lively
badinerie that Fairfax found hard going for his rusty fingers.
He became aware of repeated knocks at the street door
through this, and at last, just as he came perspiring to the end,
the bedchamber door opened and Mr. Samuel Appleton
walked in.

"Your pardon for coming in unannounced, Charlotte,"
he said. "There was no one to answer the door so I let myself in."

"Why, is Abraham not there?" Lady Mortlock said.

"No sign of him. One of the maids came up at last from
the kitchen, all suds—wash day, I take it," Mr. Appleton said
in his gentle rumble. "Didn't mean to incommode her. She
said Abraham wasn't down there neither."

"Oh, dear Lord, where is he hiding himself? He knows his
duties quite plainly, especially on a day when the other servants are busy with the laundry and can't stir," Lady Mortlock said frowning. "Hugh will be in a fury . . ."

"How is Hugh? Is he here?"

"He's abed. Well, I'm glad to see you, Father. I didn't
expect—"

"I was free of business this morning, so I thought I'd
call." Mr. Appleton sat down and nodded at Fairfax. "I
thought perhaps to see my guest here too. How do you go on,
Fairfax? Had you good entertainment last night?"

"Thank you, sir, I do very well," Fairfax said, and tried to
return his nod in a way that would convey: *Your son-in-law
is gaming mighty high. There is a woman called Lady Har-*

riet Froome to whom he seems quite as close as to his wife.
Your daughter is very unhappy and if she has a lover it may
well be Dr. Nimier or Stephen Pennant, but I don't know
which and I have had enough of being a spy . . . It was a lot
to get into a nod.

"Is it possible, Lady Mortlock, that your blackamoor has
absconded?" Dr. Nimier said.

"Why, sir, whatever makes you think that?" Mr. Appleton
said.

Dr. Nimier half-smiled. "It is surely a likely supposition.
His is not in an enviable situation."

"Well, I don't know about that, sir," Mr. Appleton said in
his considering way. "Abraham is pretty well-placed here;
there are many free men who have a worse lot. Runaways are
usually bad characters, and I can't believe that of Abraham.
I've known him for years—'twas I brought him over to England and trained him up as a house servant. Nay, I'll swear
he's a good lad. If there's been a quarrel with the master, then
he's sloped off somewhere to sulk a while is my guess."

"But do you think it a prudent, or even a kind act to bring
these poor creatures to a free country, my good sir, where
they will surely be made a prey to discontent?" Dr. Nimier
said. "As exotics they must be made vain, as slaves they must
be resentful. A dangerous combination."

"Why, if I thought that, sir, I should never bring them,"
Mr. Appleton said simply. The merchant looked very plain
and homely sitting among these fashionable people, his
hands planted on his knees, his large square-toed shoes stick-
ing out. Not undignified though, Fairfax thought. "Well, my
dear," Mr. Appleton said, smiling on his daughter, "don't let
it trouble you. Servants are always up to some tricks or other.
They wouldn't be servants else. And you are well, my dear?
You look well." He studied her, under lowered lids, but
closely.

"Never better, Father, I thank you. Lawrence has been here—you have just missed him."

"Indeed? Rare for him to be astir at this time."

"Well, he wasn't excessively lively, and didn't stay above a few minutes. Is there something amiss with him?"

"He hasn't favored me with his confidence if there is," Mr. Appleton said with a disdainful lack of interest.

"We were talking, sir, of the King and his little fright of a queen," Pennant said, "and were remarking how singular it is that they breed no scandal. Unless you have heard of any?"

"Scandal?" Mr. Appleton said quite sharply. "I never pay heed to scandal, sir, never. As for the King and Queen . . . Well, I dined but recently with His Majesty's equerry, but of course nothing of that kind was talked of."

His Majesty's equerry! Mr. Appleton brought it out casually enough, with no boastful swagger. But there could hardly have been a clearer illustration of the grand doors that were opening to him now that his family had married into the aristocracy. Fairfax saw the bashful pride in his employer's round, comfortable face.

"Perhaps, Mr. Pennant, they are simply and truly in love with one another," Lady Mortlock said. "Such things do happen, you know."

"I bow to your experience, Lady Mortlock, and I reproach myself. Where I learned such deuced cynical views of love's constancy I can't think," Pennant said. "I'm only a poor toiling musician, and know nothing of such things."

"Father, you remember Miss Sophie Vertue, I think?" Lady Mortlock said.

"Oh, I was a little awkward creature afraid to squeak when last you saw me, Mr. Appleton," Miss Vertue said. "Always lurking in Charlotte's shadow. And now I'm in awe of her all over again. How grand she's become, and how gratified you must be!"

"Well, my dear, I'm sure there is a fine husband awaiting

you somewhere," Mr. Appleton said benignly. "Who knows what destiny has in store for such charm and beauty, eh?"

Charm and beauty—but the most valuable asset for a woman in this harsh little world was fortune. Fairfax wondered about Miss Vertue. Her trim figure was fashionably dressed in brocaded silk, but there was no telling. It sounded as if she was the ward of her aunt, Mrs. Stoddart, which could mean poor relation. He thought he detected, at any rate, a note of envy for her old schoolfellow, especially when she replied to Mr. Appleton with a peculiarly acid laugh: "Who knows, indeed. Mr. Pennant, will you not play again? Mr. Appleton has yet to hear you."

They played yet again, and Mr. Appleton listened uncomfortably. Fairfax could tell that this did not come naturally to him. Asked by Pennant afterwards for his opinion, he said gravely, "Well, I hardly know, sir. I am not fond of piping sounds, in truth. I much prefer to hear a fiddle."

"Then I hope you didn't hear our orchestra at Ranelagh last evening," Pennant said smiling. "Our second violin made a noise like a sow in farrow."

"Eh—Ranelagh?" Mr. Appleton said; he had been looking thoughtfully at his daughter. "No, no, not I. I spent last night at home, looking over some accounts."

"Well, I shall have to give an account of myself to my aunt if I don't make haste," Miss Vertue said, rising. "We are to call on some frightful old German who has written something about Shakespeare . . . Dear Charlotte, it has been a joy to see you again. A pity I did not meet Lord Mortlock on this occasion, though his reputation, you know, is such that I almost feel I do know him. Sirs . . ."

"I shall see *you,* perhaps, at Ranelagh, Miss Vertue?" Pennant said eagerly.

"Good heavens, perhaps, sir, but you would do very well to pick me out of that crowd, I think—"

"'Twould not be difficult," Pennant said, bowing like a cavalier. "A diamond among paste, Miss Vertue."

"Oh, nonsense!" She was laughing as she left the room.

"So, that is the latest style, is it, my dear?" Mr. Appleton said, eyeing his daughter's hair, which was now being wound up at the crown and fastened with a pearl comb. "Very becoming. The French fashion, I should think. Curious we have to take these things from our neighbors across the Channel. Upon my word, we have invention enough in these islands."

"Perhaps the day will come when we learn our cooking from the same teachers," Dr. Nimier said. "The Englishman's attachment to plain roast and boiled is, I believe, quite a standing jest on the Continent."

"Why, I fancy that is because their victuals are so poor that they would not stand up to plain cooking. Our meats need no disguising; theirs must be fribbled and fricasseed and sauced just to be edible," Mr. Appleton said.

"My dear sir, you enchant me!" Dr. Nimier said. "I believe you are John Bull incarnate!"

"Well, there are worse things to be, I think," Mr. Appleton said sturdily. "Your pardon, sir—you are a foreigner?"

"In extraction only. My parents were exiles from France, and I rejoice in the liberties of an Englishman—if not in his cooking. Mr. Fairfax will surely concur."

"I like roast and ragout equally," Fairfax said. "My regret is that the two countries of my parentage are at war over more serious matters than cooking. At least, I presume they are. I hardly know what the cause of this continuing quarrel may be."

"Why, 'tis a matter of dominion, Fairfax," Mr. Appleton said. "Our interests about the globe must be protected, else Johnny Frenchman—begging your pardon—will grind our faces. I speak as a guardian of those interests in the West Indies, where they are most vital. In trade and commerce

France is our great, our sole rival, and must be fought—as she has been, so gloriously."

"And so much to the enrichment of men in the City, I think. Whether anyone else stands to gain for such prodigious expenditure of money and blood, I can't say," said Pennant, with a pleasant laugh.

"I beg your pardon, sir, but the successful prosecution of this war must be of benefit to the country as a whole," said Mr. Appleton seriously.

And sugar merchants especially, Fairfax thought, mindful of the conquests in the West Indies. Pennant's twinkling eye suggested that he thought the same. But it was Dr. Nimier who said, with his deepest purr: "One understands that the war was undertaken precisely to gather these rich pickings in the Indies. But may not the capture of all the French plantations make a glut of sugar, and drive prices down? That is, if they are retained . . . One hears rumors since the departure of Mr. Pitt that the peacemakers in government are prepared for all sorts of concessions. In which case, the whole war will have been a pointless enterprise, achieving nothing but a fixed enmity with an embittered France, and a probable future war with the whole of Europe against us."

"I don't see that, sir," Mr. Appleton said, thrusting out his pink lips. "The American colonies will gladly buy as much sugar as we can produce. There will be an increase, not a loss of profit."

"Ah! Then everything is justified, of course," Dr. Nimier said airily.

Mr. Appleton seemed oblivious to this sarcasm. "Certainly. Ah, but without Mr. Pitt, who knows what may happen. He was our rudder, and now we drift . . ." He got to his feet, jingling the change in his pockets. "Well, my dear, I'd best be off. I just wanted to cheer myself with your pretty face. And don't trouble about Abraham—he's sure to be lurking about somewhere. A firm word is all that's needed.

I'll speak to him myself if you have any more trouble." With his mild, slow-blinking eyes, Mr. Appleton gave a thorough look at Pennant, at Dr. Nimier, and finally at Fairfax before he took his leave.

He is wondering, as I am, Fairfax thought. Yet they're surely not likely to betray themselves with her husband sleeping in the next room . . .

"What, I wonder, does Lord Mortlock say to this matter of peace negotiations?" Dr. Nimier said.

"That you would have to ask him, sir," Lady Mortlock said.

"Of course. A man with so utterly charming a consort would not beguile their precious hours together talking of politics. Certainly I would not, if I were in his place. Such beauty must be cherished, not blighted by dullness and discord."

With a bright, unfriendly look, Pennant said: "Have you no wife of your own to cherish, Doctor?"

"No, sir. I am in a way betrothed to my vocation—like yourself, no doubt. Though I must say you seemed to admire Miss Vertue exceedingly."

"Oh, I make no bones about that. There is an open, truthful, artless quality about her that is most rare and refreshing. I always feel there is nothing worse than duplicity in a woman—do you not think so, Lady Mortlock?"

"I don't entirely know what you mean, sir."

"Why, masks, ma'am, masks—she seems this but she is really that. All show and double dealing."

"Oh, sir, you are young," Dr. Nimier said, amused. "You have yet to learn that if we wore no masks the world would be insupportable."

"Would it? Please, indulge my imbecilic youth, sir, and explain why," Pennant said, looking rather stormy.

"Because there would be no society. Imagine a world in which everyone said what they really thought all the time; in which the impulse of the moment was always acted upon, without restraint or decorum. You would have a republic of brutish savages."

"I am talking of manners, not morals," Pennant said dismissively.

"So am I. There cannot be one without the other."

"You do not agree with Rousseau's ideas about the noble savage, Doctor?" Fairfax said. "That man in a state of primitive nature is pure and happy, and only corrupted when civilization steps in?"

"As a physician I have seen the operations of nature. They are seldom kind, and people often beg me to stop them."

"And what of whatsisname — Abraham?" Pennant said. "When the slave traders plucked him, or his father, from his native shore and took him away in chains, were they doing him a favor, then, in introducing him to civilization?"

"No men are free. If not physically bound, they are slave to an idea. Or worst of all, enslaved to their own desires." Dr. Nimier uncoiled himself and bowed over Lady Mortlock's hand. "Ma'am, you are all graciousness and elegance, and only pressing business tears me away. I bid you good day." Without a word to the others, he prowled out.

"How tedious it must be to know *everything*," Pennant said, raising his eyebrow at Fairfax. "Well, I didn't choose to say so while he was here, but I remember hearing that fellow's name in a very uncivilized connection."

"Indeed?" Lady Mortlock said sharply. "And what could that be?"

"Oh, 'twas a year to two since. Some dispute with a rival charlatan over their quack remedies. Started off with them firing pamphlets at each other, but I'll swear there was a rumor that it came to drawn swords in the end. How's that for restraint and decorum?" Yawning, Pennant began putting his flute into its case. "If you ask me, the fellow looks like one of those Italian smilers in Shakespeare—the sort with a stiletto hidden under his cloak."

"You will play no more, Mr. Pennant?" Lady Mortlock said.

Pennant shook his head, smiled, shrugged. Not enough of an audience, thought Fairfax. He liked the young man, but that streak of vanity could hardly have been more plain if it had been painted down his back.

"Well, I think your new music is very fine," she went on. "I would love to hear it again. But then I daresay you think that a mere piece of tinsel insincerity, typical of a duplicitous woman, do you not?"

"I was speaking in general terms, ma'am," Pennant said, gathering up his music.

"Of course. Well, so am I when I say that the mask, as you call it, is sometimes necessary. If we do not wear the mask of cheerfulness, we are called sullen and discontented. If we do not wear the mask of politeness, we are bold-faced hussies. Indeed, I think without our masks men would not like us at all."

"Which would be dreadful for you, of course," Pennant said.

"As we are taught nothing but how to please, almost from the cradle, it would certainly be disconcerting," she said. "But perhaps then we should have to settle to being rational creatures instead."

"I cannot think you would give up the art of pleasing, Lady Mortlock," Pennant said. "It gives such power—power without responsibility. What could be better? Mr. Fairfax, glad of your acquaintance, sir. If you are ever by the Crown and Anchor in the Strand, step in—'tis where the musical fraternity meet. We'll have a glass and a song."

"When I sing, people throw glasses," Fairfax said, "but thank you, sir, I'll bear it in mind."

With the shortest of bows to his hostess, Pennant left the

room, and Fairfax realized almost with a start that except for
Boville, who was putting some agonized finishing touches to
her hair, he was alone with Lady Mortlock. Not something he
had planned, though perhaps it might be useful. She might
give something away in a tête-à-tête . . . yet on reflection he
had no great hopes. All masks, as Pennant had said, and despite those rather intriguing flashes of plain-speaking, this
was a socially adept woman. He felt her defenses would be
no more easily breached than those of her prickly husband.

"You must be tired, Mr. Fairfax, after such a night," she
said, getting abruptly to her feet. She was tall and willowy, a
graceful figure, though the glance she threw back at her reflection was full of dissatisfaction.

"The stimulating company has revived me," he said, wondering if she were giving him a hint to leave her alone.

"Hugh took you on a tour of his haunts, I suppose?"

Was she doing a little investigating on her own account?
He wondered if he should say that they had gone to Lady
Harriet Froome's, and observe her reaction . . . Before he
could reply she waved a hand and said, "Dull enough for you
to do, without having to relate it as well." Standing at the
window, she sighed, "I could leave this wretched town tomorrow without a qualm."

"For your place in Gloucestershire, perhaps? Lord Mortlock was telling me of it—"

"I'm sure he was not, unless to complain of the war taxes
on his land. As for me, I have never seen it. I daresay it is full
of portraits and monuments to the noble house of Mortlock.
Apparently there is hardly a longer bloodline in England—I
forget who was telling me. My father, probably."

"Mr. Appleton is greatly proud of the alliance, I believe."

"Who would not be? You are thinking, Mr. Fairfax, that it
was probably a typical worldly mercenary match. A marriage
à la mode."

"The world would probably call it such, even if it were not," he said.

She smiled thinly at his answer. "You are quite a courtier . . . Well, the way I see it, all marriage is a lottery. Even the most moonstruck and romantic of couples, choosing love in a cottage, are taking a monstrous risk. So is it not sensible to marry where there will be definite gratifications—compensations, if you like; where there is a style of living that one admires, a prospect of society and consequence?"

There was something in what she said, Fairfax decided, though he could not help thinking of the old jest that if you were going to be miserable, you might as well be miserable in comfort.

"I think anyone who claims to be an expert on marriage is either a fool or a hypocrite," he said. "There are as many different kinds of marriage as there are people."

She only shook her head at that—scornfully, it seemed. All right, he thought, it wasn't exactly a Solomonic piece of wisdom, but he had been up all night.

Turning from the window, she said abruptly, "I do hope Abraham has not taken it into his head to run away."

"Yes . . . I must say there were some very high words between him and Lord Mortlock when we came in, though what the matter was I don't know."

"Madame is complete," the hairdresser said, packing up his tools. "Madame is content with herself, yes?"

"Yes," Lady Mortlock said, after another bleak glance at herself in the mirror. "Madame is complete."

"And—monsieur?" Boville said, hesitating. "Will he be requiring me?"

"Oh, monsieur will not be stirring yet," Lady Mortlock said. Then a faintly malicious expression crossed her face. "But wait, though, let us ask him. Perhaps he may want his wig dressing, Boville—who knows unless we ask?"

Fairfax was on his feet. "I must take my leave, Lady—"

"In a moment, sir. Let us see if his lordship requires Boville's services." Lady Mortlock propelled the nervous hairdresser ahead of her, out of the room, and across the passage. "Knock hard, Boville—he may want some rousing." The expression of sour amusement was still on her face as the hairdresser knocked and knocked again.

Fairfax stood by on the landing, impatiently. It was all a sad business, no doubt, but he had had enough of playing pig-in-the-middle with these people. Damn it, they would have to sort out their own affairs, in both senses . . .

"No answer, madame," Boville said.

"Knock again." Lady Mortlock frowned. "Surely he hasn't slipped out again. Even Hugh has to sleep sometime . . ."

Fairfax's eye fell on the shaving gear left on the side table by Abraham. The bowl of water, brush, and wrapped towel were still there. But the handle of the razor no longer protruded from the towel. He stared, and felt as if he had swallowed a lump of ice.

"Lady Mortlock, open the door," he said.

She raised her eyebrows at his tone, very much the fine lady.

"Damn it, open the door . . ." He brushed her aside and did it himself.

Heavy curtains were drawn across the two windows, but the spring morning was bright and a dusty subterranean light fell on the large four-poster bed in the middle of the room. The bed curtains were drawn back. The figure on the bed lay sprawled across the many pillows, head back, arms spread— very much as if sleeping off a long night's drinking, in fact, and for a moment Fairfax thought his fears were unrealized. Until he saw that what appeared to be a shadow falling across Lord Mortlock's upper body was actually a great stain of blood.

Chapter Three

Lady Mortlock had followed him in. He could hear her quick-drawn breath behind him, but not until she was close enough to see the deep blood-bubbled slash across Lord Mortlock's throat did she scream.

"Qu'est-ce que c'est? Eh, pardieu, madame, dites-moi, qu'avez-vous?" Boville was babbling in the doorway. *"Oh ma foi . . ."*

Lord Mortlock's right hand was thrown out to the edge of the bed. Beside it lay the open razor, smeared with blood. Fairfax seized his wrist. The flesh was warm, but he could feel no pulse.

"Sir, run and fetch a doctor, quickly," Fairfax barked at the little hairdresser, who scuttled off at once.

"Does he live? Hugh!" Lady Mortlock cried. "Hugh, for God's sake . . ."

A natural impulse to cry out to the man, whose open staring eyes still seemed to have the alertness of life about them. But the blood in which he lay, forming a hideous shape across the whiteness of pillows and sheets and nightshirt like a mapped continent, and the depth of that terrible gash . . . Fairfax shook his head, swallowed bile.

"I fear it's no use, Lady Mortlock," he said, gently warding her away from the bed.

"My God . . ." She was shaking violently. "My God, why . . . why . . . ?"

Why did he do it? His own first thought. Yet it was swiftly borne in on him that this was not the scene of a suicide.

The razor by the right hand, for one thing. Fairfax had noticed last night that Hugh Mortlock was left-handed: in the Cyder Cellar he had idly written his name with his left forefinger in the spilled drink on the tabletop. Even supposing he had managed to cut his own throat so deeply and horribly with his right hand, there would surely have been blood on the hand. Yet there was none: both hands, wrists, and arms were unstained. No, it didn't fit.

From the way Mortlock's white unwigged head was thrown back, shaven crown thrust deep into the pillows, Fairfax surmised that someone had approached him as he lay on his back, fast asleep, had seized his forehead with one hand to hold him down and with the other hand cut his throat from ear to ear. Then that someone had left the razor by his hand in an attempt to create an appearance of suicide.

Only a cursory attempt, though, not one that would stand up to much scrutiny. The icy feeling intensified as Fairfax saw that someone had single-mindedly achieved their purpose in this room: the murder of Hugh Mortlock. They had taken the razor from the side table on the landing, stepped in here, killed the sleeping man, and walked away.

Fairfax yanked at the bellpull in the wall to summon a servant from the kitchens. Stepping back, he noticed a couple of small round objects on the rug by the bed. He bent to examine them. They were pills of some kind—large, grayish, no discernible smell. He placed them on the night table by the bed, where Lord Mortlock's purse, pocket watch, and snuffbox lay, and saw that there was an enameled pillbox there too. Opening the lid he saw several of the same pills within. What were they . . . ?

"Mr. Fairfax, I—I cannot . . ." Lady Mortlock had her

hand clasped to her mouth. He took her arm, lowered her into a chair at a distance from the bed.

"Breathe deep, Lady Mortlock. That's it. Deep and slow . . ."

"My husband is dead, isn't he?"

"I fear so. It appears to me that—it is murder."

Her eyes bulged. "But—how can it be? We were—dear God, we were in the next room . . ."

"Yes, but the door was closed, there was more or less constant talk and music . . ." A swift, determined killer had only to take the razor from the towel, step in, and do the deed with dispatch: the victim would not even have cried out. But who . . . ? He was afraid that there was an all too plain answer.

An elderly maid, with her hands damp and red from the washtub, had come toiling up at last, and curtsied into the room. When she saw Lord Mortlock she screamed ceaselessly. Fairfax gripped her arms and urged her to be calm, but she was hysterical. It was Lady Mortlock at last who stepped in. Her face was as white as her dead husband's, but there was a kind of statuesque calm about her. She slapped the maid's cheek, then held the gasping woman by her shoulders.

"Meggy. Meggy, your mistress speaks. I need you to help me, do you hear?"

"Oh, ma'am, I can't—I can't look . . ."

"You don't have to look," Lady Mortlock said, turning her away gently. "But you must let the other servants know that the master has—has been killed, and—"

"Abraham," Fairfax said. "Mr. Appleton said he was nowhere to be found. Have you seen him, Meggy?"

"Why, no, sir." Meggy gulped and scrubbed at her eyes. "I thought he was at his place in the hall, answering the door and showing the guests upstairs. Then when Mr. Appleton came, and knocked and knocked and no one opened the door to him—I came up at last and he was already in and he said

where's Abraham, and I said I didn't know, he should have
been there, and so Mr. Appleton went upstairs and I went
back to the kitchen and said was Abraham there, but everyone said no, no one had seen him. We're all busy with the
wash down there, and I'm afraid I cursed a little that he
should make himself scarce today of all days . . . Oh, sir, do
you mean 'twas Abraham did this? Oh, the filthy black, the
horrid savage, I never took to him. I always thought—"

"Hush," Fairfax said, "nothing is known yet. Meggy,
you'd best go rouse the other servants and search the house.
See if Abraham is to be found, or if anyone knows where he
can be. Quick, now."

The maid, stiffly avoiding any glance backwards at the
bed, went off muttering and sniffing.

"Lady Mortlock, was there any reason for Abraham to
leave the house? Any normal reason, I mean. An errand,
or—"

"No. In the afternoons, if I or—or Hugh sent him, then
sometimes. But in the mornings, when I receive callers, his
duty is to answer the door. He has never left his station before . . ."

But had there ever been such a quarrel with his master before? Fairfax wondered. Mortlock had even threatened, idly
perhaps, to have him sent back to the plantations . . . Fairfax
felt sick. It looked bad for Abraham.

But there was still the possibility that that was the intention, Fairfax thought swiftly. Someone who had been in the
house this morning had killed Lord Mortlock. The maids,
toiling at the laundry down in the basement with no business
on the second floor, could surely be discounted. Lady Mortlock, Boville, and he himself had remained in her bedchamber from the time Lord Mortlock had left them to stagger to
his bed until they had found him in a pool of his own blood.
Abraham had certainly been on this landing several times:
each time, in fact, that he had shown a guest into the levee

and then closed the door behind him. He had had ample opportunity to slip into Lord Mortlock's room . . .

And yet so had the other guests. Except for Mr. Appleton,
they had been shown up by Abraham, but on leaving they
had all made their own way out. Some hostesses might have
rung each time to have the visitor shown out, but Lady Mortlock cultivated a little graceful informality. Once downstairs,
Abraham would present them with their cane or whatever
they had left and open the front door for them. But in the interim, any one of them could have taken up the razor and
stepped into Lord Mortlock's room . . .

Fairfax felt a little dizzy. Yes, it could have been any of
them, Abraham included. But he had few illusions about
where a magistrate would point the finger, with a discontented, perhaps even desperate black slave having chosen
this very morning to make a bolt for it.

Indeed, why did he resist such an obvious conclusion
himself? For he did. He found himself praying that Abraham
had not run away and made himself such an obvious figure
of guilt.

"Lady Mortlock," he said, "why not go into the next
room? I'll have someone bring you brandy—and someone
should be with you. Your father, perhaps, should be sent
for—"

She was shaking her head. How young she looked: a girl.
Yet a wife, a peeress, and now a widow. Was she wondering
at these swift, incomprehensible transformations of her life?
"No, I'll remain here, sir." She gave him a straight look. "We
were separated enough in life, I think."

There were hasty noises downstairs, and in a few moments Boville came panting up. With him was Dr. Nimier.
The hairdresser gabbled that he had run up to Berkeley
Square, shouting, hardly knowing what he did, and then had
spotted Monsieur le Docteur just getting into a sedan chair
across the square. Great good fortune, was it not . . . ?

"I think I am too late here," Dr. Nimier said, taking in the scene with a swift glance. Sharp nose wrinkling, he bent over the bed, carefully drawing back his lace cuff, and placed his fingers at Lord Mortlock's throat just above the terrible wound. "Yes. My commiserations, my lady. When was this discovered?"

"But a few minutes ago," Fairfax said.

"He has not been long dead. Within the last hour. But even immediate medical attention could not have helped him, with such a wound. Carotid and jugular vessels utterly severed . . ." Dr. Nimier lifted the razor between finger and thumb, examined it before letting it lie again. "A horrid crime."

"You do not doubt it is a crime?" Fairfax said.

"I have seen suicides who have cut their own throats. Never does the scene resemble this. There are almost always small nicks—preliminary cuts—where the hand has trembled to do the deed."

Fairfax nodded. "Also, his lordship was left-handed."

"Indeed? Definitely impossible then. The incision was made from this side—that is, his left—cleanly and deeply to his right. No man could do this to himself." Dr. Nimier, after a glance at Lady Mortlock, closed the dead man's eyes. "The proper authorities must be notified. You may perhaps wish, Lady Mortlock, to have another doctor certify the death, in these circumstances." He drew himself up to his full height and met Fairfax's gaze coolly. "As I was present in the house, I must no doubt be considered under suspicion."

"Several of these were on the floor," Fairfax said, holding up one of the gray pills. "Have you any notion what they are?"

After a cursory glance, Dr. Nimier shook his head. "They are not known to me. Some druggist's compound. Lady Mortlock?"

But a delayed shock seemed to have set in, and Lady

Mortlock could only shake her head dazedly, stroking her hands back and forth as if she were washing them. Fairfax put the pill back on the night table. His first thought had been that it was the notorious "blue pill," widely prescribed as a specific remedy for venereal disease. But that was hardly a thing to say in front of the widow; and other specimens he had seen had been much larger than this.

His eye fell again on Lord Mortlock's purse, also lying on the night table.

"Lady Mortlock—by your leave?"

She nodded blankly.

"You suppose a robbery?" Nimier asked, watching him. "Yet my lord's watch is there, untouched."

Fairfax emptied the purse on to the table. A few silver and copper coins fell out, remnants of what Fairfax had lent his companion after he had lost at faro. There had also been, of course, that bill which Lord Mortlock had produced, and specifically decided to keep hold of. Fairfax had seen him fold it and stow it back in his purse.

"Something is missing," he said. "When I was abroad with Lord Mortlock last night, there was a bill of exchange in his possession. Strange . . ." He saw Nimier looking skeptically at him, thinking, no doubt, what he was now thinking himself: why would anyone take a bill which, unlike a banknote, was not payable to the bearer? And why would anyone kill to get it? It made no sense. Unless killing had been the object, and the bill had just been snatched up by someone who didn't really know what they were taking . . .

For some time hurried footsteps had been audible about the house, and now the maid Meggy reappeared.

"Abraham's not in the house, ma'am. Not a sign of him."

"What about his room?" Fairfax said. "Are his things still there, clothes, whatnot?"

"It's little enough he had, sir, but his room's just as always. He's gone. No one saw him come down to the kitchen.

Last we knew of him he was at his place in the hall. Leastways, he did come down once. 'Twas some little time before
Mr. Appleton arrived, I fancy. But that was only to bring
down the milk. The milk seller had called, and Abraham
came down to fetch the jug, and ask the cook how much she
wanted, and Cook said two pints, and then he came back
again when it was filled."

"That is twice," Dr. Nimier said.

"Yes, sir, you're right of course, but 'twas all very quick.
Abraham always sees to that himself. It's my belief 'twould
be more fitting if the milk seller came down to the kitchen
door at the back, but no, he always makes it his business to
be at the front door. On account of being sweet on her, I believe, the dirty, filthy—"

"Thank you, Meggy," Fairfax said. The milk seller calling: that must have been the knock he heard that produced no
upstairs visitor. "Has anyone any notion of where he might
have gone?"

"Why, where could he go, sir? This is his place, and he's
got no other."

True enough, Fairfax thought. It looked bad, indeed, for
Abraham.

"Abraham what?" he said. "What is his full name?"

"Oh—'tis Drake, I think," Meggy said, adding with contempt, "Not that anyone's got any call to use it."

Fairfax persuaded Lady Mortlock to leave the grisly room,
and he closed the door behind them. With Dr. Nimier and
Boville following, they returned to her bedchamber, where
she seemed to wake from her trance of shock. She had the
servants assemble before her—three housemaids, cook,
kitchen maid, and the groom and stable boy from the mews
behind the house—and Fairfax questioned them again. But
there was no doubt that none of them knew of Abraham's
whereabouts, and all Fairfax learned was that they all de-

spised him, and immediately believed him capable of cutting his master's throat.

He sent the stable boy to fetch Mr. Appleton and the groom to notify the magistrate at Litchfield Street, dismissing the other servants with a request for some brandy for their mistress. Lady Mortlock seemed content to accept his direction in this; Dr. Nimier held himself very correct and aloof, coolly recommending that Lady Mortlock should add sugar to the brandy and composing himself to wait with arms folded and elegant legs crossed.

Fairfax felt the need of a brandy himself. Without feeling that he had come to know Lord Mortlock well—indeed, he had doubts whether anyone could—he had spent a whole night in his company, ending up with a curious mixture of reluctant liking and puzzled distaste for the man. Now, to see that life so violently extinguished . . . He kept thinking of the gathering that had taken place in this room: music, gossip, some fairly acid fashionable talk, and some very cryptic exchanges—and meanwhile, at some point, the master of the house was meeting his swift death a matter of yards away. His pity for Lady Mortlock was no less for the fact that the marriage was apparently fractured by infidelity, perhaps on both sides; indeed, perhaps that made it worse.

Unless what she was feeling was relief, gladness, even triumph . . . She certainly could not have done the deed because she hadn't left this room the whole time, but it didn't take much imagination to picture her as party to a plot to be rid of her husband. On the other hand, there was the evidence of his eyes. Could such utter stupefaction be feigned? Her eyes were dry, which suggested to him that she simply hadn't taken the event in yet. It was only when Mr. Appleton arrived, bursting red-faced and breathless through the door and extending his arms with a kind of wordless cry, that the tears came. She threw herself on her father's neck and sobbed till her whole body shook.

"There, my dear. Courage, courage, child. All will be well, you'll see. All will be well." He held her with awkward gentleness, his eyes meeting Fairfax's over the top of her head, where the elaborate coiffure was coming down. "Sir, this news—I am lost, quite lost . . . We must act, we must have the law—"

"I have sent to the magistrate's office," Fairfax said, and heard at that moment voices on the stair.

"And Abraham?" Mr. Appleton said. "The boy tells me he has run for it . . ."

"Abraham is nowhere to be found, sir, we know no more than that."

The constable from the magistrate's office was an elderly man, very stout and short of breath, who came in with an almost agonized deference, lifting his feet as if he were trying to float rather than sully the carpet with his boots.

"My son-in-law has been murdered, my good man," Mr. Appleton said. "My son-in-law—Hugh Mortlock, Baron Mortlock."

It was hard to tell which was greater, the pride with which Mr. Appleton pronounced the name or the reverence with which the constable greeted it.

And yet when the constable, after some brief hushed questions, went into Lord Mortlock's bedroom, he took on more authority. Crime was his trade. He was briskly unfazed by the horror of it, examining the wound, the razor, the bedclothes, even dipping a finger into the blood to see how dry it was. He asked Dr. Nimier about his examination of the dead man, acquainted himself with the layout of the rooms, and listened to the account of the levee, the razor left with the shaving tackle on the landing, and the discovery of the body. He was attentive to what Fairfax had to tell about the pills and the apparently missing bill of exchange, and took it on himself to look through the pockets of Lord Mortlock's coat.

"And this Negro person," he said at last, eyeing the corpse

through half-closed lids as if it were a painting he were trying to judge the effect of. "No one has any notion where he
might have gone?"

"There are few places for a runaway slave to go to," Mr.
Appleton said, appearing in the doorway behind him. "If he
is a runaway . . ."

"I don't know what other name to call him, sir, begging
your pardon. And it's mighty curious that he ain't to be
found, with a scene like this in his master's bedroom."

"Yes . . . I daresay," Mr. Appleton said faintly, turning his
head away. "Yet Abraham's a good boy, you know, I'd swear
to it. I brought him to England myself, and trained him up."

The constable wiped his big perspiring face with a handkerchief. "There was a row between this Negro and his lordship, you reckon, sir?" he said to Fairfax.

"Yes, but I don't know what about. There was something
about pilfering. And there was some request, I would guess,
which Lord Mortlock seemed very angry about."

"And he made threats to ship him back to where he came
from? His lordship could do that, I take it?"

"Yes," Mr. Appleton said. "On my daughter's marriage I
made over the ownership of Abraham to her husband. Hugh
could dispose of Abraham as he thought fit. A question of
property, you see."

"I see, sir. Dear me. I think there's no doubt, sirs, that we
must track this blackamoor down, and have some frank
words with him. Perhaps, sir"—he nodded at Mr. Appleton—"you might give us a description, as her ladyship's
surely not equal to it." Lady Mortlock had remained in her
bedchamber.

"But nothing is proven against Abraham," Fairfax said.
"There were others coming and going here. After Lord Mortlock retired, there were five visitors who passed this way."

"There were indeed," Dr. Nimier said. "I was one. And so
was Mr. Appleton here."

"Aye, that's true enough," Mr. Appleton said, taking the deep but tentative breath of someone who has decided they are probably not going to be sick after all. "Aye, let's not forget that."

"Well, so I shall inform the magistrate, and I'll need the names according. But you must see, sirs, that this slave is a fugitive before the law. Here's his master murdered in his bed, while the Sambo takes to his heels. I can't say how it will look to the bench, but I know how it looks to me."

"Spoken very sensibly, my friend," said Dr. Nimier, his eyes narrowing in—what? Amusement? "Well, if I am no longer needed, I will take my leave. I am to be found at Greek Street, should I be wanted."

The hairdresser, Boville, putting his timid head into the room, asked if he might be dismissed also. The constable pronouncing himself satisfied, Dr. Nimier and the hairdresser left; the constable was about to close the bedroom door softly when he stopped and examined the handle.

"As I thought," he said. "There's blood here."

"The murderer must have had blood on his hands when he left," Fairfax said.

"Just so, sir. Hands—or gloves. The black was a footman, is that so?"

"Aye—he wore gloves and livery," Mr. Appleton said. "My friend, what do you mean to do?"

"I shall report the whole matter to the magistrate, sir. My belief is that he'll order a search for this Abraham, and make out a warrant for his arrest." Glancing at Fairfax, the constable added, "You must see, sir, that finding this man must be our first concern. And now, if I might trouble you for that description . . . ?"

"Dear me, let's see . . . A Negro man of eight-and-twenty, about five feet ten inches high, broad across the shoulders, dressed in a livery coat of blue with yellow facings and buff breeches, and he has the letters 'S.A.' branded upon his right arm. Fairfax," Mr. Appleton went on, seeming not to notice Fairfax's frown, "I would go attend on the magistrate myself, but I have a duty here"—he indicated the door of Lady Mortlock's bedchamber—"a father's duty. She is quite alone. Will you go with this man and give the magistrate whatever information he needs, and find out what is to be done? I place my trust in you entirely. I shall be here, with my poor daughter, when you are done." He shook his head. "Abraham . . . I cannot quite believe it. But no matter— whoever took away the life of my son-in-law must pay the ultimate penalty."

Fairfax wished that the magistrate at Litchfield Street had been the famous "blind beak" John Fielding, whom he knew pretty well. Still, Mr. Saunders Welch, the man who presided here, had a similarly good reputation as one of the handful of fair-minded reforming justices of the capital. Also, he had an unusual background: he had been born in a workhouse, and started life as a parish apprentice. It might, Fairfax thought, make him more sympathetic to the plight of a fugitive slave, or at least not so prompt to condemn.

Sympathetic he certainly found the man, who, after being closeted some time with the constable, received him in his office-cum-study. Mr. Welch was a man in vigorous middle age, with heavy-lidded eyes that seemed to have observed a world of sorrow, and he listened attentively to everything Fairfax had to tell him. But he was at pains to point out that no amount of sympathy for Abraham Drake's predicament, or that of his fellow slaves, could make him appear less culpable in this case.

"You must consider my resources here, Mr. Fairfax. With a handful of constables, and with the hostility of much of the population, I and my fellow justices must listen to and re-solve every complaint that comes before us, from a dispute over market rights to the treatment of an apprentice by a brutal master. You have seen, no doubt, the queue of petitioners in my waiting room. And we must also somehow prevent crime from taking over the metropolis, which at times, such are the number of assaults and burglaries, robberies and affrays, seems a very likely eventuality. Now if a crime is committed and no one is caught red-handed, then we must rely on those few men, on the doubtful system of rewards for information, and on the goodwill of the public. It might be different if we had a body of police of the Continental model, but I cannot see the English ever sacrificing their liberties to that extent. So in a case like this, one must look to the likely culprit—"

"Likely, but not certain," Fairfax said. "Others were there, sir, as I have explained."

"But none fled the scene, with such apparent . . . guiltiness. Yes, that is a different thing from guilt, but we must proceed on what is likely. In any event we can do little until this slave is traced and found. If he can give a satisfactory account of himself then the matter is somewhat altered. Believe me, a crime of this kind—the murder of a man of such high estate"—a wry look touched the magistrate's face—"will be dealt with in no dismissive spirit. And in that spirit I have no choice but to make a warrant for the slave's arrest, and order that a search be made for him. There are indeed few places he could go. In the riverside districts, perhaps, he would be least conspicuous, as there are many of his race there. In the meantime I shall arrange for an inquest upon the body of the late baron for tomorrow. You know, of course, Mr. Fairfax, about the workings of the law, and how stiff-jointed they can be."

"You know me, sir?"

"Your father was the late Justice Fairfax, was he not? Mr. Fielding has mentioned you. He took an interest in your recent exploit up in Stamford—the matter of the highwayman there. You would seem to have inherited your father's astute-

ness. Perhaps also his impatience with the occasional ob-
tuseness and muddleheadedness of the law?"

"Perhaps. I know very little of this Abraham Drake, sir,
and if he is a murderer then I would not see him escape justice. But I am concerned that he should *have* justice, and I
fear that as a Negro slave he will not get it."

Mr. Welch inclined his head; impossible to tell whether
the grave and careful man agreed with him. "Well, sir, as I
have said, your qualities are known to me, and I will respect
whatever you have to tell me. *Is* there more that I should
know?"

Fairfax hesitated. The matter of his investigations as the
gentleman from Yorkshire was delicate. Lord Mortlock was
dead, but his sorrowing widow remained . . . "Well, I betray
no secrets when I say that it was a household lacking in har-
mony. As for Lord Mortlock, I knew him only the one night,
but I think he was far from an easy man—in any area of his
life."

"Hm, so one hears . . . A man likely to excite enmity, you
think?"

"Well, there was one alarming instance." He told the story
of Sir Anthony Spicer and the refused duel. "Yet Sir Anthony,
of course, was not there this morning, nor anyone known to
him, as far as I can tell. Though there was another curious
matter. Last night Lord Mortlock was in possession of a bill
of exchange for forty pounds, drawn on Martin's of Throgmorton Street. But it was not there this morning, when his
body was found."

"You are sure he brought this bill home?"

Fairfax thought back. He had, of course, dozed a while in
The Finish . . . Yet Mortlock had seemed to make a point of
keeping the bill, and he couldn't imagine him giving it away
in that place. "I'm almost positive. He was adamant about
keeping it; he made quite a parade of it when we were at
Lady Harriet Froome's. That is—her private assembly."

Mr. Welch smiled thinly. "I know of the noble lady—and her faro bank."

"Lord Mortlock seemed somewhat at odds with the man who runs the place—a great soft-spoken brute named Griffey."

"Luke Griffey. Aye, I know him well too. The faro bank is far from the worst of Griffey's activities. A thoroughgoing villain, but difficult to pin down. A great pity that our nobility will associate with this demimonde, but so they will. Pardon me, sir, but if you suspect Lord Mortlock's death came about as the result of some criminal intrigue, I must have more than this. Even if it is possible that the slave was a tool of some such intrigue, our best course remains to net him and put him to the question."

Fairfax nodded. "Very well, sir. I confess that my ideas are vague at best. And yet—"

"And yet if you should come across something germane," the magistrate said, getting to his feet, "I will, believe me, listen very readily. As I said, Mr. Fairfax, my resources are strictly limited. So consider that you always have my ear, sir, for anything not *entirely* fanciful."

Well, it was as good as he was going to get, Fairfax thought, thanking the magistrate and taking his leave. It certainly seemed that "innocent until proven guilty" was not a legal formula that applied to black slaves—the reverse, in fact. But if he were going to find Lord Mortlock's murderer, he mustn't let crusading zeal get in the way of an objective assessment of the facts.

Weary, jaded, and headachy as he was, and with few illusions about the morality of the people he was mixed up with, Fairfax nonetheless vowed it to himself as he headed back to Hill Street: he would find this killer. He was better placed than anyone; he had spent the last night and day deep within the Mortlock circle, and had seen and heard much that was suggestive and mysterious. Moreover, he could not forget the sight of the dead man: not so much the blood and horror, frightful as that was, but the sheer *purpose* about it. He had seen such things before, but never with such an atmosphere of arrogance about them. There lay the true loathsomeness — the sin, he was tempted to say — of murder: the inhuman arrogance, the horrible presumption and pride. Someone stood in the murderer's way, so they were erased. No matter what the motives of the killer — and he knew that these could be desperate, tragic, even in some way "honorable" — there was always this egotism gone out of control.

Well, Abraham Drake had certainly had reason to want Lord Mortlock "out of the way." The threat to ship him back to the plantations . . . Unenviable as his lot might be as a house servant to a demanding master, it could not compare to the purgatory of plantation labor. And yet how serious had that threat been? It had seemed to be a furious response to whatever Abraham was asking of him.

Trollops. He remembered it now — his brain must be slow from lack of sleep. *Dangling after these trollops* had been Lord Mortlock's characteristically gracious phrase. An amorous entanglement of some sort, then, of which his lordship had not approved. Rakes could often be the greatest prudes, of course, but there must have been more to it than that to have made Mortlock so angry.

At the same time he remembered what Meggy had told him about the milk seller, and how it was Abraham who always dealt with her. If the young man had a paramour, then she was surely worth approaching first of all . . . Mounting the steps to the Mortlock house once more, he noticed a chalk mark on the front doorpost: three strokes with a line across. It was common for street traders to keep a tally of their customers' purchases thus. So the knock had come some time after Lawrence had been shown up, and before Mr. Appleton's arrival — by which time Abraham was gone.

The milk seller, then, had probably been the last person to see the slave before he disappeared . . .

It was Meggy, still tearful, who answered the door to him. He took a moment to look around the hall. Near the linen chest, in a small alcove, he noticed a bentwood chair — probably, he thought, a footman's seat. Meggy confirmed it.

"Aye, that was where he took his ease, betwixt answering the door. It was her ladyship who had it put there. Pampering I call it. As if standing by wasn't good enough for a savage like him!"

"That will do, Meggy." It was Mr. Appleton, coming down the stairs. "Mr. Fairfax, step in here if you will."

They went into the dining room, large and grand enough for a banquet, but musty and chilly from disuse. Mr. Appleton, very much at home, fetched brandy from a cabinet. Well, it had very probably come out of his pocket, Fairfax thought, gratefully accepting a glass.

"I have sent for a surgeon to make a thorough examination, and a laying-out woman to clean the — to clean Hugh and be with him. Charlotte insists that she be left alone for a while. What could I do? At such times a mother's care is missed." But Mr. Appleton looked as gentle as any mother as he sipped at a little brandy and sorrowfully shook his white-wigged head. "I would have given anything to spare her such a blow, but there, 'tis vain to question Providence. Well, sir? You saw the magistrate?"

Fairfax related his interview with Mr. Welch. Mr. Appleton, normally so shrewdly attentive, seemed distracted, his eyes wandering around the lofty room and the rococo writhings of plaster and gilding.

". . . And so there will be an inquest tomorrow, and the constables are to search for Abraham Drake, sir; it seems we must wait on events."

Mr. Appleton abruptly drank off his brandy. "Perhaps. But I also know of your exploits, Fairfax. That is partly why I entrusted you with such a confidential—'mission' last night. Though of course that is by the by now."

"Is it, sir? Perhaps. But perhaps those matters you were concerned about have a bearing on this shocking event."

Mr. Appleton gazed with raised eyebrows. "You think so? Well, well . . ." Nodding, he emitted a sibilant, almost sound-less whistle through his teeth, a habit of his. "You have an-ticipated my question in a way. Do you think Abraham capable of this act? Of course you did not know him as I did. I knew him from a boy—and that makes it hard for me to see him as a murderer."

"If there were no one else who could have gone into that room then I would have to accept it. Yet as the act *could* have been committed by anyone who came and went to Lady Mortlock's levee—"

"Including myself," Mr. Appleton said with a faint smile.

"Exactly. Of course Abraham must be found, if only be-cause we do not have his account of things. But there are . . . other possibilities, yes, sir."

Sighing, Mr. Appleton let his eyes travel around the room again. "There is much to do . . . People must be informed, 'twill be the most shocking news in society. Then there is a funeral to be arranged. Hugh had no close family living, but I myself shall ensure that the occasion is all that is fitting for the scion of a noble house."

Still in love with the grandeur and consequence of it all; the human mind was remarkably resilient, Fairfax thought.

"Charlotte must not be troubled, that is my chief concern. Charlotte must be protected at all costs . . ." Mr. Appleton came sharply out of his abstraction. "Fairfax, hearken to me. I want the killer of my son-in-law found. I do not, perhaps, need to tell you how gratifying my alliance with the house of Mortlock is. It may be that my gratification was not entirely shared by Hugh himself. He was in some ways a difficult man."

Fairfax inclined his head, remembering Lord Mortlock's slighting attitude to his father-in-law.

"It may also be that—on a personal level—the match was not an entirely happy one. But to lose Hugh like this—for Charlotte to lose her husband like this—it is an outrage, sir. Will you use all your efforts, Fairfax, to discover who is responsible? That may mean flushing out Abraham. He may be our bird, and if so, then so be it; but he may not. I leave the matter in your hands."

"I shall consider it a privileged duty. But I must ask, sir, for liberties that you might not normally allow. For one thing, I will have to speak with utmost frankness with your daughter—and your son, who was also here this morning."

After a fractional hesitation Mr. Appleton nodded. "Of course. I would ask only that Charlotte be left in peace for the time being. The poor child suffers greatly, and is not to be pressed."

"Of course. By your leave, sir, I'll talk to the servants. I know the constable has examined them, but they may have been frightened in his presence."

And another person who will have to talk frankly, Fairfax thought, is you, Mr. Appleton. You are quite as much under suspicion as the others . . . After all, he thought as he went down to the kitchen, Samuel Appleton stood to gain from Lord Mortlock's death in at least one regard: there would no longer be a drain on his purse from his son-in-law's extravagances. Not that that should have been such a great difficulty for a man of Mr. Appleton's wealth . . . at least, as long as the wealth was intact. Could it be that he was in financial straits? The boom profits of war taking a plunge, perhaps, with the stirrings of peace? That was worth investigating. Unless, of course, the merchant had some other motive against his son-in-law—had discovered something so appalling that he felt compelled to put a violent end to him. Yet he couldn't imag-

ine what that would be. Mr. Appleton had seemed prepared
to hook a lord for his daughter at practically any price.

In the big stone-flagged kitchen the copper still bubbled
and there were heaps of damp linen everywhere, but un-
derstandably the servants had abandoned the laundry for
solemn-faced gossip over a dish of tea. Meggy took it upon
herself to answer Fairfax's question, or rather not to answer it.

"The milk seller? Why, she's had this milk walk for a year
or so, I'd reckon. What her name is I couldn't say. I've better things to think of than common hawkers and their doings.
She brings the milk and that's about as far as—"

"Her name's Kate Little," said the youngest and lowliest
of the maids, who looked as if she herself had been rubbed
small from scrubbing the huge pans that hung on the walls.

"Why, how should you know that?" Meggy asked with a
sniff.

"Because Abraham said. He used to talk about her." The
little maid's voice was timid.

"Did he now? Fancy," Meggy snorted. "Well, I can say to
my pride that I never listened to what that unnatural creature
had to say. Kate Little, indeed. I'll warrant she must be a
bold-faced hussy, to put up with the moonings of such a
black-faced devil as that—"

"Do you know where she is to be found?" Fairfax asked
the little maid gently.

"Her father keeps a milk cellar over by the Haymarket,
Abraham said."

"Thank you, you've been greatly helpful." Fairfax smiled.

"Hmph! Fancy you knowing such things. You'd do better
turning that mangle, I think, than listening to what don't concern you," Meggy said to the little maid acidly.

"They know most who talk the least, I often find," Fairfax
said, leaving them.

So could Abraham be hiding out with this milk seller, for

whom he seemed to have a taking? Possible, though if he were really bent on escape it was a pretty warm trail to leave. Well, Fairfax thought as he left the house, at least I will be stealing a march on the constables. And if it is only to find a cringing fugitive with blood on his hands, then so be it. Yet he hoped it would not be so, if only to prove the repulsive likes of Meggy wrong.

The brightness of the cold day surprised him, but, of course, it was not long past noon. The day felt more advanced because he had seen so much of it. A strange life he was leading! He wondered if rumor was already carrying the tidings of Lord Mortlock's death around the town, to be toyed with over the chocolate cups as the newest and most diverting sensation. A man with a bad reputation coming, it might be said, to a fittingly bad end. But then which of us, he thought, could truly say they deserved a good end? Hugh Mortlock had been a rakehell, a gambler, neglectful of his wife, and tyrannical to his servants—or so it appeared, at any rate—and seemed also to have played a dubious part in digging the grave of at least one impressionable young man. Yet Fairfax had been conscious of no brimstone whiff of evil in Mortlock's company—only the familiar scent of compromised, fallible humanity. Perhaps his senses were at fault. One thing was for sure: it was a human being who lay butchered among the brocade bed hangings at Hill Street, and neither puritan morality nor town tattle could be allowed to obscure that.

Chapter Four

He took a chair to the Haymarket. Here in the purlieus of St. James, carriages bearing coats of arms jostled for space with drays and wagons and with the lacquered sedans of high-class bawds about their business of procurement and assignation. As in most of the older London streets, there was a warren of poor alleys and yards behind the main thoroughfare, and here a sweep's boy, like a skeletal monkey, pointed him to a fetid hole called Bellman's Court, where Little's milk cellar was to be found.

The cellar served as a pointed reminder of why Fairfax avoided milk in the capital. Steep steps led down to the room, which was beneath the premises of a sausage maker. No sign advertised the cellar's trade: a rancid cheesy reek did that. Fairfax found the door at the bottom of the greasy steps ajar, and pushed it open when no one responded to his hallo. A single rush candle feebly lit the cellar room, revealing the pails, tin measures, and wooden tally sticks of the milk seller's trade, as well as a few pieces of furniture, including a narrow bed with a rag-work quilt, which might have been the only spot of color in the dingy dwelling, had it not been for an extraordinary structure that stood by the opposite wall. A few moments' scrutiny revealed this to be some sort of old showman's booth, partially dismantled and placed so as to form a partition across one side of the room. Gaudy curlicues could still be seen on the faded planking, ornamented with peeling gingerbread work, and there was a ragged curtain to which a few sequins still clung—and which, Fairfax saw now, was being held back by a gnarled hand.

"What would you have, sir? We have fine fresh milk and the very best cream . . ." The high singsong voice spoke the words mechanically. Fairfax's first thought was that the old man who came squinting and tottering out from behind the curtain was blind. A blast of gin-soaked breath corrected the impression. The man peering up into Fairfax's face, and rubbing his palm expectantly on his corduroy breeches when he saw that the visitor was likely to have money, was blind drunk, or had been. And not very old—perhaps scarce sixty—but ingrained dirt made the seams and wrinkles in his foxy face look deeper.

"What'll you have, sir? I was just taking my rest, sir, or such rest as my malady allows me, but my daughter will serve." Staggering, he gave a glowering look about the cellar. "She's here, or should be . . ."

"I have the honor of addressing Mr. Little?"

"You do, sir. You do have that honor," the man said with shaky dignity, and then, grimacing, "Leastways . . . depends who wants him, sir."

"Really I think it's your daughter I seek. If she is Kate Little, the milk seller."

"*I'm* the milk seller, sir," the man said, drawing himself up to his full shrunken height. "This is my milk cellar—and so I'm the milk seller. See?" He seemed mighty pleased with this formula. "And only the best, sir, from Jack Little's. You've heard of overwatering, and frothing milk up with snails to make it look fresh, I daresay, but there's none of that here. We deal with the houses of the quality, sir. Testimonials to that effect—"

"I believe you. But I am looking for Kate Little—"

"She should be here, ods rot her," Jack Little said, making a fierce dart around the cellar and fetching up unsteadily against the painted booth. "I thought she was here—I'll swear she was. What's she done, eh? You tell me, sir—trust me for it, I'll leather her. Plays fast and loose with me, she does, on account of my malady. 'Twas my malady obliged me to give up the traveling theatrical line, sir," he tapped the painted panels. "You admire it, I see. The finest puppet show ever to grace Southwark Fair. Signor Solera's *Fantoccini*. I kept the name, sir, after I bought the concern. And I keep the remains here out of sentiment, sir. It takes the edge off my malady—as a glass of toddy has been known to do, sir, it must be said . . ."

The old man gazed lovingly at the money Fairfax drew from his purse.

"As I said, I'm looking for Kate Little, though she's done nothing wrong, as far as I'm aware. All I want is to ask about a man she may know—"

"What, Kate? Ask me, sir. I'll know anything she does. A man, is it? Well, there's the black. He's been here. Not that anybody could want him, and so I've told her—"

"A black man? Name of Abraham?"

"Aye, that's it. Taking our good Christian names off us, an' all," Little said, spitting on the floor, and nearly toppling over with the effort.

"When was he here? Today?"

"Might well have been," the old man said, scratching his jaw and eyeing the money still in Fairfax's hand. "Might well have been today, sir—my memory lets me down, on account of my malady. But he's surely been here, dangling after Kate—Lord knows I've leathered her for it—and it could well have been today, sir. Or yesterday. Whatever pleases you, sir . . ."

Wondering how much reliance he could place on the word of this dislikable old drunkard, Fairfax handed over a shilling and was about to ask where Kate could be found when a shadow fell across the doorway.

"Here she is, idle sliving creature, never where she's wanted!" Little scuttled into his partitioned den to stow his money like a monstrous squirrel, then came back shaking a palsied fist. "And a gentleman wanting you—keeping him waiting till bull's noon . . . !"

Fairfax thought he saw a flash of alarm in the eyes of the young woman who entered the cellar, a basket over her arm. But it was quickly gone, replaced by what seemed an habitual expression of gentle, slightly sleepy placidity. Kate Little was a handsome though big-boned and slow-moving girl, with a fine fair complexion unmarked by smallpox and a mass of thick, dark brown hair that she looped up with a clean, slightly unsteady hand before coming forwards. It was easy to see why she found custom in the genteel districts, where an uncomely milkmaid would lower the tone.

"Well, where've you been?" her father snapped.

Yes, thought Fairfax, where had she been . . . ?

"Just upstairs to pay our rent, Father," she said in a deep, soft voice. "And across the way for bread. Only he'd sold out, and he's only just begun baking again." She laid the empty basket down on the rickety table.

"Useless—useless, lazy article!" Old Little shook his fist, drooling at the mouth. "Time was, sir, when I would have sat down to cold meats and best butter at this hour, and in a clean neckcloth and bands too, every time . . . You do not see me as I once was, sir," he added loftily, brushing down the stained front of his waistcoat, "not as I once was."

Strange creatures we are, Fairfax thought: vanity is always the last thing to go. "Miss Little, my name is Fairfax. I've come from the Mortlock house in Hill Street, which is on your milk walk, is it not?"

"A damn good walk; cost ten pounds to buy it," Old Little muttered.

"Hill Street. Yes, sir," his daughter said, her expression flat and unsurprised.

"Miss Little, I need your help. I act for Mr. Appleton, Lady Mortlock's father. A servant belonging to the house has gone missing. His name is Abraham Drake."

Kate Little turned and reached up to a high shelf, on which there was a stone jar. "I think there's a drop left here, Father. Yes. There's a tot for you." Having given him the jar, she moved away from her lip-smacking parent. "Abraham Drake. Yes, sir?"

"His master Lord Mortlock is killed. That is why Abraham is sought."

"Aye, I know. About Lord Mortlock."

"How?"

"Why . . . it is all round the streets. My morning milk walk finishes at Berkeley Square, sir, that's where I heard it. Someone came shouting for a doctor there. People were standing out of doors to see what was amiss. The news soon got round, sir."

Probable enough. "I see. But you do know Abraham?"

"Oh, yes, sir."

Fairfax saw Jack Little's cockerel eye swivel towards them as he maundered over his gin.

"And you have seen him today?"

"Yes—when I brought the milk to the Mortlock house this morning. I knocked as usual, and 'twas Abraham answered as usual. He took two pints, and I went on to my next house, sir."

"What time would that have been?" he said, realizing at the same moment that people of Kate Little's station had no watches or clocks, and did not reckon time very exactly.

"Midmorning, I daresay. Usual time."

"And you have not seen Abraham since?"

"Oh, no, sir."

Fairfax glanced over at her father; so, he saw, did she. But the old man was savoring his gin, eyes closed.

"Yet Abraham Drake has been here, has he not? Isn't he your sweetheart, Kate?"

Calm and stolid, she said, "We've—come to know each other pretty well, sir. He's been here sometimes. But only when he's free, sir. When he's out on errands in the afternoons, just for a little while. And sometimes of a Monday evening. His mistress would let him have Monday evenings, sir, sometimes."

That was interesting. "This was Lady Mortlock's doing?"

"Yes, sir. He was fond of his mistress, I believe."

"Was?" Fairfax said sharply. "How do you mean, was?"

She licked her lips slowly. "I don't mean nothing by it, sir."

He hesitated. He didn't like to browbeat her; it looked as if she put up with enough of that from her wreck of a father . . . Who was now, he saw, creeping towards the steps, hand tightly clenched around what he guessed was the shilling he had given him.

"Abraham," he mumbled. "Taking away our good Bible names. Dirty black-faced heathen—I've warned her, she don't listen." At the top of the steps he sniffed the air, then whined: "Cold, mortal cold. Cess and shit take it, 'tis always cold. I want my greatcoat. Where's my greatcoat?"

With the faintest of sighs, Kate said: "In the pawnshop, Father. Where you took it."

"I never did!" Little growled, swaying on the steps and offering for a moment the pleasing prospect of his tumbling down and breaking his head. "Never . . . Why, sir, look at me. Do I look like a man who's ever seen the inside of a pawnshop?"

Fairfax was spared the difficulty of answering, as the old man lurched up the steps and out of the cellar door with a last foulmouthed reference to the cold.

"When you spoke to Abraham at the door of the house today," he went on, "did he say anything of being unhappy there? Of running away, perhaps?"

"No, sir." With a bare shrug she added, "Where would he go?"

"We know he quarreled with his master. I believe the quarrel was over you."

Her round face showed no more response than if he had spoken in Latin.

"You're poor," he said. "It's plain. Did Abraham ever try to help you?"

"Well. Perhaps a little," she said after a moment. "But that's the way he is, sir. He's a good man."

"Is he? You must understand this, Kate, the importance of it. Lord Mortlock has been murdered—his throat cut while he slept in his bed. And Abraham has disappeared. You see how it appears?"

A tremor seemed to pass over her face, but all she said was, "I don't know about that, sir. All I know is Abraham is a good man."

"But if he is a runaway—and so it would appear—then that will be a hard blow for you, will it not? As you are fond of him."

Quite simply and informatively she said, "I'm accustomed to hard blows, sir. And I don't know what else I can tell you. Except that the Abraham I know is a good, kind man, quiet and thoughtful. Sometimes his feeling heart runs away with him, perhaps. But he's not a hating man, even if—" She lowered her eyes. "Even if sometimes it's a wonder he ain't."

Fairfax studied her face. "Well, you should know there is a warrant for his arrest. The constables will be looking for him. They may well also come to you. And they may press you to discover where he is."

Kate shrugged. "I can't tell you what I don't know."

Fairfax took out his purse. "Will you take this? Please?

For your time. I . . . I also gave some to your father. Which may not have been wise."

For the first time she smiled faintly. "No matter, sir. He's no better nor worse when he's—treated, so it don't signify. He'll sleep, at any rate." She went to the booth and pulled back the curtain, began tidying the frowsy bed within, then straightened and gave him a look that was again touched with a faint smile. "Pretty, ain't it? He bought it from an Italian, years ago, when I was little. It didn't last long. He hadn't quite the temper for the traveling, and the takings . . . didn't last. They were good days, though. I remember them."

As he left Bellman's Court, Fairfax's mood was grim and a little gloomy.

Kate Little might have been telling the truth; it was difficult to judge, with that impenetrable placidity. If she was not, and if she did know where Abraham was—if he had indeed come in the first instance to her—then she was hardly likely to give it away. It was plain that she did love him, and love had its own loyalties. Still, if she suspected that her man had been responsible for a horrific murder, would she still protect him? Perhaps she would . . . but he preferred to see it as another small mark on the credit side of Abraham's character.

Well, he was hardly in a position to bully it out of her, nor to mount a twenty-four-hour watch upon the milk cellar in case she could lead him to Abraham. He was stuck as far as that side of the case went. But there remained the five people who had come and gone to and from Lady Mortlock's levee, any one of whom might have taken up the razor and slipped into Lord Mortlock's room. Mr. Appleton and his son Lawrence could easily be approached, as he was living under their roof. Then there was Dr. Nimier and Stephen Pennant, Lady Mortlock's suitors, as he had come to think of them. Not that anything loverlike had passed between either of them and their hostess, as far as he could tell; yet he was sure

that the lover of whose existence Mr. Appleton had had his
suspicions was one or the other. And then, perhaps most
enigmatic of all, there was that pert, rattling, bright young
woman named Sophie Vertue. Overbright, he would have
said, as if compensating for something. Niece and ward of
Mrs. Stoddart, the Blue Stocking hostess. It was years ago
that he had gone, as a poor young scribbler, to one of her receptions, and he had felt too conscious of his obscurity and
his shiny worn sleeves to do more than squeak the odd word.
But never mind, it was time to presume upon an old acquaintance.

At Mrs. Stoddart's town house in Hanover Square he found
the ladies just returned from calling . . . some frightful German who had written about Shakespeare, he recalled Miss
Vertue saying. He found Mrs. Stoddart, at any rate, apparently refreshed from her encounter with the Teutonic scholar,
and full of agreeable reassurances that she remembered Fairfax perfectly, though she clearly didn't know him from
Adam.

"Well, my dear sir, you may know that I hold my receptions still, whenever I am in town, and whenever the
wretched state of my health permits me. I hope to see you at
my next, which will be on Monday. Johnson will be here—
that I can positively engage for."

It would be good to see his old mentor again, Fairfax
thought, thanking her, but of course all depended on the outcome of this business.

"Will you drink tea?" Mrs. Stoddart went on, ringing the
bell. "Some will not at this hour, which I think a nonsensical
affectation. Let us be natural is my premise, let us be natural
in all things."

Fairfax had stopped to eat at a cookshop on the way there,
but he gratefully accepted the offer of tea; he would need all

the stimulants he could get as his long night began to tell on him.

"My niece will join us, I'm sure. She's just this moment changing out of her morning habit—she's young, of course, and particular about such things, as Lord bless me so was I, more years ago than I care to count. Sophie, my poor late sister's child, you know her perhaps?"

"I have had the honor of meeting her just this morning," Fairfax said. "Indeed it was on that account that I wished to speak to Miss Vertue—"

"An enchanting creature, is she not? Such bloom and freshness! It is, I assure you, a very great delight to me to have her with me, though I must regret the occasion of it." Mrs. Stoddart leaned forwards confidingly. "There was never a sweeter creature than my poor sister—indeed I see her in Sophie sometimes, and cannot forbear shedding a tear—but it must be said that she lacked in prudence what she owned in beauty and tenderness of nature. She might have made any number of good matches, but her heart was captured by a man who, whatever his personal recommendations, was not of a sort to gratify an anxious parent or a solicitous friend. Mr. Vertue had much grace, ease, and address, but those things did not make him any less a dancing master, without money or connections. Heyday! they managed pretty well, all things considered, and Sophie speaks of her parents with the warmest admiration, but there's no denying that there was not the fortune or the society that there might have been. And when they died within a month of each other—estimable devotion, a true case, I believe, of breaking hearts!—some two years since, Sophie was left an orphan with only a small portion. Well, I have added what I can to it—my own chicks, you know, have flown—and to continue the avian metaphor, I have taken her under my wing. A scrawny and bedraggled sort of wing, no doubt," she concluded, laughing cheerfully, "only you're too polite to say so!"

Fairfax laughed with her, aware that some quarters of fashionable society laughed at her, not for any scrawniness, for she was a sturdy-looking woman despite her talk of her health, but rather for the way she bedizened her horsey fifty-year-old plainness with such outfits as this—a sack gown with vast hoops and layers of flounces and a headdress featuring a roll of false hair, a pompon and a medley of pearls, feathers, and jeweled ribbons. Yet, though she gave the impression of never caring about anything very deeply, there was something likable about her, as about her old-fashioned drawing room with its uncomfortable straightbacked chairs and brimming bookcases.

"I'm sure she has greatly flourished," he said. "I was struck as all were at Lady Mortlock's levee by her vivacity and charm. Unhappily—"

"Lady Mortlock—aye, that is the daughter of old Appleton, is it not, the sugar merchant? Sophie was telling me of her remarkable elevation. I remember the child but indistinctly, as a friend of Sophie's youth, but then one meets so many people. They do say, of course, that that marriage was, ahem, solemnized at the altar of Mammon rather than Venus, but then the town always talks so. For myself, I never judge. Let us each be happy in our own way, and to the devil with what others may think."

"Alas, the marriage is not to be proved one way or the other. Lord Mortlock is dead, Mrs. Stoddart, found killed in his bed this very morning."

"No! God save my soul! Oh, and his too, of course. Dear me, that news is so very shocking it has betrayed me into barbaric superstition . . . Why, he cannot have been above thirty. For myself I believe I never spoke a word with him beyond good day, but then our circles were not of the sort to touch. Quite the rakehell, they say. His father, Black Peter, I remember pretty well—he trod on my train when I was quite a youngling, at a rout in Pall Mall, and then gave me a round cursing as if 'twere my fault. Not that I minded—I learned a good many interesting new words. And I always think society would be the poorer without such originals as that; I can tolerate anything but dullness. But killed, you say? Why, who would do such a thing?"

Fairfax hesitated. "I believe there is some suspicion against a servant who has yet to give an account of himself. But nothing is certain yet. That was partly why I sought out Miss Vertue again, on Mr. Appleton's behalf, to acquaint her with the news, and to discover whether she can recall anything from this morning that may help—"

"Oh, I'll warrant you Sophie will have marked anything unusual—she is prodigiously observant. If it had been me you would be out of luck; my sight is shorter than a mole's nowadays. It has its advantages, you know—my coach takes me past the most hideous slums and ash heaps, and I see only a vaguely pleasant prospect of hills!" Mrs. Stoddart laughed heartily and began pouring the tea, which had been brought by a yawning footman with his stockings half down. "But dear me, Sophie will be quite distressed—for her poor friend, I mean."

"She was not, I gather, acquainted with Lord Mortlock himself."

"Not that I know of, but then it is not my habit to direct her acquaintance. Very remiss of me some might say, but I say no: let young minds breathe and blow and take root in whatever soil they fancy. We are far too anxious to protect our young from mistakes, it seems to me. Without accident and mischance life would be utterly mechanical! A mistake can be quite as fruitful as something dully designed. Why, you know that half of Shakespeare's most piquant lines are probably misreadings from corrupt texts. The freedom I allow Sophie, you know, is only the self-responsibility that any rational creature must possess. I only play the deus ex machina and swoop down from the wings when absolutely

necessary. I instance when we were at Bath last season. I
gave Sophie quite as much liberty as she could desire — and
'twas a kindness, after all, for I was much occupied with
treatments for my health. I trusted her to choose her own society, and to act according to the principles that her own good
sense and natural feeling dictated. Now some might say I
was wrong, as it came to my ears at last that she was getting
herself talked about. Aye, some unsuitable attachment, conducted without the propriety and ceremony that society
somewhat irrationally demands. She did not wish to speak of
it to me when I questioned her — as was her entire right —
but I had her assurances that nothing immoral had taken
place. I saw that youth and inexperience had led her perhaps
to avowals that she might regret, and deemed the best course
was to take her away, enlarge her views, afford her a variety
of prospects, and let remembrance take its chance with novelty. So we went to Bristol Hotwell, and then on up to Scarborough, and at last back to town. I made no stipulations
about correspondence. Sophie and I have remained the best
of friends, and I still place no proscriptions on her. I believe,
you know, that I acted rightly after all, though some who
have more tyrannous notions of guardianship would not
agree."

So Miss Vertue had got herself into some romantic entanglement at Bath . . . He remembered Lawrence Appleton
saying at the levee, in his tactless fashion, that there had been
some talk about her. But where did that leave her in relation
to Lord and Lady Mortlock?

He looked up to see Sophie herself coming in, her already
round eyes widening further at the sight of him. Breathless
eyes, he thought, if there could be such a thing.

"My dear, here is a gentleman with the most dreadful
news," Mrs. Stoddart said eagerly. "He has come from Lord
Mortlock's house —"

"Mr. Fairfax, we had the most delicious music there this

morning, did we not? How do you do, sir? I did not think to
see you again. Mr. Fairfax, you must know, Aunt, played
most brilliantly with Mr. Pennant—the gentleman I was
telling you of who leads the music at Ranelagh and who has
written an opera and, oh, an oratorio on the story of Ruth, and
it is the most affecting thing—"

"Aye, child, I quite thirst to hear it. I am devoted to music,
you know, Mr. Fairfax, and a few years since I was invited to
contribute some verses for a scena to be set by Mr. Handel,
only he died before . . . But my dear, you will never believe—Lord Mortlock is killed, and your poor friend a
widow. Is it not the most shocking thing, and will you have
tea?"

Sophie Vertue went sensationally white, then flushed to
the roots of her hair. There were young ladies who cultivated
blushing as an art form, but Fairfax had never seen such a
startling change of color before.

"How killed?" she said faintly, sinking into a seat.

"Lord Mortlock was found in his bedchamber with his
throat cut," Fairfax said. "It was not a suicide."

Sophie looked at her hands. "Well. Nothing could be
worse than that. A suicide, I mean . . . Yes, tea, I thank you,
Aunt. Self-slaughter is the most dreadful end, though, is it
not? For one knows that in that case the poor wretch left the
world in despair, which is so—"

"Aye, my dear, very true for the moderns, though one
must not forget that for the ancients, and the Romans of the
Republic especially, suicide was frequently a noble act for
which a man was highly honored," Mrs. Stoddart said, pouring tea.

Extraordinary creatures, Fairfax thought: they could turn
anything into a debate.

"This appears nothing less than cold-blooded deliberate
murder," he said, watching Miss Vertue carefully. "Which I
think is bad enough. He was found just before noon, and had

been killed, it seems, while Lady Mortlock's levee proceeded in the next room."

"Poor Charlotte!" Miss Vertue said, after a deep drink of tea. "Not even married half a year, and now she must put on widow's weeds. I feel for her most dreadfully. How does she bear up?"

"She is greatly shocked, of course. Mr. Appleton is with her. I am dispatched to discover what I can—"

"But who can have done such a deed? A man lying innocently in bed—I never heard anything so monstrous!" Sophie cried.

"It makes one shudder indeed, like Hamlet's father murdered sleeping in his orchard: 'Sent to my account with all my imperfections on my head,'" Mrs. Stoddart said, quoting in a deep, rolling voice.

"The question of who could have done it is one I am charged with answering," Fairfax said, "and to that end—"

"And also *why,* surely," Sophie said. "Why would anyone want to kill Lord Mortlock? I know of his reputation, of course. But I am sure he cannot have been as bad as report would have it. Indeed, I'm convinced of it."

"There is some suspicion—unfounded as yet—on the black footman at the Mortlock house, name of Abraham Drake, who has disappeared. I wonder, Miss Vertue, whether—"

"Yes, I recall him. He showed me upstairs—very civil I thought. He used to be at the Appletons', did he not? Why, the poor creature, what can he have been thinking of? They will hang him—"

"That may be, though I've read that some of these tropical natives, when faced with the certain prospect of execution, can will themselves by trance into an easeful death," Mrs. Stoddart said, while Fairfax wondered if it were possible ever to finish what you were saying in this company. "I have the volume somewhere . . ."

"And when you left the levee, Miss Vertue," he said, almost shouting to make his voice heard, "was Abraham at his station in the hall?"

"Why, certainly, and opened the door for me very civilly, I think . . . Lord, I hope this poor creature is not suspected simply because he is black, sir! You cannot be so barbarous in your views—"

"I have no views, and seek only information," Fairfax said firmly, doing a little interrupting of his own. "A man is dead, and someone in that house this morning killed him."

To his surprise Sophie Vertue's great eyes filled with tears, which she made no movement to wipe. "What a terrible word—'dead'—and what a terrible world it is!"

"You never met Lord Mortlock, I think?" Fairfax said.

"Never. And now never will . . . What a world . . ." Wistfully blinking her wet eyes, Sophie drank tea.

"Aye, a world of tears," Mrs. Stoddart said briskly, "and divines would have it that this is because of the Fall, and no other. But surely, without going to the lengths of the Frenchman who wished to see the last king strangled with the entrails of the last priest, one may say that we humans have *made* it so—"

"Did Charlotte love him?" Sophie said to Fairfax, abruptly.

"I knew the Mortlocks but recently," he said as honestly as he could after a surprised moment. "So I can't say."

"I hope she did. Because love remembered, though lost, is a great resource—don't you think, Mr. Fairfax?"

"I think it is better retained. Well, if you can think of nothing else that may help, Miss Vertue—"

"I wish I could. But of course you know I was not the only one there today, sir. There was quite a gathering of company, not that they were people I knew at all well. Young Lawrence, of course, I remember from when Charlotte and I were girls, a dear awkward creature . . ."

"Mr. Pennant?" Fairfax said. "You were acquainted with him before?"

"I believe I had met him, briefly, in some connection. I am quite an enthusiast for introductions, you know. I find people so vastly interesting that I sometimes wish I could meet everyone in the world which is sheer nonsense of course—"

"You did not know Dr. Nimier, however?"

"I never met him before today. But I was most struck with him—he seems to have the most brilliant mind, don't you think, sir?"

No, Fairfax wanted to say: he had found Nimier altogether too pleased with himself, and he liked to think that his own mind was at least equal to that of the overbearing charlatan . . .

"Nimier?" Mrs. Stoddart said. "Why, the man is everywhere. 'Tis since the Princess Augusta took him up, though his list of fashionable clients does not stop there, by all accounts."

"You have consulted Dr. Nimier yourself, Mrs. Stoddart?" Fairfax said.

Mrs. Stoddart hooted with laughter. "Not I. He don't deal with my sort of ailments, sir, from what I've heard. Intimate and confidential, I think, are the words that describe his type of practice. Of course that's only rumor, but then if his dealings *are* intimate and confidential, no one will talk of them openly, will they?"

"Mr. Pennant made reference to a pamphlet war with another quack . . . ?"

"Aye, I remember it. Took a very nasty turn. Both were puffing some patent medicine of their devising, and accusations flew. I believe the rival went so far as to say that Nimier's nostrum was more likely to kill than cure, not an uncommon slander, but Nimier took it amiss, and they do say it came to a duel at last."

"What became of the rival?"

"That I don't know, but Nimier seems to rule the roost alone now, at any rate." Mrs. Stoddart blinked her short-sighted eyes at him. "Why, my dear sir, you must be considering Lady Mortlock's guests this morning in the light of *suspicion*. How very awful and diverting! Sophie, my dear, *you* have not turned murderess, I hope?"

"Oh, Aunt, we mustn't joke about such things," Sophie said with an earnest look. "Think of poor Charlotte."

"Oh, but I do indeed. We must send her something—I have a volume somewhere of rational reflections by the best philosophes that I found a great comfort when Mr. Stoddart expired. And you, my dear, you should go and see her as soon as may be, for your vitality, I am sure, would cheer anyone's spirits—"

"No," Sophie said, with a sharp agitation, Fairfax thought. "No, Aunt, I could not—I think I had best not intrude just yet."

"Well, I have intruded here long enough," Fairfax said. "I am to be found at Mr. Appleton's at Leicester Fields, Miss Vertue, if you should think of anything that may be of help."

Unfair thoughts, as he came away from Hanover Square—comparisons between the life led by Sophie Vertue and that led by Kate Little. Leisure, comfort, and amusement on one side; labor, poverty, and dullness on the other. If they had anything in common, he thought, feeling himself growing strict, it was the vacancy where parental support and responsibility ought to be. He liked Mrs. Stoddart, but he did not think he would like to be a young person in her care—or rather, he would probably like it too much. Mrs. Stoddart's shortsightedness, he thought, was more than physical. And that diffuse, careless kindness was no kindness at all if it meant allowing her young ward to go off and hurt herself all she liked.

This business of an affair—an indiscretion, perhaps, was the term—at Bath last season . . . He would have dis-

missed it but for the knowledge that Lord Mortlock had
been at Bath last season also. It was where Charlotte Appleton had met him, and been whisked into marriage by her
eager parent: September, he recalled Mr. Appleton saying,
had been when they had returned to town with the engage-
ment in the bag (not that that had been Mr. Appleton's
term). Could it be that Sophie too had met Lord Mortlock
that season, and that there had been an affair, an involvement of some kind?

Well, Sophie was plainly an ardent and impressionable
girl, and Hugh Mortlock did not have a reputation for scrupu-
lous conduct. It was not beyond possibility to imagine it . . .
Then Mrs. Stoddart, belatedly awakening to the fact that her
niece was the subject of gossip, had taken her away on a tour
of various other healthful spots, only returning this week to
London. Where Sophie would discover that Lord Mortlock
was married, and to a girl who was her old schoolfellow but
was far her superior in fortune . . .

A jealous fit, then? The rage of a young disappointed
heart, beating in the breast of a girl whose hectic emotional-
ism was not only plain to see but had also been plainly en-
couraged by her upbringing? Fairfax realized that his
thoughts had led him to supply a motive for Sophie Vertue to
have gone into Lord Mortlock's room and cut his throat. All
that was needed now was to imagine her actually doing it . . .
and he couldn't, quite. There was definitely some conceal-
ment about Miss Vertue, for all that fresh-faced candor, and
there had surely been something pointed and insinuating
about some of her remarks to Lady Mortlock at the levee.
But he couldn't find a firm platform for suspicion of her as a
killer.

But she had thrown some light on his task in another way.
Finding out the *why,* as she had said, was crucial—perhaps,
indeed, it was his only way of proceeding in this case. Because all of the people who had left the levee could equally

have done the deed; there were no vexed questions of alibis and whereabouts, as far as he could tell. Perhaps the murderer had counted on that. It made investigation mighty difficult.

At the Crown and Anchor in the Strand he asked where he might find Stephen Pennant, and the various fiddlers, pipers, and singers who gathered there treated him to the sort of answers that probably appeared very witty after half a day's hard drinking (on the moon, up a tree, under the table with the bishop), until a crab-faced German correcting a score on a table swimming with ale gave him the information he wanted.

Ranelagh: the most genteel of London's pleasure gardens. He went there by water, taking a boat from Exchange Stairs. Ranelagh, like its more rackety rival, Vauxhall, was the venue for concerts, balls, firework displays, and ridottoes, as well as a public resort where anyone who could afford the half-crown entrance ticket could stroll in the evening among the lantern-festooned trees, mingle and gawp, and try to guess which were the fine ladies and which the courtesans. At this time of day the gardens with their gimcrack "Chinese" buildings looked a little forlorn, with only a couple of gardeners repairing hedges and gathering litter. The place Fairfax wanted was the circular hall called the Rotunda. For sixpence a yawning attendant overcame his reluctance to let him in.

The great round room, one hundred and fifty feet across, empty as it was, lent a fine acoustic to the orchestra rehearsing on the central dais. A pity, Fairfax thought, they would not be heard to such good effect when the Rotunda was filled with company, who, in between taking tea in the arched side boxes, would promenade round and round the floor in their finery. The effect, both visually and aurally, would not be unlike a cattle market.

Stephen Pennant was leading the orchestra, a small ensemble of strings, oboes, and horns, from the harpsichord. Fairfax knew that rehearsals were a rare luxury for London musicians, who sometimes performed a new piece on their first sight of it, but a glance at the other figure on the dais told him why this extra care was being taken. He recognized the porcine features of Mrs. Benaglio, a singer of great renown and greater girth. She had tyrannized opera stages for many years now, and was no more young than slim; if you knew Italian, the words of the Handel aria she was singing could only raise a gray smile — they were the sighs of a maiden pining away to a shade for love of a shepherd. The voice was still intact though, and so, judging by the anxious concentration of the musicians, was Mrs. Benaglio's notorious temper. Fairfax sat down to listen next to a tiny man who introduced himself in a whisper as the singer's husband. That would be her fourth or even fifth, Fairfax reckoned. Perhaps she smothered them turning over in bed.

"Bravo! Bravo, *carissima*!"

The singer was all smiles as her husband led the applause. Then Stephen Pennant, standing up at the keyboard, made the mistake of mildly suggesting that they run over the da capo passage again. The stamp of Mrs. Benaglio's foot made the music stands rattle. She stomped, protesting, off the dais, her husband jumping to his feet with a shawl and a flask at the ready.

The interruption gave Fairfax his opportunity. While the singer sulked, he waved Pennant over.

"Why, Mr. Fairfax, damn you for a closefisted old lickpenny, could you not wait and pay your half-crown to come in this evening? Well met again, sir," Pennant laughed, shaking his hand. "Not that people *listen* in the evenings, devil take 'em. 'Tis all one jabbering, chattering, fan-rattling gallimaufry and you may as well be playing to a set of monkeys."

"A look from Mrs. B. should silence them . . . Mr. Pennant, might I speak with you privily?"

"Eh? Oh, surely, sir. Step in here. Aye, she's a Tartar," Pennant said, leading him into one of the side boxes, "and I'd gladly strangle her if my hands were big enough. I swear that necklace she's wearing is made up of the severed cods of all her husbands." Pennant licked his lips and gave Fairfax a covert, speculative look. "You have a message for me, perhaps, sir?"

"A message? No . . . I bring news of an unhappy sort. Lord Mortlock is dead."

He left it at that for the moment, and watched the young man's face. Pennant started, then frowned and glared at Fairfax, almost as if he were angry with him.

"Damn you, what do you mean by such a jest?"

"I would be damnable indeed if I could jest about such a thing. Lord Mortlock was killed this very morning—struck down with his own shaving razor while he slept."

As he related the tale, he admitted to himself that Stephen Pennant looked genuinely horror-struck. Shocked at the deed; or shocked that Fairfax had come to question him about it?

"Dear God . . . How is she? Lady Mortlock?"

"She is—as you would expect."

Pennant nodded, then glanced over in sharp irritation at the dais, where the violinists were amusing themselves playing a jaunty jig. "Well, I can only say that I am sorry, though I hardly knew the man. Dear God."

"You know Lady Mortlock rather better, I think."

After a dry-mouthed moment, Pennant said, "What do you mean by that, sir?"

Fairfax shrugged. "Only what I say."

"Look you here, Fairfax, I'm not a fool. You must have your reasons for bringing this to me—"

"You were at the house this morning when Lord Mortlock

was killed. Also . . . you seemed to expect a message a moment ago, which suggests that you are—concerned in that quarter. I don't know, Mr. Pennant—I know nothing except what I am told."

He held the young man's gaze for some moments. At last Pennant shifted and with something like a pout said, "Well, I daresay. 'Tis just a damnably odd flabbergasting sort of thing to fling at a man when he's peacefully making music . . . And as for telling you anything, my friend, there's simply nothing to tell. Aye, I was there this morning right enough, but I certainly didn't take a razor to Hugh Mortlock. Why, what sort of monster do you think I am, to go cutting the throat of a man I hardly know?"

"You have been, I think, quite a frequent visitor to the Mortlock house? Your reception there would seem to suggest it, and—"

"Aye, and what if I have? Lady Mortlock's fond of music, and I supply it and conduct the odd lesson. I'm asked to play at half a dozen houses. Why, man, this is a base insinuation and—"

"I was going to ask, as you had been often at the house, what you knew of Abraham Drake, the footman who went missing this morning."

"The black?" Frowning, Pennant began to cool a little. "Well, I have seen him often enough. Never paid much heed to him, in truth."

"You noted nothing unusual about him this morning?"

"Not I. 'Twas he showed me upstairs as usual, and then later old Appleton comes in saying the black wasn't at his post, as you know yourself, and I saw no more of him. If he's the man you're after, you know, I can't help you. I wouldn't know him if he passed me in the street. Mighty barbaric how the West Indian merchants treat these fellows, no doubt, and all the rest of it, but upon my honor 'tis not my affair." He glanced over his shoulder. "It looks as if madam grampus is ready to resume . . . You'll forgive my shortness, Fairfax, but in truth no man likes to be accused—"

"I was clumsy, I think," Fairfax said, thinking: *But I have accused you of nothing.* "It is a most tragic and perplexing matter, and of course Mr. Appleton is desperately anxious, on his daughter's behalf, to have it resolved. I won't keep you— if you could just tell me about this young man, Richard Spicer. I have heard his name mentioned in connection with Lord Mortlock more than once now."

"Spicer? Well, there's another tragedy if you like. As I said this morning, I was at school with him and had seen him here and there since he came to London. Oh, 'tis an old story: a young man turned loose in the city with a little money and grand notions about cutting a figure as a rake-hell. I thank God, you know—and this may sound deuced holy and conceited, but never mind—I thank God for making me musical. Because it fixed me on something. Aye, I've lived it high in my time, but never as an end in itself. That's the worst thing about that way of living, it seems to me: not that it's dissipated, but that there's nothing to it. Dicing and drinking and whoring just for the sake of it—'tis poor thin stuff to make a life out of," Pennant said, rubbing his fingers and thumb together expressively, "poor thin stuff indeed."

Thinking of the bleary, dreary morning he had spent with Lord Mortlock in The Finish, Fairfax had to agree.

"I'd heard Spicer was living beyond his means, and was seen about with Mortlock. No great wonder in that: the man was supposed to be the prince of rakes, and a young rip like Spicer would surely want to attach himself . . . Well, on Tuesday morning a cow keeper going home found the poor fellow lying in a shady spot in St. James's Park with a pistol by his side and a ball in his brain. There was no suicide note or anything like that. All that was known was that he'd come to his lodgings in the small hours of

Tuesday morning, spoken to his landlady a little, and then
said he was going out again. There was no money on him
and his rooms were chiefly furnished with creditors'
bills . . . An old story, as I said: it came out at the inquest
yesterday. They summoned me because there was a half-
written letter to me among his effects—a begging letter,
alas—and there was really no one else to deal with matters
in the first instance. His friends in London were of the fair-
weather variety, I think, and his only family was an old
uncle out in the country who had to be sent for. I saw him
at the inquest—a doughty old squire of the Roger de Cov-
erley sort. Seemed quite broken up."

"Sir Anthony Spicer."

"That's the name. Well, you know of the matter, obviously," Pennant said, looking faintly displeased.

"Only in part. Thank you, Mr. Pennant. My apologies
again for disturbing you. You have had your fill of shocking
news of late, I daresay."

"Aye, 'twas a sad waste, a sad shameful waste," Pennant
said reflectively, and then, jumping to his feet, "Not that I
saw a great deal of Spicer, you know. Different circles."

"Where can I find you, if need be?"

Pennant stared at him. "St. Martin's Lane, by the sign of
the Grapevine," he said at last. "If need be, sir. But I can't see
how the need will arise."

His face was remarkably cold when it stopped being imp-
ish and twinkling, Fairfax thought. And as if he knew it, Pennant halted on his way to the dais and smiled.

"By the by, sir, have your interrogations taken in Miss
Vertue, that charming creature who was there this morning?
Lucky fellow, if so. She is the most enchanting angel there
ever was, don't you think, sir?"

"Miss Vertue is charming, indeed, though I know her but
slightly. You rest your judgment on a more intimate acquaintance, perhaps?"

But Pennant only repeated, with an airy smile, "Enchanting angel, enchanting!" and went back to the orchestra.

He was not smiling as he sat down at the harpsichord, however, and Fairfax doubted that Mr. Handel had ever written such a thundering discord as that which Stephen Pennant crashed out on the keyboard as he left the Rotunda.

Chapter Five

Masks: a world of masks, Fairfax thought as he disembarked at Exchange Stairs and walked up to the Strand. The people he was dealing with breathed subterfuge, subtlety, dissembling, and artifice. What held society together, after all, but an elaborate system of seeming? You proclaimed yourself the obedient servant of someone you despised, you professed yourself ravished by an evening of thumping dullness, you presented your sincerest compliments and made your humblest apologies . . .

As if in eloquent illustration of his thoughts, a grand lady was stepping down from her carriage at the door of a mantua maker's. The hoops of her skirt were so vast that she had to push it out of the carriage before her; the stays were laced so tight across her bodice that her bosom was just under her chin. Her hair was frizzed and teased and powdered ice-blue. Her face was white with lead paint and dotted with felt patches, she wore false eyebrows of mouse skin, and she was variously hung about with jewels, fan, flowers, muff, and reticule, all of which left her about as much freedom of movement as a set of fetters.

There was a real flesh-and-blood person underneath there, somewhere, Fairfax thought. But, as with the people he had met today, the real person was not easy to get at. Pennant was the same; for all his frank openhanded manner he was giving nothing away. Not consciously, at any rate, but Fairfax felt he had had some revealing glimpses. If he had to lay a bet on the identity of Lady Mortlock's lover, he would put his money on Stephen Pennant.

A simple love triangle? Perhaps. But there was also the matter of Spicer, the luckless would-be rake. The young man's uncle had been plain about where he placed the blame for his nephew's end. Did Spicer's friend, Stephen Pennant, harbor a similar bitterness? He had spoken as if they were not very close, but that might have been pure policy. Whatever the truth, it was easy to find abundant reasons for Stephen Pennant to have killed Lord Mortlock.

As for the Spicer business, he wondered if there was more to that than he knew. The verdict of the inquest had been suicide. Were there no suspicious circumstances surrounding young Spicer's death, which had been so swiftly followed by that of the man who had been his gambling companion and, it seemed, corrupter?

Fairfax's fingers had been toying with the slips of paper in his pocket for some minutes before he realized what they were. Sir Anthony Spicer's cartel — the formal challenge that Lord Mortlock had refused. Taking them out, he found that the address was still intact: *The George and Blue Boar, Holborn.*

The writing was shaky, and Fairfax felt a keen pang of pity for the fierce little man as he made his way to Holborn. Another pang, when a chambermaid showed him down the endless creaking passages of the great inn to Sir Anthony's room, where he found the man sitting by a cold grate, his arms loose by his sides, his gaze hollow and incurious. The room with its old box bed and musty paneling was a cheerless place, the afternoon light leaking dimly through the leaded panes.

"Sir Anthony, I wonder if I might speak with you. We have met but briefly; my name is Fairfax."

Sir Anthony gave him a mild and absent look. "A mistake, perhaps, sir," he said. "I know scarcely anyone in London."

"Last night. Lady Harriet Froome's house at Covent Garden. I—"

"Oho, I have it!" Immediately transformed, Sir Anthony was on his feet, the bristling terrier again. "You were with that highborn rapscallion Mortlock, I remember now. Well, sir, what is it? Hey? Has the brute decided to accept my challenge, is that it? I would like nothing better—ods bobs, I am ready whenever he chooses—name the time and place, sir, where I may have my satisfaction . . ."

Fairfax held up his hand. "It is nothing of that sort. Lord Mortlock can make no challenges. He is dead, Sir Anthony, killed this morning."

Sir Anthony stared at him, lips trembling. After a moment he went unsteadily to the table, where a brandy bottle and a solitary glass stood.

"I am anticipated, then. I am not sorry," he said in a low voice. Brandy slopped onto the warped oak as he poured. "I am not sorry, sir. If you are his friend then I—I should not perhaps say it in your hearing. But I can't help it. And to be frank, if you *are* the man's friend, then—then the worse for you, sir."

"I knew him a little," Fairfax said, in some perplexity. His friend? Not really, but it was a melancholy reflection to think that there was no one the dead man could call a friend. "Sir Anthony, Lord Mortlock is murdered. He leaves a young widow."

"I pity her," Sir Anthony said, drinking deep and gasping. "On all counts. Who killed him?"

"That we do not know. But—"

"But justice must be served, eh? Well, I thank you for the information, sir. It is of great—great interest to me." He gave a glassy smile. "You surely cannot expect me to howl vengeance for Mortlock's blood. You know well that I sought to spill it myself."

"Under the conditions of a duel, which, quibbles aside, are very different from the cold-blooded way Lord Mortlock met his death. Someone cut his throat as he slept."

The little man was breathing heavily. "I won't weep for him, Mr. What's-your-name. Don't expect it. 'Twas a cowardly act, no doubt. But there, he played a coward's part with me last night, did he not?"

Fairfax held his eyes. "Did he?"

Sir Anthony set the glass down with a bang and wandered over to the window. Iron-shod wheels and hooves on the yard below made a constant commotion. "So, I am suspected of this horrid crime, am I? I am a little old to be turning housebreaker, but I will state my case, if the law wants me."

"There is no question of that. Someone who was in the house at the time must have been responsible. But I am investigating Lord Mortlock's death, and I would esteem it a favor if you could clear up certain matters for me. I'm sorry to press upon a painful point, but they concern your nephew."

"Why, what do you know of Richard?" Sir Anthony said hotly, tossing his head.

"Nothing, or very little. Yet I keep hearing his name."

Sir Anthony emptied his brandy glass and went over to a small trunk. He lifted the lid and gazed into it. Fairfax saw a few clothes and papers.

"These were his effects. They amount to very little." The little man frowned, his lips working convulsively. "I bury him tomorrow morning. Then, I suppose, I travel back to Hertfordshire. My place is at Riseley. The estate has been in the family for many generations and I seldom leave it. Very quaint and rustic it would seem, I daresay, to people of fashion, but I cherish it all the more for that."

Fairfax realized with an unpleasant start that Sir Anthony must see him as just such a person: he had been in the company of Lord Mortlock, and he was still dressed in the dandified suit he had worn for the occasion.

"I had hoped that Richard would, after a long and well-spent life, at last lay his bones down at Riseley, as I shall do. Instead I must put him in a city plot, and go home . . . And that's the end of Richard."

"He was your heir?"

"Aye, aye. My heir," Sir Anthony said quietly. "I have been a widower many years, without children. The baronetcy dies with me, of course, but my estate and fortune would have gone to Richard, as my nearest kin. He was my brother's child. He was orphaned at fourteen and so I stood guardian to him. Through a friend I procured him a post with the East India Company when his schooling was done. Richard was eager, and I thought it promised well, for he needed perhaps some—some settled course to steady him. But he did not take to it, and against all my persuasions came back to London and commenced living the life of a . . . I suppose the word should be 'gentleman.' A life of folly and peril, I would say." Sir Anthony stooped and lifted a coat from the trunk. It was of brown velvet with gold frogs and embroidered tails. One sleeve was torn at the seam, and there were dark stains along the back. Seeing Fairfax's grimace, Sir Anthony said, "No, no. This is the coat he was wearing when he was found, but that is dirt. The ground was muddy in St. James's Park, I would hazard." He laid the coat back in the trunk. "For the rest, it is mostly tradesmen's bills and notices of debt. How quickly, sir, a man may dig himself into this pit . . ."

"Did Richard appeal to you for relief?"

Sir Anthony did not look at him. "He commonly drew on

my credit, knowing that my name is good for a great deal. But there were also direct appeals, which I was not always able to satisfy. At least, my hope was to bring him round to an understanding that he could not go on living like this." Sir Anthony slammed the lid of the trunk shut violently. "My hope was vain."

Fairfax did not exactly see it all, but he had a fair notion of what Richard Spicer had been about. "Living off the reversion" was the usual term for it. Baldly, it meant spending the money that would be his when his uncle died.

"I know that we make our own choices in life. But a young man of good qualities does not become an abandoned wastrel without some devilish encouragement. I knew Mortlock's reputation. My heart misgave me when his name appeared in my nephew's letters. When I came to London, a very few inquiries confirmed my suspicion, that Mortlock had made a hapless protégé of Richard, and paved the path to his ruin. At the inquest I heard that he had spent his last night in company with Mortlock, at the house of that vicious peeress in Covent Garden. That hired ruffian of hers was there to testify. Aye, says he, Mr. Spicer honored our establishment with a visit that night—bah, the stink of it! Corruption in powder!"

"But Richard, I understand, stayed much later at the gambling house than Lord Mortlock on Monday night."

"What of it? More time to be fleeced in."

"Hm. And he lost that night? Griffey said so?"

"Lost? Of course he lost! No one wins at those damnable places. It was, I fancy, one loss too many. Sunk in debt as he was . . ." Sir Anthony sat down heavily. "And so he walked into St. James's Park and took his own life. I was sent for: an old schoolfellow of Richard's met me. He had been doing what he could."

"Stephen Pennant."

"Aye. I wish Richard had had more such friends . . . So,

the inquest declared him a suicide. Of course, it could not say
murder—not the indirect kind of murder that I saw behind it.
You think me wild, exaggerated in my suppositions. Well,
perhaps. I confess I was a little unmanned when I came to
that gaming den last night. But I did blame Mortlock. I believe—I firmly believe—that things would not have been as
they were without that man's baleful influence. Oh, yes; he
may have left earlier on Monday night, but he was not done
with Richard yet. Because Richard met him again, at a place
called Bob Derry's Cyder Cellar." Sir Anthony made a face
of distaste. "The potman of this—this establishment testified
at the inquest. Richard had come in at about one in the morning, and sat with Mortlock. The fellow thought Richard gave
him a note of some kind."

Fairfax's pulse quickened. "A note?"

"Something like that. It must have been some form of
promise to pay. He surely numbered his corrupter among
his creditors. A man of Mortlock's means must have been
able to prime the pump in that way. No doubt he'd always
get his investment back—from that creature at Covent
Garden."

"Lady Harriet Froome."

"Naturally. From what I have heard, and from what I
have seen, Mortlock was no better than a procurer. He
brought foolish young men to her gaming table, and received—well, payment in return." Sir Anthony sniffed.
"Her favors. I speak only of hearsay now, but it appears
mighty probable. Well, 'tis of no account to me now.
Richard is gone, and . . ."

"Lord Mortlock also."

Sir Anthony nodded. "Perhaps you should not be surprised, sir. If ever there was a man to make enemies . . ."

True enough, thought Fairfax, but whose was the enemy
hand that had wielded the razor? It could not have been that
of Sir Anthony, whose hatred of Hugh Mortlock was open

and undisguised. But Sir Anthony had given him tantalizing food for thought, all the same.

"Might I ask you one more question, Sir Anthony? It is an odd but not an idle one. Do you have any dealings with one Martin's of Throgmorton Street?"

Sir Anthony stared. "Yes. They are brokers of good repute: I occasionally draw a bill on them. Why?"

Before Fairfax could speak there was a knock at the door.

"I beg your pardon for intruding, sir. I wouldn't think of it, only . . ." The plump, motherly lady hesitated, seeing Fairfax.

"Come in, Mrs. Lyme. What is it? This, sir, is Richard's landlady. The last person to see my nephew alive, I believe," Sir Anthony said with a harsh smile.

"A very pleasant young gentleman," Mrs. Lyme said, performing a nervous curtsy. "I shall be lucky to find another such to take my rooms, I'm sure. That is — when I . . ."

"Never mind, Mrs. Lyme. You must live, you know. We must all live," Sir Anthony said bleakly.

"That's so, sir, you're in the right of it, and 'tis only on account of that matter that I make so bold as to trouble you . . ." Mrs. Lyme's fluttering hands fiddled with the strings of her lace cap. Then she folded them in front of her, taking a deep breath. "'Tis the matter of the rent, sir. The rent that's outstanding on Mr. Richard's account. If it were a small amount, I'd gladly . . . Only he was much in arrears, sir. He was very apologetic about it when I — the last time I saw him, poor gentleman. But he said he simply hadn't a penny to give me. And now . . ."

"What is the sum, Mrs. Lyme?" Sir Anthony said, taking out his purse.

"Four pounds and eight shillings, sir," she said faintly.

In silence Sir Anthony counted out the money into a pile on the table, then walked away from it.

"There," he said, looking out of the window. "Please, take it, madam."

"Thank you, sir. I wouldn't think of presuming, only—only as a lone and unprotected woman . . ."

Sir Anthony waved a hand. "Please, please. You will not be the last creditor I shall have to satisfy, Mrs. Lyme."

"Ma'am, may I ask you—that night when Mr. Spicer came home, how did he seem?" Fairfax said.

"Why, I can't say, sir," the woman said, hastily slipping the money into the pocket of her apron. "I declare I don't like to think about it."

She didn't mind thinking about the money, though. "Please try."

"Well, 'twas as I told the inquest. He'd been out since before noon, and came home at about two in the morning—I was astir, as it happened, on account of my dyspepsia. Shocking it is, it starts here, and goes round in a circle . . ."

Waiting up to dun your tenant for rent, Fairfax silently amended. "Go on."

"Well, he came in and greeted me pleasantly enough, and said he wouldn't be able to oblige me with the rent as he hadn't a penny in the world. As an unprovided gentlewoman under the necessity of letting her chambers to keep body and soul together, sir, I have to say I'm sadly accustomed to the, ahem, excuses of single gentlemen . . ." She bobbed an apologetic curtsy in the direction of Sir Anthony, who was moodily staring out of the window. "But in truth there was no doubting poor Mr. Spicer that night. He was usually a spruce sort of gentleman, but he was as downcast and draggle-tailed as ever I saw him, and he could only shake his head at me when I—well, when I took him to task a little, only as a kind mother might, sir, about his manner of living. Well, then he went into his room, to go to bed as I thought, and I was ready to draw the bolts and try to take a little rest myself, not that I was likely to get any. But after a while he came out of his room again, with the strangest sort of smile on his face—yet not a smile neither—and he told me that he was going out again. At this hour? thinks I; but I was too surprised to speak. And so he went out then, and turned on the steps, and said to me, 'I'm going to buy some gloves.' Just that, as I told the inquest, and off he went. It made no sense, of course, for where would he get gloves at that time even if he had money, and so they took it as showing how his mind was foxed and disturbed, poor gentleman, with what he was going off to do. And that he chose not to do it under my roof I take as the last instance of that delicacy of conduct he always showed—"

"Enough!" barked Sir Anthony, coming away with a jerk from the window and advancing on them with balled fists. "Must I hear this again? Is it not enough that Richard is . . . Madam, you are done here, and you too, sir, and I will have no more . . . I cannot command myself—get out, get out!"

They got out, and Mrs. Lyme gave Fairfax a reproachful look on the stairs, as if to say it was all his fault, before tit-tuping off at speed.

Fairfax bent his steps towards Covent Garden. What he had learned was enigmatic in itself, but taken together with his memories of the gambling house last night, and the curious matter of Lord Mortlock's missing bill, it set off a train of ideas that might, he thought, lead somewhere interesting.

In the light of the gray afternoon the Cyder Cellar was surely one of the most unappealing spots in creation, Fairfax thought. He trod gingerly on the sawdust of the empty bar parlor, which judging by the smell covered various unmentionables. Although the potman, a baby-faced bruiser in a leather waistcoat, remembered Fairfax being here last night, he was reluctant at first to speak to him until Fairfax took a chance and said he came from Mr. Saunders Welch. Invoking the name of the magistrate made the man lurkingly cooperative.

The potman had a good memory, no doubt as a result of keeping a continuously close eye on his seedy clientele.

"'Tis just as I told at the inquest. The young gentleman came in here about one on Monday night. Lord Mortlock was in his usual seat, and the young 'un goes over and joins him. They had a glass or two together, and then the young 'un goes off."

"They did not leave together?"

"Lord Mortlock stayed put. Well, you know him, I daresay: he's an all-nighter."

"Was," Fairfax said. "He's dead."

"Is he now?" The potman squeezed a wad of tobacco in his mouth and chewed pensively. "Well, we'll miss his custom. But there, our custom does drop off that way. A short life and a merry one, eh?"

"I heard something about a note being passed."

"Aye, the young 'un gave Lord Mortlock a note or some such. I saw that plain. His lordship puts it in his pocket nice as you like. No concern of mine. It's things being slipped out of pockets without the owner knowing about it that I have to look out for. The beaks would gladly have us clapped shut for a disorderly house if they could. *You* know."

"You didn't see this note clear or close?"

"Not I. Settling accounts, I daresay. Like a man does when he's flush, if he's honest."

"Flush? You mean Spicer had money?"

"Aye, he had money," the potman said casually, stepping nimbly on a cockroach that was scuttling across the sawdust. "He settled up his bill here before he left, cash down. Just as well as he'd run up quite a score, and I'd been reckoning to speak to him about it. Settling accounts, like I said. Leaving things tidy, that's my guess. Then off he goes and blows his head off, poor bastard. I've never understood it myself, but these youngbloods will take a fancy to do for themselves. I remember an old dandy who always wore two pocket watches, and was the biggest whoremaster about the Garden; he piped up one night that he wanted to kiss all the wenches he'd ever had, which took quite a time as you'd imagine, but he did it, and then he took a tavern room and called for hot water to wash his hands, and then he shot himself in the breast, smiling."

"Spicer had money . . ."

"Well, his purse was a-jingle, I remember that. Speaking of which . . . Lord Mortlock's a dead man, is he? Heyo . . ." The potman went to a slate hanging behind the bar and, after a regretfully grimacing moment, wiped it clean. "Had a wife, didn't he? Well, I ain't about to go dunning her."

Which just went to show there was a good side to everyone, Fairfax thought, thanking him and leaving the Cyder Cellar with a new spring in his tired step.

So, Richard Spicer had come home penniless at two on Monday night, or rather Tuesday morning. But at one he had been in the Cyder Cellar, and apparently with plenty of money. Lord Mortlock had seen him there, and been given a note which Fairfax had no doubt now was the bill drawn on Martin's of Throgmorton Street—probably repayment of a loan. Earlier they had been at Lady Harriet's faro table together, and Spicer had stayed on to gamble . . .

Thinking back to last night, Fairfax was sure there had been a very pointed meaning to Lord Mortlock's cryptic taunting of Luke Griffey. Richard Spicer must have won on Monday night, he thought, perhaps even broken the bank, and Lord Mortlock knew it because he had seen him afterwards and shared in the largesse. Why then had Mortlock made a parade of showing that bill, and why had the sight of it plainly disquieted Griffey? And where was the bill now?

Lady Harriet's house was close by. Less malodorous than the Cyder Cellar, it still had the musty unloveliness of a night haunt exposed to daylight. The thug footman blinked like a mole as he showed Fairfax upstairs, past the empty gaming room and up to an overheated apartment full of chinaware and gilded trinkets on spindly tables, painted silk screens, peeling-gilt girandoles, and moth-eaten damasks. A macaw shrieked at him from a pagoda-shaped cage. Lady Harriet Froome reclined amongst cushions, her hair in curlpapers, a tea table at her elbow; there was a bottle of gin next to the teapot.

"The gentleman from Yorkshire," she said in a heavily ironical tone. "It cannot be sixteen hours since you were last here, sir. May I take it as a tribute to my powers of enchantment?" She laughed in a forced, weary way, and Fairfax saw that the skin around her brilliant violet eyes was red and puffed. "Be seated, sir. If you are come to amuse me, you are doubly welcome, for God damn me I am in need of it."

As he sat down the macaw screeched again, as if to alert him to the book that lay open on the chair. He removed it, seeing that it was Crebillon's *La Sopha,* a notorious novel in which a sofa tells the racy story of the things that have happened on it. He knew because he had made a pirated translation of it at a penny a page, years ago.

"I wish I could, but I fear my business will not admit of it. That is to say, my news—"

"I know it," she said, stirring restlessly. "If you mean Hugh. I have heard. It is all around the town, of course. Delicious, is it not?" She watched his expression, then laughed with a yelp that set the macaw shrieking. "To die in bed, I mean, full of wine after a good debauch. What could be better?"

"To have another forty years, perhaps."

"And grow old and haggard and have to be lifted to stool like a drooling baby. No, no, the manner of Hugh's going suited him. I envy and salute him!"

"Yet you've been weeping, Lady Harriet."

"I weep at anything, my dear sir. A play, a song, ecod, a peeled onion will do it. Oh, I was fond of Hugh, certainly. Doubtless in the Yorkshire wilds such things would not be countenanced, but the fact is the attachment clapped upon 'em by a parson at the altar is not the only one that subsists between men and women of the world. And so, how goes it with that little chit he married? Will she look prettier than ever in her widow's weeds?"

"Lady Mortlock is shocked and distraught as you would expect. The first concern of the family must be to bring the person responsible to justice. And as you feel the loss yourself, Lady Harriet, you share in that wish, I'm sure."

She shrugged. "The talk is that it was a black servant who took to his heels after. It appears probable enough to me. That is, unless that little grocer's daughter put her gallant up to the job. Come, never tell me you haven't heard *that* talk about her. 'Twould be more surprising if she did *not* have a beau — a pretty miss queening it in silks before all comers, and left to her own devices by a husband who . . . well, who was hardly loverlike in his attentions." She darted a covert glance at Fairfax, who kept his face impassive. "Oh, but who gives a fig for justice? What does it mean, really, except something we all hope to escape?"

" 'Use every man after his desert and who would 'scape whipping?' It's one view."

"That is Shakespeare no doubt. No use quoting poetry at me, sir; I am entirely prose, all the way through." Lady Harriet went over to the macaw's cage and began poking her finger through the bars, withdrawing it teasingly each time the bird tried to nip.

"You never met the young Lady Mortlock?"

"Faith, 'tis hardly likely. And what did I think when Hugh married her? I thought it a charming notion. Much as if he'd said he was going to set up a new carriage with lacquered trim and yellow wheels! Oh, it was a Smithfield match, of course, but what other kind can a sensible man make?"

Smithfield—the livestock market. "Well, it obviously did not deprive you of Lord Mortlock's company. He came here just as before, presumably, and presumably introduced his friends just as before. He was very valuable to you, I gather."

Her look was hostile. "If there are fools in the world, sir, then folly is what they'll seek and find. Just as a man going abroad without hat and cloak will catch cold. The gentlemen Hugh brought here were overjoyed to come. It was what they wanted. All he did was assist people to get what they wanted—not so bad, hey?—and obliged me into the bargain."

"Ah. Yet he was not a man, surely, to do favors."

"Well, let us say he *owed* me them . . . Besides, Hugh was tickled by it. He liked seeing men become what they really are, beneath all the mummery and pretense."

"Your faro bank has lost two of its best customers lately. Dark times. Will you survive the triple blow?"

"I always survive . . . Triple? Is there another death I should know of?"

"No. I mean that Richard Spicer won on Monday night, did he not? Lord Mortlock kept hinting at it and now I'm sure of it. Spicer stayed on late, gaming alone against the bank, I imagine, and he won heavily. Even stripped the bank, perhaps."

"Oh, my dear sir, I can't recall. Mr. Griffey concerns himself with that—I am only the hostess at our little gatherings—"

"Two men are dead, Lady Harriet, and that makes me a little impatient with this genteel fiction of yours. I think you know very well that Spicer won here on Monday night — as Hugh Mortlock knew it."

Pale and thin-lipped, she faced him. Ah, he thought, there was the earl's daughter, staring down the impudence of the commonalty. "You force me to repeat, sir, you must ask Griffey. Or do you dare only to harass women with your impertinent questions?"

Before he could answer, her little boy came running into the room. Lady Harriet held out her arms.

"Ah, my darling, you have on your new bonnet! Let me look at you, you cunning creature . . ."

The boy hesitated a moment, cocking a solemn look at Fairfax, before running to his mother's arms. Pale and compelling eyes . . . Lord Mortlock's eyes, in fact? he wondered greatly.

Lady Harriet was embracing the boy and kissing him. A certain element of parade about those caresses, Fairfax thought.

"Well, I will disturb you no longer. Where can I find Mr. Griffey?"

The look she gave him over the boy's curly head was surprisingly hateful. "He has a private room on the ground floor. Would you like me to ring, sir?"

"I'll find my own way."

He was almost out of the door when she called him back.

"Mr. Fairfax. Before you judge me, consider what it is to be a woman in this world. We cannot do what men do freely. We cannot *do* at all, in truth; we simply are. We exist as a sort of goods, and mighty perishable ones at that: one touch and we are spoiled, apparently, yet how carelessly we are traded, used, and discarded, as if we didn't bruise at all."

He bowed. He admitted the truth of it, but disliked being seen as in need of the lesson.

Going downstairs, he saw a familiar figure crossing the hall to the front door.

"Lawrence!"

Lawrence Appleton gave a sort of cringing start before turning and assuming his usual expression of awkward nonchalance.

"Oh, Fairfax. Just fancy. How goes it, m'dear fellow?"

"You've heard the news?"

"Shocking, ain't it? Aye, I went home this afternoon and the servants were all full of it. Poor Charlotte, eh? Still, Pa's with her and all that. Shocking. I was never so amazed at anything. Shows you can't really trust the poor blacks, you know. Well, I must be going." He had crammed his hat on his head and made a gangling exit before Fairfax could speak.

"It is indeed a most dreadful piece of intelligence," came a familiar husky voice. Luke Griffey stood huge and square in the doorway of a room to the left. With his hands tucked under his coattails, his red waistcoat tight against his paunch, and an expression of peculiar smugness on his scarred face, he looked like a sinister shopkeeper. "You came, perhaps, to acquaint Lady Harriet with the news. Unhappily it has reached us. Dear me. It is a lesson for us all, I think," he went on blandly.

The room beyond him, Fairfax saw, had the look of a bar parlor strangely transplanted into this aristocratic old house; even the light in there appeared subterranean, as if it were a night cellar.

"Sad indeed. Your custom is certainly"—he recalled the potman's apt phrase—"dropping off of late, Mr. Griffey."

"Custom, sir? I don't understand."

"It's in regard to your custom here," Fairfax said, ignoring this, "that I wanted to ask you something, Mr. Griffey. You remember young Mr. Spicer, of course. On Monday night—the last night of his life—he gamed here and, I believe, won handsomely. He took away a goodly amount of money from your establishment, did he not?"

"That I couldn't say, sir. When gentlemen choose to play here, 'tis entirely their concern—"

"Nay, that's humbug, you must think me a fool. You keep a faro bank here, and a book on it. I think Richard Spicer did very well out of that bank on Monday night. He left here flush—but he went home with nothing."

"Merciful heavens," Griffey sighed, "'tis ever a matter of wonder with me how these young gentlemen contrive to spend their money—"

"Even Covent Garden offers nothing at two in the morning to spend a small fortune on. Every penny, gone. And by dawn he was dead. Singular, eh?"

"Again, I couldn't say, sir."

"Perhaps your book will be more communicative."

"My private accounts, sir, are my business and no one else's. And pardon me"—scarcely moving, Griffey somehow *loomed* over Fairfax in the most significant way—"but I'd like to see you or anyone attempt to spy on them, sir. You've no power. And pardon me again, but there's nothing to stop me throwing you down the front steps, Mr. Fairfax, speaking theoretical, I mean."

"I have, as you say, no power," Fairfax said, trying not to feel intimidated by the bulk of the man. "Only a powerful curiosity as to what happened to Spicer's winnings. Or most of them. One sum is accounted for, oddly enough."

They stared at each other. Griffey's thick hands moved restlessly.

"I don't know what you mean, sir," he said, his voice smaller and softer than ever. "But I have a fancy you're trying to cross me. When I'm crossed, I'm cross, which ain't like me, as I'm a placid sort of soul as a rule. I'm known for it, in fact. But when I'm crossed, I *am* cross, sir, don't doubt it."

"I don't doubt it," he said with a slight bow, and went to the front door. He could hear a faint female voice singing upstairs. At the last moment something made him look around. He found that Griffey had stolen to within inches of him, as silently as if he had levitated. With a long wheeze which Fairfax identified as a laugh, Griffey opened the front door with a flourish. "Dear me," Griffey huffed, "you are not such a country cousin after all, sir. You plainly know the first rule of this city: watch your back. Always, sir, watch your back."

Chapter Six

Evening was descending on the city when he returned to the Mortlock house, and already in the western squares the thrum of social life was beginning: carriages rumbling out from mews passages, stacked heels and malacca canes rapping on the flagstones, the torches of linkboys sputtering into life in the damp sooty air. Fairfax fancied he could hear, like the sound of sea in the distance, a great murmur of busy tongues all across the city, quickened by a new and most titillating scandal.

Meggy admitted him to the silent house.

"No, sir, no news. No sign of that murdering rascal, anyhow. There's comfort, though: the undertaker's women are here, and his lordship's been attended to proper. And they'll never lay out a better, truer man!"

Fairfax wondered what Lord Mortlock would have made of this shining virtue that death had conferred on him.

"Is Mr. Appleton still here?"

"He went home a while since, sir. Mistress would insist. I must face it alone sooner or later, says she. Of course, she's got me to look after her. And the doctor's with her now."

"The doctor—?"

Nimier: he came at that moment down the stairs, straight-backed and correct, inching a pair of skintight gloves onto his elegant hands.

"Mr. Fairfax." Nimier looked at him as if he knew everything he had been about today. "Sir, you are indefatigable."

"I might say the same. You found Lady Mortlock well?"

"Tolerable. I have no time to speak with you now," Nimier said, consulting a gold watch. "You will, I'm sure, wish for an interview. I am at your disposal on the morrow, sir, as early as you please. You know where to find me."

He was gone as swiftly as a cat. Fairfax fancied he hardly needed to have Meggy open the door for him: he looked as if he could slip through the crack.

Upstairs, in the cavernous drawing room, Lady Mortlock stood at the window. She had changed into an evening frock of buttercup-yellow satin, as if in defiance of mourning. A nearly empty glass of wine stood nearby.

"Dr. Nimier came to see me—to offer his services as a physician—it was good of him," she said rapidly. "He gave me a sleeping draft, though I do not think I shall take it."

"He is not your usual physician?"

"I never saw him as such before today." She scooped up the glass and drained it. "I know him by repute, of course."

Fairfax nodded, but he was suspicious. The last thing Nimier lacked was confidence, but to impose like that . . .

"What is the draft? Some valerian compound, perhaps?" He looked around expectantly.

"Oh—I don't know. I had Meggy take it downstairs." She met his eyes, looked away.

"I see . . . She tells me there is no sign of Abraham. Still, I suppose he cannot hide forever. Of course, the hiding itself gives an appearance of guilt, but it need not be so. If he is innocent, and has heard what has happened, then he is just as likely to hide because of the weight of suspicion falling on him. Lady Mortlock, please tell me: do you believe Abraham Drake to be the killer of your husband?"

"How can I answer that?"

"Honestly. And as a woman who, I think, was generally

kind to him, and did not treat him with the abuse and contempt that seemed to be his lot from master and servant alike." As she did not speak he added: "Lady Mortlock, you know this matter will be most publicly aired. The magistrate will be thorough. All the questions surrounding such a crime must be answered . . . and I fear voices will not be lacking to accuse you of some complicity in your husband's death."

She lifted her face, its shape beautifully traced with amber in the firelight. "And why, pray?"

"Because—because the marriage was known as an unhappy one."

"Oh, good heavens, then half the spouses in England would be murdered if that alone were a reason," she rapped out, then gave him a crooked smile. "I do not care what people say about me, Mr. Fairfax."

He admired that, while doubting it was strictly true. Everything from her headdress to the decoration of this house proclaimed her a slave of society, if a willing one.

And then she surprised him utterly. She did something he had never seen a lady do: she sat down on the floor by the hearth, gathering her legs gracefully under her and resting her head on the arm of the chair.

"I always used to sit thus by Father's chair when I was a girl," she said. "I have never found such comfort since. Strange how it comes back . . . Is it not a pity, Mr. Fairfax, that childhood is not a *place,* which we could revisit when we wished? We must leave it so completely behind . . . If I were to meet the learned men of the Royal Society, I should say to them: make me a country of the past! *That* would be something worth . . ."

Too much mind, he thought, for this brittle and facile world. And too much heart—or too little? He didn't know, though he knew that at that moment he could have fallen in love with her himself very readily. Which made the behavior of her late husband all the more inexplicable.

"I knew Lord Mortlock but briefly," he said, taking a chair. "I knew his reputation, of course. From this little knowledge, I am trying to find a reason why someone would kill him."

"Someone other than Abraham, you mean?"

"Until Abraham is found, and can tell his story, nothing is certain . . . I keep coming across this matter of Richard Spicer, however. Perhaps it is not germane, but I should tell you that last night a man named Sir Anthony Spicer, the young man's uncle, challenged your husband to a duel. He was very passionate, not quite in his right mind, and Lord Mortlock mercifully declined the challenge. But Sir Anthony does most earnestly blame Lord Mortlock for bringing his nephew to a ruinous end. Do you know anything of this?"

"I never saw this Spicer. I used to hear his name sometimes, no more. That was how it was with Hugh's companions. You were the first exception."

"Monday night was when Spicer last went a-gaming with Hugh. Early on Tuesday morning Spicer was dead. Did Hugh speak of this matter at all? Can you think back to that time?"

"Why, there is nothing to tell. On Monday night Hugh went out, as usual, with no word of where or when he would be back, and I remained here."

"Alone?"

"No. On Monday I enjoyed a musical evening here, with Mr. Pennant and my brother Lawrence." She spoke distinctly, with a faint edge of indignation.

"Indeed . . . I gather you sometimes give Abraham his freedom on Monday nights. Was this such an occasion?"

"It was. Once Hugh had left, I gave Abraham the evening off. I felt a little liberty would benefit him. And as I said, I had company—Mr. Pennant and my brother."

"And when did Hugh return?"

"At some late hour—I couldn't say when as I was abed. I saw him in the morning, and he had nothing out of the common to say then. That was how it was, sir. Married people can live very . . . independently. Hugh certainly never confided in me. If he had . . ." She seemed to lose whatever she was going to say in a rapt contemplation of the fire, then stirred and smiled faintly at him. "Forgive me, I have offered you nothing and you must have had a long and tiring day of it. Let me get you something to drink."

"Thank you, I do very well." Again he felt at that moment that he could have loved her: her offer, striking suddenly on his deep tiredness and perplexity, almost brought tears to his eyes. And then he thought: am I a sentimentalist? She is young and charming and pitiable, and so I am as ready to fancy her the Good Woman as to label Lady Harriet the Bad Woman . . . Truth, he thought, was rarely so simple.

"This quarrel between Lord Mortlock and Abraham," he went on, shaking himself, "seems to be to do with the milk seller—Kate Little is her name. I suspect a romance. Lord Mortlock did not approve?"

"Oh, I knew Abraham was sweet on her. There was a fuss about some food going missing from the pantry—Abraham treating his paramour, apparently. It was a triviality, though Hugh chose not to think so."

"Would Hugh have allowed Abraham to marry, do you think?"

"Out of sheer tyrannical willfulness and pigheadedness, probably not," she said with uncontrollable bitterness. "You think that was Abraham's wish? He never spoke of it to me—but then, I'm not the master. Well, 'tis possible. Hugh—I think Hugh would have raged about it. And then forgot his rage the next day. I can't believe . . . I mean, Abraham is a *servant*." The loftiness was unaffected. "These should be minor matters."

Exactly his thought on witnessing Mortlock's quite disproportionate anger that morning . . . "You first met Lord Mortlock at Bath, I think."

"Yes. Last autumn. Father had a grippe and was trying the waters. Hugh had been there some weeks. He had spent part of the summer at his place in Gloucestershire, only some eighteen miles distant, but had tired of it and taken a residence at Bath. He had no pleasure in hunting—a thing I liked in him."

"Did you know that Miss Vertue was at Bath then also?"

She shook her head, still looking at the fire. "No. I never saw her, but then there was a good deal of company wintering there. And Father—well, Father was chiefly concerned to pay our addresses to Hugh, as soon as he found he was at Bath. That was his one aim."

"And yours . . . ?"

"I was very eager to meet him. Certainly. I had long heard of the name Mortlock, from my grandfather's stewardship of the family estates. When our own family rose to an eminence whereby we could meet Hugh socially, it was highly gratifying." She looked at him. "I am my own woman, sir. I was not forced into anything."

Except, Fairfax thought, by that pride and ambition that must have been in the air you breathed from your very cradle . . . And who, after all, did anything truly out of free will? The sum of all our past actions and influences stood at our back, impelling us forwards, lifting a foot here and an arm there just like a puppeteer.

"You were close to your grandfather?"

"I was still a child when he died, but I loved him dearly."

"And he you, plainly. He left you a large legacy. How, I wonder, does your brother regard that?"

"Oh, sir, there's no harm in Lawrence, believe me." Again that amused, faintly contemptuous dismissal. "He is very much a boy, and we rub along pretty well together . . ." She rose gracefully to her feet. "Mr. Fairfax, my husband is dead. It is a thing there is no preparing for—it is the world turned upside down. But I *must* accustom myself to that. I am a widow now. That is the future wherein I must walk. The past may not be edifying . . . there may be mistakes and regrets. But it is still the past, and so it is dead too. We must make our lives anew each time we wake, must we not?"

"A heavy responsibility," he said, getting up. "May I ask you one more thing—the pills that were at Hugh's bedside. Do you really not know what they were for?"

"No. I cannot conceive. Hugh never—never took any care of his health." For the first time tears stood in her eyes.

Thanking her, he bowed and left.

Mr. Appleton kept a good table, and Fairfax was glad of it when he at last returned to Leicester Fields. His employer, eating little himself, allowed Fairfax a little space to replenish himself with food and wine before plying him with any questions. Mr. Appleton was one of those rare people with whom one could be restfully silent.

"I have received several messages of condolence already," he said at last. "From quite high company. Dear me. It is gratifying, though one could wish the circumstances different . . . And so you saw Charlotte again, sir? I was chary of leaving her, but she was insistent; she is a strong-minded girl. How did she strike you?"

"Quite strong, as you say, sir . . . Actually, I found her not alone. Dr. Nimier had been to see her."

"Indeed?" Mr. Appleton pursed his lips in his soundless whistle.

"As a medical man, I presume."

"Yes . . ." Mr. Appleton lifted his glass, then set it down untasted. Difficult for him, Fairfax thought. His suspicions about his daughter's infidelity were thrown into new relief by the murder of his son-in-law. The slander—if slander it was—voiced by Lady Harriet today would find an echo on many lips: had Lady Mortlock been freed from her marriage by an obliging lover? Even the notion of a tacit complicity on her part cast a horrible shadow.

It was, of course, only talk, nothing proven. But that the question of his daughter's lover was uppermost in Mr. Appleton's mind was plain.

"Charlotte must be protected," he said. "She is in a vulnerable position. The rumors of which I spoke before this happened—the suggestion that she had allowed herself to be, ahem, swayed by an insistent admirer—are made newly pertinent. It is all very delicate and must be handled with discretion." He blinked at Fairfax expectantly.

"If your daughter has a—an admirer, I suspect it is either Nimier or Stephen Pennant," Fairfax said. "There is much in the behavior of each that gives me ground for suspicion. Nimier I have yet to talk to. But proof is obviously difficult to procure in such a—delicate matter."

"Of course," Mr. Appleton said, thoughtful. "Of course . . . I am glad you appreciate the delicacy of the situation, Fairfax. Naturally the search for young Abraham continues to take precedence. Damn the boy, what did he mean by it? I mean this flight of his—even assuming nothing about his guilt or innocence."

"As I remarked to Lady Mortlock, he may be hiding in fear of accusation, even if he is guiltless. He surely has no happy expectations of how the society of his masters will deal with him. I have talked with the milk seller at the Haymarket, Kate Little, who it seems pretty certain is his sweetheart. I have a strong fancy that she may have seen him today, possibly even knows where he is to be found. But she is close as an oyster. The loyalty of love can be an unbreakable barrier."

"Oh, she's the one, is she? He was talking to me last evening, in a roundabout way, about such a matter. Servants are allowed followers in most households, and there's no harm in it, is there—things like that? I simply told him to mind his work, and not trouble his head about such things."

"I see . . . Last evening, Mr. Appleton?"

"Aye. Aye, I went over to see Charlotte, you know. A father's fondness."

"Your pardon, Mr. Appleton, but at the levee this morning you said that you had spent last night at home, going over some accounts."

Mr. Appleton drank his wine. "So I did," he said, nodding. "Yes. That was how I chiefly occupied the evening. But I went over and spent a little time at Charlotte's house. A man of affairs can get dull if he does not refresh himself with female company." He smiled. "You are quick, Fairfax. You do well to be; I'm pleased. Nothing but the most dogged attention to the truth, I think, will resolve this terrible business."

True indeed, thought Fairfax, and if people did not *tell* him the truth, then no amount of doggedness would provide answers. Though lies too could be revealing. At any rate, he had caught Mr. Appleton out in one. Or an omission of truth, at least. Perhaps not important, but it made prominent a fact that they were both aware of, and choosing not to mention— the fact that the murder of Lord Mortlock could easily have been committed by Mr. Appleton himself.

Fairfax wondered about those accounts. Were they heavy on the debit side? Had there been further subsidies to Lord Mortlock's extravagance which Mr. Appleton had decided could no longer be borne? Or was his troublesome son-in-law about to embroil him in some deeper trouble that Fairfax had not guessed at? Possibilities . . . Indeed, Mr. Appleton's close involvement with the Mortlock destiny should have made him a first suspect: everyone had an emotional center, and his was right there in the grand house at Hill Street.

And yet Samuel Appleton had promoted the marriage as his heart's desire; having his daughter as Lady Mortlock was plainly the crowning achievement of his life. Fairfax just couldn't make the leap from there to cold-blooded murder.

"Nimier . . . Pennant . . ." Mr. Appleton mused, motioning the footman to refill Fairfax's glass. "Nimier I know only by reputation; he has the entrée to some very high circles, I hear. As for Pennant—is he known?"

"He is a musician of some promise, I think. But without family or influential connections, which in all the arts is a handicap."

"Hm. He seemed very attentive to Charlotte's young friend, Miss Vertue."

"Yes, I have seen her today. She had nothing to say of that. Indeed, I did not know what to make of her."

"Oh, there can be no harm in such a delightful young creature, surely," Mr. Appleton said with a wave of his hand. "Only the usual little vices of her age and sex—a little vanity, a little giddiness."

Finding this rather too chucklesome, Fairfax said severely, "Crimes are only little vices writ large, sir. There remains of course one other of the company at the levee—Mr. Lawrence, who is proving rather elusive."

Mr. Appleton grunted, then again when there came the sound of the street door. "Talk of the devil," he said with peculiar emphasis as Lawrence came in, "and he appears."

"Lor', what a day and no mistake," Lawrence said vaguely, sitting down, then adding, "Oh, Pa, there's a hackney at the door wants paying. I'm clean stripped, I fear—"

"You have not even money for a hackney? You had an adequate sum of me on Monday, Lawrence." Mr. Appleton dug in his fob and passed a coin to the footman. "Pay the man, will you? What the devil do you do with it, boy?"

Lawrence swallowed a glass of wine and immediately beckoned for another. "Well, you know . . . How does poor Charlotte do?"

"She bears up, I think," Mr. Appleton said, frowning.

"And how," Fairfax said, "does Mr. Griffey do?"

"Eh? Oh, him . . ." Lawrence avoided his eyes. "None of that fish for me, only the chicken—fish gives me the gripes. Supposed to be digestible, ain't it? Curious thing. I fancy my innards must be different."

"Mr. Griffey, Lawrence?" Mr. Appleton said.

Perhaps it was unfair to sound him out in front of his father like this, Fairfax thought, seeing Lawrence's grimace. But the young man *was* damned elusive.

"Oh, I was at Griffey's house earlier. Well, in truth it's Lady Harriet Froome's place—she keeps a faro bank there. A gaming house, you know. Why, *he'll* tell you," Lawrence concluded, pointing at Fairfax with his knife.

"The place I visited with Lord Mortlock," Fairfax said. "A regular haunt of his, I think."

"And *your* regular haunt, Lawrence?" Mr. Appleton said with raised eyebrow.

A pertinent question, Fairfax thought, watching Lawrence. The young man shrugged, then half-choked and swigged wine. "Oh, I've passed the odd hour there. As I said to you last night, Fairfax, I have a score to settle up with Griffey."

"A gambling score?" his father said.

"Aye. I was wondering if I might speak to you about that, Pa. The fact is, I'm pressed just at present—devilish pressed." Lawrence tried to give his foppish chuckle, but he looked pained, Fairfax thought, as if the pressure were a physical reality.

"I see," Mr. Appleton said with weight. "And so that is your business with this—this Griffey. An ill name, I fancy. And the lady's is not much better . . ." He glanced darkly at Fairfax. "At least I think I see . . . unless there is anything else you have to tell me, Lawrence?"

"Why, wh-what should there be?" said Lawrence, his eyes bulging until they resembled those of the dressed fish on the table.

"Come, you were there today when Hugh—when Hugh was killed. We must all put our heads together over this, boy, 'tis no light matter. Your brother-in-law is horribly killed and the culprit must be found."

"Don't ask me. What should I know? Lord, I believe I wasn't there above ten minutes."

"Aye, indeed, and why *were* you there?" Mr. Appleton said. "Morning calls are scarcely your habit."

"Oh, I just wanted to see Charlotte about something. 'Twas not of any consequence. And then—then I went away."

"Abraham was at his station when you left?" Fairfax said.

"Eh? Oh, yes. He was at the door. Some tradeswoman was there on the steps."

"A milk seller."

"I think so. That is, I wouldn't know a milk seller from a coal man, in truth," Lawrence said with a fatuous smile. "All alike to me, you know."

Mr. Appleton's square shoulders twitched in irritation. "Don't be a fool, boy. What else?"

"Why, nothing. She was just on her way, I suppose, but they were lingering about making sheep's eyes at each other. You know how servants are. Seemed to liven the fellow up, anyhow, for he was mighty down in the mouth before. Truth to tell, you know, girls of the common sort are all a-dangle for the black fellows. Novelty, I suppose." Lawrence winked at Fairfax. "Want to see if they're that color all over, perhaps—"

Mr. Appleton put down his knife with a clatter. "What more?"

"Oh—nothing," Lawrence said, jumping. "I came away . . . and that was all. You know, when I heard what had happened, I was never more amazed. Still and all, the world is a deuced odd place, eh? Deuced odd. Any more of that wine?"

Mr. Appleton not only turned away from Lawrence but actually shifted his chair around, as if he found his son's company unendurable. Somewhat to Fairfax's surprise, he began to talk of his West Indies estates, warming to his theme when the cloth was taken away and the port bottle circulated. There was much of interest in this—Mr. Appleton waxed rhapsodical on the beauty of the Jamaican sunsets, made the flesh creep with tales of the effect of tropical diseases on European constitutions and of the depredations of runaway Negroes who had taken to banditry in the hills—but Fairfax could not forget what this colorfully described world was based on.

"How much," he found himself saying, interrupting Mr. Appleton in midflow, "would a slave of Abraham's age cost?"

"I would say twenty-eight to thirty pounds," Mr. Appleton said after a moment. "The war has pushed prices up, as with most things. Come, sir, I know that look. I have seen it on men's faces before; but you must own that we do not live in an ideal world. Labor is the common lot of mankind, and always has been. And there have always been varying degrees of freedom likewise, going back to antique times. The Greeks and Romans would have seen nothing strange or unjust in one people being set above another, by reason of that people's greater power and energy; they would have seen it as the inevitable way of things. Of course there are abuses of the system, though you will see no worse in coal mines here in England, and for my own part I insist on an enlightened treatment and a degree of comfort, as far as possible. Overkindness, of course, can lead to trouble and discontent."

Fairfax doubted that overkindness was the besetting sin of the Jamaican plantations. But it was an argument he could not hope to win. Nor could he even press it as he wished, simply because Mr. Appleton was, or soon would be, his employer. He was not owned by this man, he was free to quarrel violently with him and walk out of his house, but he also needed to earn a living, and nothing else had presented itself this year. He was stuck.

Instead he said: "Do you think that's what has happened with Abraham?"

"I should be sorry to think it," Mr. Appleton said, with a misty look into his port. "It may be that living among the luxury and liberty of our society has raised up an ungovernable and resentful spirit in that young man . . . But I always approved him as a very amenable good-hearted fellow, and I should be sorry to think it. Poor Abraham!"

Fairfax craved bed and sleep, and soon asked to be excused. He had only just lit the second candle in his bedchamber and taken off his coat, however, when there was a tap at the door and Lawrence slipped in.

"Still awake, eh, Fairfax?"

"I have not got to bed yet."

"No. No. Damned fagging business, undressing, ain't it? Fair knocks me up sometimes." Lawrence stood tapping an empty snuffbox and gawking round the room. The young man was acting very strangely; there was no doubt about it.

"Was there something you wanted to talk to me about?"

"Ticklish. Very. That's a rather good coat, you know— who's your tailor? Well, never mind. The ticklish thing is— well, I'm in low water as you may have fathomed, m'dear fellow, deuced low water, and what I need—"

"I cannot supply," Fairfax finished. "I have no means of my own, Lawrence. I was engaged by your father as tutor, though he found another occupation for me: a thing I think you had already guessed."

"Ha! I did smoke you, as it happens." Lawrence looked momentarily pleased with himself; then his face fell again. "That's no good then. Cock's life, 'tis a pesky world . . ."

"Lawrence, what is this all about? And why are you really

seeing Luke Griffey? You must know that it has a suspicious
whiff about it."

"Eh? Eh? 'Pon my honor, Fairfax, I don't follow, strike
me but I don't!" cried Lawrence, looking about him almost
wildly.

Was he that much of a fool? Fairfax doubted it. He was
certainly very afraid of something. "You know what sort of
man Luke Griffey is, Lawrence? The King Street house is the
more genteel side of his operations, by all accounts."

Lawrence nodded, giggled faintly, and swallowed.

"If you have let yourself become—beholden in some
way, pushed into some intrigue by this Griffey, then for
God's sake you must reveal—"

"Nothing!" Lawrence's voice broke on the word. "It's
nothing, damn it all, nothing. Devil take it, you are the most
suspicious fellow I ever . . . 'Tis a mere question of money,
Fairfax, as I said. Money—that's all it comes down to, and I
must—I simply must have some, you know, a man can't get
by . . ." Dropping his voice to a whisper, he said, "I hoped for
something from Charlotte today, in truth; she's generally
openhanded, if you can get her alone. I didn't mention it with
Pa by, because he don't care for me bothering her . . . Ain't
it the most scandalous thing that money should be such a
plague to a fellow, when there's folk about with plenty of it?
Ain't it, though? Never mind." He gave Fairfax a look at
once crestfallen, wry, and furtive. Then with a hunch of his
bony shoulders he was gone.

Well, Fairfax thought, his sister was one of those folk with
plenty of money. But it seemed likely that her marriage to
Hugh Mortlock had denied Lawrence access to it. If Mortlock had stopped her from indulging her brother, then it
could only be of advantage to Lawrence to have his lordship
out of the way. All came down to money . . . Fairfax wondered about that. Yet in spite of the curious matter of the

missing bill, he somehow doubted that it *did* all come down to money in this case.

He lay in bed, but exhausted as he was he found some gloomy and self-pitying thoughts a barrier to sleep. Tomorrow — Friday the twenty-sixth of March, 1762 — was his thirty-second birthday. No great matter, but there was a heaviness on his spirit. No one to know or care about the day of his entrance into the world . . . In an odd way, he felt that Lord Mortlock was the person he had been closest to here, and he was dead. The only other bond he felt was with Abraham Drake. An offensive comparison perhaps; he was hardly in the slave's position. And yet he felt a touch of empathy with the man who led an existence here without friends, without rights, without a soul to speak for him. And as for those snatched moments with the pretty milk seller who came to the door . . . he understood the value of those. A time, however short, when you could be *yourself* — how vital that was to the soul!

He knew because last year he had found the woman who was for him — and not for him. Cordelia Linton was God knew where now; it didn't matter. She was a married woman. Unhappily so, he knew, but nonetheless, marriage was forever. Unless one were very rich and highly placed and could manage the trouble and expense of divorce, which had to go before Parliament, and which utterly destroyed the woman who was party to it. A pipe dream. In fact, the whole matter of Cordelia was one he must simply forget. It was self-torturing folly to think of it.

And yet his thoughts of Cordelia were somehow mixed up with his intense wish to prove Abraham Drake innocent. To prove it, perhaps, simply for the sake of those snatched moments, the sweetness of which he knew. In this way, the quest, which had already seized his restlessly inquisitive mind, engaged his heart too.

Prove Abraham innocent . . . Unfortunately, it would

mean proving something else: that one of the visitors to Lady Mortlock's levee today—Mr. Samuel Appleton, young Lawrence, Miss Vertue, Dr. John Nimier, or Stephen Pennant—was going to bed tonight with murder on their conscience.

Chapter Seven

Word came the next morning that the inquest upon Lord Mortlock's death was postponed. The coroner had been detained on a visit to Essex by a broken carriage wheel, and plainly it was felt that his deputy would not do for a case as grand as that of the murder of the fifth Baron Mortlock.

Mr. Appleton soon made ready to go to his daughter. "All I can offer are a father's grieving condolences," he said. "And I know from the loss of my own wife that sometimes solicitude can be like chafing on a wound. But I must be with her and do what I can. Perhaps then I will go on to the magistrate's house and see if there is any news of Abraham. You, I believe, Fairfax, mean to talk to Dr. Nimier today."

"Yes, he expects me at his rooms in Greek Street."

Mr. Appleton buttoned his broadcloth coat, soundlessly whistling. "I hardly need urge you, Fairfax, to use your utmost penetration and discretion in attempting to discover . . . whether there is anything about Dr. Nimier I should know." His ruddy cheeks darkened a little. "Now, of course, is not the time to press my daughter to—to unburden herself. No. We must proceed as best we can."

They left the house together, Mr. Appleton taking a chair, Fairfax setting out on foot for Greek Street. His birthday was, at any rate, bright if cool, a breeze stirring the ever-present miasma of the refuse-heaped streets, splashes of sunshine falling on the colorful forest of hanging shop signs and reflecting in horse troughs and the glasses of lumbering carriages.

Entering Greek Street, he saw John Nimier himself some fifty yards ahead. The doctor was coming out of a tall house on the left in company with a lady clad in satin, her face veiled. Nimier escorted her across the road, nimbly avoiding the horsedroppings, to a crested carriage waiting there. Wand-slim and courtly, he handed her in, then stood talking to her through the window, retaining in his the gloved hand that rested on the sill.

Not Lady Mortlock's hand, anyway, Fairfax was sure of that: the lady was shorter and plumper. One of his grand patients no doubt. The street door of the house Nimier had left stood slightly ajar, and after a moment's thought Fairfax darted up the steps and slipped inside. Stealing a march, however slightly, on that ever-prepared and impenetrable gentleman was something he couldn't resist.

He found himself in an austerely whitewashed hall, looking at a bust of Hippocrates and a surprised manservant.

"Dr. Nimier is expecting me," he said, brazening it out. "My name is Fairfax. Is he in?"

The manservant showed him into Nimier's consulting room and asked him to wait. The room was large, richly carpeted, and ostentatiously set about with wonders. A fully articulated human skeleton grinned at him from the corner. One wall was taken up with glass cabinets containing more articulated bones, death masks, mummified remains, and something that Fairfax's appalled eye recognized, after a moment, as a fetus near to its full term, floating in a jar of spirits. There were curios and bibelots aplenty too, fragments of Egyptian and Etruscan ware, statuettes including a Buddha and a Greek Priapus, the head damaged but the member thrustingly intact. Greek men had a lot to live up to, Fairfax thought. The window gave onto the street; a peep showed him that Dr. Nimier was still preoccupied with the lady in the carriage.

As he thought: the curtain at the back of the room concealed a door. He tried the handle and found it unlocked.

A private study, less showy but more interesting. There were chemical retorts, jars of liquid and powder, and new-baked pills set out on earthenware dishes. He examined one, sniffed it.

Was this the same preparation as the pills by Lord Mortlock's bedside? Somehow he had mislaid the one he had purloined, he realized, cursing himself, but it certainly looked similar. He replaced it and went over to the desk, which was neatly set out with a diary or daybook in the center.

An unwarrantable intrusion, he thought, and then, Damn it, and opened the book. Under today's date he read, in a tiny and somehow secretive script, two entries: "Visc. Barford" and "Mr. F. Cave."

The first must refer to Viscountess Barford, he thought—the woman in the carriage, no doubt. She had a name for promiscuous affaires . . . The other entry defeated him for a moment until he realized that that word "Cave" was lightly underlined. *Cave*—Latin for "beware." Mr. F. must be himself. It was not unpleasant to think of himself as someone to beware of, and it was certainly highly revealing. Nimier did have something to hide. He flicked back the pages, and his eye lit on an entry at the bottom of the page for Tuesday, three days ago. "L. Mort., 8:00."

His heart thumped loudly. Did this mean he had met Lady Mortlock on Tuesday—here, or elsewhere, perhaps? He riffled the pages, but nothing else caught his eye. A folded note next to the book, however, did. He recognized the handwriting as soon as he opened it.

Sir. I beg leave to wait upon you at noon today, at your

chambers. The matter is equally urgent, important, and confidential. Yours, &c, Samuel Appleton.

The note was dated the twenty-sixth: today. Mr. Appleton must have sent it over first thing this morning. Curious! Fairfax listened out but could hear no sounds of Nimier returning. He laid the note down, his glance falling on the oddest thing yet: a monk's cowled habit thrown across a chair. Picking it up, he found a domino mask beneath. A masquerade costume, of course. He remembered Nimier at the levee talking of the masquerade he had been to at Ranelagh . . .

"I would not like to be thought of as mocking the monastic tradition. Though popish, it accomplished much of good."

Nimier had appeared right behind him without a sound. Fairfax still had the costume in his hands. Damn the man, he moved like a phantom . . .

"But the costume was not my choice," Nimier went on with an urbane half-smile. "It was sent to me with a masquerade ticket by a lady who wished me to join her at Ranelagh on Tuesday. Being from the country, sir, you have perhaps not heard of this quaint custom—in imitation of the Venetian habit, I suppose. Moralists do not like it, but I am not so severe. There. I have satisfied your curiosity on that matter. Perhaps I may complete your satisfaction, Mr. Fairfax, by answering your questions, which I am quite willing to do. You were not compelled, I think, to pry in this way. I must mention, however, that anything that touches my private and confidential relation with my patients is strictly *hors de question.* My Hippocratic oath as a physician requires nothing less. I offer to help you, sir, as a favor, not an obligation." Nimier gestured to the door. "Shall we?"

So much for stealing a march on him. Fairfax felt like a reprimanded schoolboy, and willed his cheeks to stop burning. In the consulting room Nimier prowled over to the glass case and dabbed at some faint fingerprints with a scented handkerchief.

"I see you have been admiring my preserved infant. It still lies in the in utero position, you will note: the exact position, curiously enough, that we adopt in moments of the worst extremity of fear or suffering. I remarked a starving beggar-boy in the street the other day, who was curled up among some straw in precisely this posture. And so, how goes it with your quest, sir? The black has not turned up, I suppose?"

"No. But there are still many unanswered questions besides that. Perhaps — as you are so good as to offer to satisfy my curiosity — you will tell me the identity of the lady who sent you the masquerade ticket."

Nimier's eyelids crinkled in amusement. "My dear sir, she did not disclose her identity. Anonymity is the entire point of the masquerade. But come, I know what fish you are angling for. Milord Mortlock is murdered, and I was there, so your busy brain is hunting about for connections. Well, I must repeat myself. I attended Lady Mortlock's levee because I had heard much of its elegance. I am welcome at many such gatherings, sir: I move in high circles. I was not disappointed, however, in what I found."

Fairfax did not believe him. "And your acquaintance with Lord Mortlock? I may be in error, but when we arrived at the levee he seemed — struck by seeing you there."

Nimier spread his thin scrubbed hands. "I cannot comment on that. All that I am free to tell you I tell."

"You once fought a duel, is that not so?"

"Indeed. That is no secret, or no more a secret than such things usually are. Yes, sir, I fought, and with swords. It is truer to the custom's chivalric origin. Pistols are machines, and make the contest arbitrary. You cannot close with your man."

"What was the outcome?"

"My opponent was wounded. I spared his life, on pain of his retracting his slander and libel, which he did."

"The slander and libel concerned your professional standards?"

For the first time Nimier looked slightly uncomfortable. "A medical man cannot be too careful of such things. His treatments, his compounds, they are his honor—"

"And what precisely do you treat, Dr. Nimier? I do not think such opulence can come from bone-setting. Do you specialize in venereal infections?"

Nimier looked down his nose, lips curling. "Let us say, sir, that if you have been wounded in the service of Venus, I may be able to be of assistance. Come, Mr. Fairfax, is that it? Is that the reason for your furtive explorations? You had only to say, sir—"

"I think you are making fun of me, Dr. Nimier." Fairfax cut him off.

"No. But where your curiosity becomes mere inquisitive impudence, sir, I must stop you. I have an important and lucrative practice to maintain, and I will not see it jeopardized by baseless, meddlesome insinuations." Nimier went to the door. "Did I kill Lord Mortlock? I say I did not. But if you wish to demonstrate that I did, Mr. Fairfax, then I shall be diverted to see how you manage it. Diverted up to a point, anyhow. My patience is not unlimited, and when I am out of patience I am a bad enemy."

There was a tap at the door, and the manservant put his head round.

"A lady, sir."

"Thank you. I will see her at once. Mr. Fairfax was just leaving."

Well, the picture of recent events was filling in, at least. And the figure in the foreground was surely Lady Mortlock. Technically guiltless she must be, wholly innocent she perhaps was, but all the lines of this baffling pattern seemed to converge on her.

Monday evening—a music lesson with Pennant and Lawrence. Wednesday evening, when he himself had toured the town with Hugh Mortlock, she had been visited by her father. Tuesday evening . . . well, was it Nimier who filled that gap? Had Lady Mortlock—or "L. Mort"—sent him the masquerade ticket, and met him there? It was damning evidence if so—damning insofar as it suggested a clandestine affair, doubly damning if one saw the meeting as the occasion when a murder had been planned . . .

Even without that worst construction, he found his regard for Lady Mortlock dimming. To think of her with Nimier . . . For he truly hated that man—his poise, his inhuman confidence. Jealousy, perhaps, he thought. John Nimier, with no more advantages of birth, fortune or education than he, was wealthy and independent and waited on by the great.

So the intense suspicion he felt towards Dr. Nimier was perhaps misleading, because personal dislike was mixed up in it. And by the same token, was his admiration of Lady Mortlock making him overkind to her?

He didn't like that thought. He prided himself on his even-handedness. The trouble was, there were limits to how firm he could be with a woman who had just been made a widow. Not to mention a peeress and the daughter of his employer . . .

Well, that was another question: Why was Mr. Appleton visiting Dr. Nimier today? Was he doing a little investigating on his own account? In which case, did he not trust Fairfax—or was he playing some double game of his own? Solid Mr. Appleton was apparently less two-faced than these society creatures with whom he was dealing . . . but then, of course, homespun plainness itself could be a disguise. Suppose Nimier knew something, and Mr. Appleton knew that he knew it . . .

Fairfax's head ached. This was like moving in a world of mirrors. Perhaps he should remember the rule of Occam's razor: entities are not to be multiplied. The word "razor" gave him a bracing reminder: a man had died horribly, drenched in blood. Whatever veils were drawn across his eyes, he must not lose sight of that.

Meggy showed him into the Mortlock house, and gave a sort of simpering cringe at the sound of raised voices coming from the drawing room.

"Perhaps, sir, you'd care to wait in the small parlor while—?"

Fairfax ignored her and barged into the drawing room, where he found the usually mild Lawrence in such a passion that he took no notice of the visitor.

". . . Of course you've got it to give, damn it all! Why, you said yourself you're seeing your banker today! You're hardly poor, Charlotte—don't come *that* with me, least of all *now*. Good God! I can't believe you'd refuse me. Devil take you women, you're naught but a parcel of designing rogues, not fit for . . . But you're different, Charlotte, you're my sister, damn it, and you can't—"

"I beg you not to talk of this anymore, Lawrence," Lady Mortlock said, turning away from him, pale to the lips. "I have not been ungenerous in the past—but I have many things to think of, and this is hardly . . . this is hardly the time."

She glanced at Fairfax, but her brother, pink-cheeked and graceless as a thwarted boy, still took no notice. "I must have it," he said, and flung himself down on a sofa, folding his arms. "I shan't move from here till I do. I am in earnest, sister, you know. I shan't move."

"Dear, dear, the maids will have to dust round you, then," Lady Mortlock said with a weak laugh, but there were tears in her eyes as she said to Fairfax, "You have come to trouble and torment me too, have you, sir? There is room on the sofa, you know, if you wish to adopt the same tactic."

"Forgive me, Lady Mortlock, I have only a few small questions . . ." He glanced awkwardly at Lawrence.

"Speak on, sir," she said. "My brother, you know, is only part of the furniture."

"Well . . . I simply need to establish some recent events involving yourself and the late—and Hugh. Just to be clear. Monday, you have told me, was your musical evening; Wednesday your father spent the evening with you here. But Tuesday . . ."

Lawrence spoke up. "Tuesday evening Hugh was gambling at White's till late. I saw him there. He was playing French ruff, and he was a hundred guineas out when I dropped in." He pursed his lips, giving his sister a triumphant look. "That's what Hugh was up to that night, at any rate. What of yourself, Charlotte, eh?"

"I cannot recall. I—I truly cannot, and"—she drew herself up, in a tearful attempt at haughtiness—"and I will not be badgered like this, in my own home. 'Tis sheer insult and impertinence. I have done nothing wrong—I swear before God I have done nothing wrong, and—and you will please leave, both of you, just go away . . ."

She ran off, choking back sobs. Fairfax listened to her feet on the stairs and the slam of a door. He bit his lip. Not what he wanted at all . . . His eye fell on Lawrence, still lolling on the sofa.

"God's life, man, is this a time to be deviling your sister for loans?"

"Eh? Well, damn it all, she is my sister. What about you? You're deviling her with questions, ain't you? Mighty rum, when it's Abraham who's the one they're after. Unless you've took a fancy for her, eh? Oh, none of my business if you have, m'dear, only she's out of your reach, I fear—"

"You are offensive, sir," Fairfax said whitely. "I do what I am employed to do. That is a consequence of having to earn one's own bread, and I count it no disgrace, certainly no more disgrace than begging for funds from everyone you meet."

To his astonishment, Lawrence Appleton's eyes bulged and he let out a sob before covering his lips with a trembling hand. "I know it," he said. "Damn you, Fairfax, I know it. I don't want to be—the way I am. God knows I don't . . ." He choked back another sob. "But I can't help it. The flesh is weak, don't it say so in the Bible? I really can't, and there are worse things than what I do. I swear there are worse fellows than me and . . . Oh, I am sorely pressed, Fairfax—I declare I am absolutely squeezed and I don't know what I shall do short of drowning myself like a damned unwanted puppy . . . Not that they drown themselves, you know, silly notion—"

"Lawrence, are you being threatened by Luke Griffey? If so, the law may help—"

"Not the law!" Lawrence wiped his eyes, shuddering, then got to his feet. "They can do nothing—nothing. Obliged for the thought, though, my dear fellow. Heyday! I never meant to shout at Charlotte, you know. Only sometimes that little miss ain't as straightforward as she likes to pretend. There's a deal to be said for having a pretty *way* about you, and she's always had it. Well, I'll get nothing here, I fancy, not today at any rate." Lawrence's eyes narrowed and he looked sidelong at Fairfax. "All depends, you see. Now on *Monday* evening, she had money to give, oh yes, very readily."

"The musical evening?"

"That's the one. Now I ask you to judge—Monday evening, she slips Abraham a few shillings to take himself off, and there's a couple of guineas for me to do the same. Aye, I was here, for a space. Pennant started his lesson, lots of scales and those other things—like artichokes—"

"Arpeggios?"

"That's the ones. Oh, she was cunning about it. Invites me over, you see. Then when I gets restless with all the jangling and fallalery—I can only abide so much of it—she says I can go if I like, and points me to some money on the mantelshelf." Lawrence tapped his nose, going to the door. "Oh, yes, I can see as far into a millstone as another. Mind, you don't have to take my word for it. Ask Pennant."

And with that he was gone. Fairfax lingered a moment, mulling over what Lawrence had told him. Then he went out to the hall and stood irresolute, wondering if he should try to seek another interview with Lady Mortlock. But he doubted she would speak to him now . . . So much for firmness. Again he looked round at the hall, the portrait of Black Peter at the foot of the stairs, the linen chest, the alcove with the chair where Abraham would sit; again he tried to picture Abraham stealing downstairs after the murder, opening the door, leaving the house for the last time, slipping off to whatever hiding place he had found in the great city . . . And then in turn he tried to picture the guests at the levee, each coming downstairs to the empty hall and leaving the house while the music and talk continued upstairs, one of them a little breathless, perhaps, a little appalled and exalted, having just deftly and smartly extinguished a life. Which, which . . . ?

Damn it, he *would* find out. Going out, he halted at the foot of the steps, something making him glance up at the doorpost. Kate Little, he saw, must have called this morning: her tally was chalked up there, two strokes with a line through. He looked again at the mark she had made yesterday: *three* strokes, with a line through. He assumed each stroke meant a pint of milk delivered . . . yet hadn't Meggy said she had brought two pints yesterday? Abraham had brought the two pints down to the kitchen—yes, he could swear it.

Curious. Kate Little didn't look the sort to cheat her wealthy customers with false tallies. Probably it was a trifling matter, but he bore it in mind. He certainly intended talking to the milk seller again before he was done. For now, though, he was going to act on Lawrence's advice. "Ask Pennant."

"He ain't astir yet." The landlady of Stephen Pennant's lodgings, behind a hosier's in St. Martin's Lane, blew her nose on her apron. "I won't walk up—I've got the ague. And the screws. 'Tis hardly fair. You can walk up and wake him if you like. 'Tis more than I'd care to do. Wicked temper when he's liverish. Irish, you see."

Life was simple, Fairfax thought, going upstairs, as long as you remembered that the French were licentious, the Irish temperamental, the Scots mean, and the Negroes irredeemably savage . . .

Stephen Pennant *was* stirring—at least, he was lifting himself groggily from the pillow when Fairfax knocked and went in.

"Mr. Fairfax." Pennant sat up and scratched the short fair hair on his unwigged head. "I wasn't aware that I'd begun holding levees, but there, 'tis a novelty. I fear I don't make such a pretty sight as the ladies do . . ." He swung his slender legs out of the bed and put his feet gingerly to the floor. "By God, my tongue's like a barber's strop."

"Forgive me. I wouldn't disturb you without good cause."

"That sounds a trifle ominous. Oh, take a seat, sir, if you can find one." The room, not large, was half taken up by a spinet, and there were heaps of music manuscripts everywhere. Pennant pulled a morning gown over his nightshirt. "Let me guess: yesterday's tragic news. Poor Lord Mortlock having his quietus made with a bare bodkin. Bad business. But I verily believe, Fairfax, that I've told you everything."

"It was not so much the events of yesterday as the events of Monday evening I'm curious about. Apparently there was a musical party at Lady Mortlock's."

"Aye, so there was." Pennant rubbed his eyes with the heel of his hand. "I give Lady Mortlock a little musical instruction from time to time. She has a good touch upon the keys, and taste, but little confidence as yet. We play exercises, sing catches—"

"I hear the party was reduced to two."

Pennant gave a frowning smile. "You hear a lot, don't you? Do you never catch a chill, pressing your ear to all those keyholes? Or does the thrill compensate, perhaps?"

Fairfax wouldn't be rattled. "My dear man, there's no use in either of us climbing up on our moral high horse. I like you, and don't particularly want to find out anything discreditable about you. But my business is the murder of Lord Mortlock, and any lies or half-truths I come across are bound to make my ears prick up. I'm not a magistrate or a constable; I'm a good deal more agreeable than they are likely to be, for one thing, so you may as well talk to me, because I'm not going to go away."

Pennant looked hard at him for a moment, then laughed. "Spoken like an honest man, sir, or a good imitation of one, which is the best one can expect in these times." He rooted among the papers and came up with a bottle. "Will you drink with me? Aye, an ungodly hour, I know. Well, you want to know what goes on, naturally enough. And now I hold up my hands"—he did so—"and tell you, honestly: with Lady Mortlock, nothing."

Fairfax studied him. His skepticism must have shown.

"Oh, I've paid my compliments, made my bows and pretty speeches, right enough. Only because I knew such fooling wouldn't be unwelcome in that quarter. Come, it was plain the marriage was a sheer expedient. Title for her, money for him. A common story. One poached on no preserves by admiring—flirting even. It was never any more than that."

"And yet"—Fairfax tried to keep his look pleasant—"you have been alone with her. On Monday evening, at least.

But she is a married woman, and even in townish circles that is surely—"

"Damn it, I know how it looks. And I tell you . . . Well, look here. Before you set me down in your little book as Lady Mortlock's illicit beau, take note of this. Lady Mortlock spent the whole of Tuesday evening with a man, at the masquerade at Ranelagh. That man certainly wasn't her husband, and it certainly wasn't me, as I was leading the orchestra the whole time. Now"—Pennant took a drink of canary from a smeared glass—"ask yourself, my friend, whether you do not have the wrong sow by the ear altogether."

The masquerade . . . It was confirmation, then, of a sort. "Who was this man?"

"My dear fellow—*masks*. Besides, I saw nothing; I was occupied with the orchestra."

"Then how can you be so sure?"

"Because I was told it, by Miss Vertue. *She* was at Ranelagh that night, and got near 'em, and she had no doubt that it was Lady Mortlock." Pennant made a sour face, or it might have been the wine. "Deep in tête-à-tête with some fellow the whole time."

"What was this man wearing?"

Pennant blinked. "Eh? Oh, I don't recall. You'd have to ask Miss Vertue."

"When did you hear this? You mean you are an intimate of Miss Vertue's?"

"No, no. Well . . . she was present at the inquest on poor Spicer on Wednesday. Aye, I don't know why, but she was about, and she spoke to me after. Lord Mortlock's name kept coming up, and she wanted to know about him. I told her as much as I knew: that he lived high, that he'd lately married the daughter of old Appleton, the Midas of sugar. Oh, I know her, says she—old schoolfriends, you know. And then she pipes up that she'd seen her the very night before, at Ranelagh—swore it was her—with this fellow. Well, that

certainly wasn't her husband she was with, thinks I. Mortlock wouldn't be seen dead there, and besides, everyone
knows why liaisons are kept at the masquerades—'tis a by-
word for vice . . ." Pennant poured more canary. "So you see.
This is trading in gossip, perhaps, but as you seemed to suggest that there was something more than mere acquaintance
between me and Lady Mortlock, I must point out that the evidence points elsewhere. To *whom,* I don't know."

Nimier, Fairfax thought: who else? Lady Mortlock's
keeping a secret rendezvous with Nimier would certainly
suggest that he was the lover . . .

And yet, there was something about this young man that
was a little too pat, a little too smug—beyond the general
smugness of young men, rather. And what about this business of Sophie Vertue attending the inquest on Richard
Spicer? Where did that fit in?

"I think," Fairfax said, "I will have that drink after all. I
am thirty-two today, and allowed a little indulgence."

"Today? Why, sir, many congratulations!" Pennant said,
looking for another glass; and Fairfax could see him thinking: *My God, how dreadful to be that age* . . .

"The inquest, then, was your first meeting with Miss
Vertue."

"Aye, that was it. Oh, she's the most charming creature, is
she not? Now, if you were to suspect the state of my affec-
tions towards *her,* then I might be put to the blush. I certainly
hope for a renewal of that acquaintance . . . But as for Lady
Mortlock—why, what would I be doing paddling in such a
forbidden lake as that? I am a great fool, I know, but not an
entire fool. Your very good health, sir."

"And yours." Fairfax drank, his mind teeming. Thoughts,
and doubts . . . Pennant's behavior to Lady Mortlock at the
levee had had a definite pique about it. The pique, perhaps,
of a jealous lover who had heard about her rendezvous with
another man? Or if not lover, then obsessive admirer? Could

it be that Lady Mortlock was leading the two of them, Nimier and Pennant, some kind of amorous dance? Discontented upper-class wives had been known to while away their boredom thus. And the fact remained that she had shuffled both Abraham and her brother out of the way when Pennant was there . . .

"Well, I thank you for your time, and for the good canary wine," Fairfax said, setting down his glass.

"Glad to oblige, my friend. My apologies for the picturesque squalor, by the by — I shall move on from all this some day. *Ruth* will lead me, perhaps," Pennant said, tenderly patting a bound bundle of manuscript music. "Well, she may, though it's a rash man who puts his fortune in the hands of a woman." He grinned, raising his glass in valediction.

Aye, my friend, you are too self-satisfied by half, Fairfax thought as he left, and for all you've said, I still think there is something going on between you and Lady Mortlock — in fact, I'd double my stake on it.

Of course there remained the mystery of the man she had met at Ranelagh — Nimier? And if so, why? The only thing he felt sure of was that no one was going to come out of this well.

He headed back to Mr. Appleton's house because it was the merchant's custom to have a cold collation at noon, and he was hungry; he also felt it was time to do some plain talking with his employer.

Lawrence, he found, was there before him. Again he was greeted by the sound of loud voices, but this time, dismissing the footman, he stayed in the hall to listen.

". . . I'm your son, Pa, and a son has a claim on his father's purse, don't he? Well, don't he?"

"Be silent, sir. You disgrace yourself and me with these outrageous clamors. I have told you there is no money for

you. Have you no shame, to persist with these intolerable demands? I'll hear no more of it, not a word more, Lawrence."

The parlor door opened and a heated-looking Mr. Appleton came out. Lawrence pursued him.

"I'm your son! Don't that count for anything, damn it? I
notice you had money to give to Nimier this morning. *That's*
all right, I suppose, but when your own son asks you—"

"How dare you! You have been at my account book. You
have pried into my private records, sir, and you had no business—"

"Oh, come, Pa, you always griped at me for not taking an
interest. That was what you had planned, after all. Charlotte
would lift you into society, while I would carry on your
wretched trade, and the boys—what, one for the navy and
one for the army, perhaps? All neatly planned out. Very well,
I've peeped into your precious accounts, and interesting
reading they make."

"Mr. Fairfax," Mr. Appleton said stonily, "leave us, if you
please."

"I think I had better stay, sir," Fairfax said.

Mr. Appleton glared at him, then transferred the look to
his son. "You have acted in a most shocking, underhand
manner, Lawrence. I wish I could say it surprised me—"

"I have to! Don't I have to, Pa? When am I ever considered? You didn't even make me a party to your little secret
about this fellow"—Lawrence gestured at Fairfax—"who I
knew pretty well must be the new tutor, or was supposed to
be before you had him running round like your lackey. But
oh no, I wasn't to be told . . ."

Fairfax had noticed before that it was dangerous to stand
near a quarrel; you were always likely to be hit by a flying
insult.

"Oh, no, leave the boy out of it," Lawrence went on, his
voice shrill like an overblown flute, "he's of no account, not

he—always Charlotte, Charlotte, from the day I was born, and—"

"Lawrence!" Mr. Appleton held up a warning finger. "Are you a man, sir?"

Lawrence swallowed. "I'm just saying it's not fair—"

"Are you a man, sir?" Mr. Appleton repeated, fixing his eyes on his son's, though Lawrence tried to shrink away. "Are you a man? And have you aught to say to me, as a man? If not, then get you gone."

His face scarlet, Lawrence turned and stalked out, crashing the front door behind him.

Mr. Appleton, shaken out of his normal placidity, took several deep breaths before saying, "I asked you quite courteously, I think, to leave us, Mr. Fairfax."

"I hope I was courteous in my refusal, sir. And I hope you understand that my position is made intolerably difficult when some secrets are revealed to me and not others."

"Secrets?"

"You have given money to Dr. John Nimier? Or was what Lawrence said not true?"

Mr. Appleton made a face. "I recompensed Dr. Nimier for his time, that is all, and it is my habit to enter all my cash transactions in a daily account. A very good habit, sir. I recommend it to you. Yes: I have been to call on Dr. Nimier. As a father, sir. A father . . . Will you embarrass me by forcing me to repeat what was painful to mention in the first place? You know well that there were rumors circulating about Charlotte before this. Now Hugh is killed, the rumors may be—darker in tone. As a father, I want no breath of new scandal to touch her at this dreadful time; and I want to make sure that those who are, ahem, in her immediate circle, know it."

"I see." Paying Nimier, then, to keep his distance. Or was there more to it? What exactly did those accounts reveal?

Was Mr. Appleton in financial straits, as he had wondered before?

"It was your own information, Fairfax, that led me to believe that Nimier *may*—I only say *may*—have been behaving improperly in regard to my daughter. And that is why I spoke to him, as a concerned father."

"Well, he was certainly at Lady Mortlock's last evening," Fairfax said. And now I've heard more, he thought: a meeting at that nursery of scandal, a masquerade. But he wanted to follow that trail by himself. He could be secretive too . . . "But I believe there is equal or greater reason to suspect the—the behavior of Stephen Pennant. Indeed, I am sure of it."

"Pennant, eh?" Mr. Appleton looked thoughtful.

"He denies any greater degree of intimacy than the usual compliments that are acceptable in such circles as Lady Mortlock moves in, but—"

"Compliments?"

Damn the man, Fairfax thought, never mind this puritanical alderman stuff. He must know perfectly well that the world into which he has sold his daughter observes the moral code of the polecat . . . "Yes, sir, and I'm sure you know what I mean. Though I must say Pennant seems quite happy to . . . keep his distance. Of course, a direct approach to Lady Mortlock herself, asking her flat if there was any inappropriate relation—"

"No." Mr. Appleton was sharp. "Such an approach must certainly not come from you, sir. If anyone . . . My daughter is but newly widowed, Mr. Fairfax, and is not to be roughly handled." The merchant consulted his gold watch. "Well, you have been plain, sir. I respect it, where some other employers might resent it—though there are limits beyond which I will not go. However, I thank you for your diligence. And lest you accuse me again of being secretive . . ."

I never did, Fairfax thought. Well, all right, I did.

". . . I may as well tell you that I called in to the magistrate's house and learned the news, which is precisely nothing. The constables are searching among the blacks who congregate in the river districts, but they of course are no ready friends to the law, and the task is a hard one. Poor Abraham!" He shook his head. "Well, I to my study. There are cold meats in the dining room if you are hungry. What do you intend this afternoon?"

"Well, I hope to find Miss Vertue more receptive to questions: she was somewhat overwrought yesterday."

Hardly seeming to listen, Mr. Appleton nodded and went away with his lips soundlessly whistling.

Fairfax made a hasty meal in the empty dining room, while his mind chewed over the latest tidbits: Mr. Appleton covertly visiting and paying Nimier; Lawrence apparently so desperate for money that he was even driven to an uncharacteristic self-assertion. All comes down to money . . . Making no sense out of it all, Fairfax picked up a newspaper that lay folded under a chair. It was Wednesday's *Daily Post.* Turning past the gossip of the court and the accounts of new "beauties" and their conquests, he came to a page of advertisements and found to his surprise that it was incomplete. Something had been raggedly torn from the bottom of the page. The columns were filled with situations vacant and wanted, coaches and horses for sale, cures and treatments and lonely widows, valuables lost or stolen—these with appeals for their return "and no questions asked." Which the law frowned upon, as an incitement to criminality, he knew. Back in the days of Jonathan Wild, the so-called "Thief-taker General" who had controlled London's underworld while ostensibly serving the law, such advertisements had proliferated. If something was taken from you, you applied to Wild, who would do his best to recover it for you for a small fee. In fact, he had all the thieves and robbers under his thumb: he would handle the stolen goods and sell them back to you, whilst the luckless thief lived in fear of Wild turning him in to the authorities, who, in turn, depended on him to secure them convictions. Wild had been hanged at last, and laws had been passed to prevent such abuses, but the advertisements still appeared. Was the piece that had been torn out one of those? Fairfax wondered. Impossible to tell, as the advertisements had been randomly ordered by the printer.

A curiosity indeed—but a meaningful one? He couldn't tell. He told himself again to bear in mind the rule of Occam's razor, and set out for Hanover Square.

"Mr. Fairfax! You come opportunely, for this is a time of wonders indeed—sensation upon sensation! I half expect to see a lioness whelping in the streets, and ghosts that squeak and gibber, as the poet has it!"

Mrs. Stoddart hailed him from her study, where she was kneeling among a pile of books with dust on her prominent nose.

"I seek a line in Milton—at least I think it is Milton—that came to my mind as wonderfully apt for the moment, but no matter. Did you see that remarkable child on your way in?"

"Miss Vertue? I did not. Is anything amiss?"

"I would not call it so, though the poor creature is in a taking, there's no doubt of that. But she will find it *such* food for the growing soul, I think, and we can regret nothing that nourishes us so. Well, I will tell the wondrous tale. Here has been Mr. Stephen Pennant, the young musician, not twenty minutes ago: quite breathless and disordered, but full of the most impetuous gallantry. One could not help but smile upon it, or at least I could not, for I love a spontaneity of feeling above everything. In he came, and introduced himself to me as briefly as may be—not that I minded it, for it dispensed with ceremony, which is so very unnatural—and then craved a word alone with Sophie; in short, he has made her the most ardent proposal, here and now! What do you think?"

"I . . . A very great surprise."

"And all the more beautiful, I think, for it! He was, he said, so struck, so absolutely entranced by Sophie, that he was emboldened to brush aside convention—indeed, he couldn't help himself, he said—and throw himself at once before her and beg that she would consider his suit. A proposal, there and then, in the most romantic manner! There certainly was a thorough disregard of convention in it, and he was conscious, he said, of presuming on a *very* short acquaintance. But what does that matter? For myself, I think a couple may know each other a single day, and run away and be happy for the rest of their lives. Indeed, 'tis likelier than if they have come to know one another first!"

"True," said Fairfax, who did not think this true at all, and indeed thought it the stupidest thing he had ever heard an adult person say. "But pray, what was Miss Vertue's response to such an unexpected avowal?"

Mrs. Stoddart smiled. "She wept. She told him, as best she could, that the proposal was not to be considered, and insisted that he leave. This he did, with the reluctance of an ardent lover and the protests of a passionate heart. But really poor Sophie could not bear it, and she shed many a tear on my shoulder. Love, she said, was dead for her, utterly dead; she had no intention of ever giving her heart, and such a proposal could only awaken the most painful sensations in her breast, so painful indeed that she had hardly been able to give him a coherent answer, beyond telling him to speak no more of it and be gone, if he truly had any of that warm regard for her being that he professed." Mrs. Stoddart's shortsighted eyes shone with the drama of it. "Well, I could only assure her she need do nothing that would cause her pain, and told her I was very sorry that she should feel herself to be dead to the tender passion. I asked, indeed, why she should feel so, but not in such a way as to demand an answer—not I; I make it a rule never to trespass upon the sacred ground of her feel-

ings. And when she said she couldn't tell me, I didn't press
her. She said she couldn't speak of it any more, and must go
out. I would have had the carriage made ready, but she
wouldn't stay for that. And so she went, poor child, no doubt
with such a clutch of feelings at her heart that to be within
doors was intolerable. Ah, I remember those days! And so
here you find me, sir, my head still quite ringing with it. I had
only just digested yesterday's terrible news. Hard upon the
heels of death comes this—almost as if to say that life must
go on. I do not mean the conceit unfeelingly; Milton has the
thought much more succinct, if I could only find the passage . . ."

   She would do better to look for her niece, he thought, then
reproached himself. Thirty-two was rather young to be a cen-
sorious prig. Besides, was Mrs. Stoddart's benign neglect
worse than Mr. Appleton's industrious meddling?

   He had an idea, at any rate, of what Stephen Pennant was
up to. He also had an idea of where Sophie Vertue had
gone—an idea that brought other ideas in its train. He
thanked Mrs. Stoddart, and left her among her books.

Chapter Eight

At the George and Blue Board Inn he found he was not the only person who wanted to see Sir Anthony Spicer. There was a whole gaggle of folk gathered in the narrow paneled passage outside the door of Sir Anthony's room. Ostlers, maids, the innkeeper—and at the front, with her hands pressed against the timber of the door, Sophie Vertue.

Fairfax edged his way through to the innkeeper. "What goes on here?" Sophie Vertue turned wide, haunted eyes on him.

"The gentleman's locked himself in, sir. He's in there, all right, but when the maid showed this lady up to see him, he turned the key in the lock and won't answer. The maid says he was acting mighty strange this morning, and there was"—the innkeeper lowered his voice—"a pistol on his table, in full view. You know the gentleman, sir?"

"Yes. He was but recently bereaved, and greatly distracted . . ."

"He lost all that he loved," Sophie said huskily, her hands still pressed to the door. "I fear for him . . ."

Fairfax felt the catch of the door, and was about to charge it open when the air was rent by the sound of a shot. A maid screamed. Sophie closed her eyes and beat her fists weakly on the door.

And then while the shot still echoed, there was a rattle at the lock and the door opened.

Sir Anthony Spicer stood hunched and pale, regarding the gasping onlookers with unfathomable eyes. Behind him, Fairfax saw a pistol on the floor. There was a scorching smell of powder.

"Well, well. There are a good many witnesses of my final humiliation," Sir Anthony said with a gray spectral smile. "I think, innkeeper, that I have caused a little commotion under your roof. I apologize for it. I had in mind a foolish notion, but no matter: I am too much of a coward for it. Be assured, my good man, that there is no damage to your fittings, and that I will make no more trouble for you." Sir Anthony patted down his cravat with a trembling hand. "Ah, Mr. Fairfax, you too. Quite a meeting."

Fairfax signaled to the innkeeper that it would be all right, and presently he, Sophie, and Sir Anthony were left alone at the door. Sophie was gazing at the old gentleman with a rapt, almost trancelike expression; as he noticed it he frowned.

"Well, young woman? Do I know you?"

"You may have—seen me at the inquest," Sophie murmured faintly. "But . . ."

"This is Miss Sophie Vertue, Sir Anthony," Fairfax said. "Who I believe had hopes, or expectations, of being your relation some day."

"What?" Both started at his words.

"Why, as bride to young Richard. That's so, isn't it, Miss Vertue?" Fairfax said. "The man you met at Bath—the attachment that Mrs. Stoddart thought it best to discourage. That was Richard Spicer."

Sophie nodded slowly, turned to Sir Anthony. "I am honored to meet you at last, sir. Richard would speak of you, and it was always my hope to meet you in—in different circumstances from these." She put out her hand, and after a moment Sir Anthony took it wonderingly.

"May we come in?" Fairfax said. "I think we all have need of a frank talk . . ."

Inside he bent, picked up the pistol, and laid it on the table. Seeing Sir Anthony's expression, he said: "You called it cowardice, Sir Anthony. I call it courage. What is facing each sunrise, except courage?"

Sir Anthony shook his head. "You know nothing, sir . . . but that is not your fault. Oh, I did not believe I would do it. I primed and loaded and steadied my hand—but all I could do was fire into the floor, and throw the damnable thing from me. God curse me for a fool . . ." He groped at a sheet of paper on the table, half-covered with writing, and screwed it into a ball. "Well, never fear, I am not about to do anything more. I am resigned."

"Richard's death was tragedy enough, sir," said Sophie, clearly and firmly. "Yes. It's true"—she glanced at Fairfax— "and I hope you will not think the worse of me, Sir Anthony. I have been debating whether to speak to you, and today my heart was so sore . . . At Bath in the autumn I met your nephew Richard—and we fell in love."

Sir Anthony stared at her. "I had no notion he had been at Bath."

"He went there only for a short stay. He was tired of London, he said, and needed to refresh his spirits."

And temporarily escape his creditors, Fairfax thought.

"Our meetings were conducted clandestinely—oh, but animated only by the purest spirit of love, sir. The attachment had many things against it. Richard explained that he was— like me—an orphan, and not in a position to make promises, as he was not yet settled in the world, and dependent on the favor of a relation. A relation who . . . who was not pleased with him."

Sir Anthony gazed at her, with an expression as if he were trying to follow the tune of distant music.

"At last my aunt heard rumor of the attachment, and

though she is the kindest of guardians to me, and pressed me to no confessions or undertakings, she thought it best to carry me away from Bath, and trusted that absence would either confirm or undo what a tyrannical proscription might only force to an unnatural growth. So she reasoned, at any rate. For my part I was quite decided: Richard was the man above all others that I could love, and would wait for, and it was on those terms that we parted, with I am afraid a great many tears on my side, and a sorrowing fortitude on his. But he was adamant that it would be unfair to hold me to any promise while his own fortune was so undecided. While I traveled with my aunt to Bristol, Scarborough, and other places, Richard and I wrote one another frequently — at least, I poured out my heart often in letters, for that is a woman's way, and he wrote me warmly from London, though the trouble of sorting out his affairs meant it could not be as often as he wished . . ."

She paused for breath, looking at Sir Anthony, who smiled at her with sad kindness. "I see, my dear," he said. "I think you loved my nephew very much. Tell me, do you have a portion?"

"A little money comes to me when I am of age," she said. "Not a great deal."

Sir Anthony nodded and gently gestured her to go on.

"Well, at last my aunt was ready to return to London — you may imagine my joy at that! — and our return was set for last Sunday. I wrote Richard so, and when we came to my aunt's house late on Sunday night, I found waiting for me a sweet note from Richard, with two tickets for the masquerade at Ranelagh on Tuesday. I was easily able to persuade my aunt that they came from a female friend welcoming us back to London society, and so we went to the masquerade, and I of course was dreadfully on the watch for Richard, certain I would know him at once despite masks — his graceful carriage and his most musical voice . . ."

"There, my dear," Sir Anthony said, patting her head. "There. 'Tis told. You could not see him there, of course. Dear, dear."

"No. He had—he had died in the early hours of Tuesday morning, by his own hand. But I didn't know that; and of course because the relation between us was secret, no one thought to tell me. The evening of that masquerade was, I think, the longest of my life. I went home wretched, and in the morning, despite some prideful suspicion in my heart that he had deserted me, I applied to his landlady, and learned the truth. And so all the joyous hopes that I had carried with me for almost half a year were—blasted."

Sir Anthony sat down heavily. "I wish I had known this."

"Oh, believe me, sir, Richard had no intent to deceive, not in any underhand way. He was just so sorely unsettled about his future that all his proceedings had to be circumspect. I knew that he was . . . well, looking about him for something to settle on, as it was far from his nature simply to wait upon the inheritance that would someday be his . . ."

Her voice faded, and she blushed. There was a world of sadness in Sir Anthony's eyes, and Fairfax wondered whether it had really been far from Richard Spicer's nature to do that—whether, in fact, he had not lived his dissolute life simply waiting and hoping for his uncle to die.

"I know he found it hard to settle to anything," Sophie went on in a lower tone, "but I also know that he would not have come to the end he did without being badly led astray. His letters talked of Lord Mortlock as his frequent companion, and when at the inquest I learned of his habit of gambling, and the debts he had run up, then I could not help but see this Lord Mortlock as his bad angel. I blamed him, most bitterly, and hearing that he had married my old schoolfellow Charlotte Appleton, I went to her levee, hoping to—I know not what: see this monster, take the measure of this man who could play with human lives so callously. But I did not see him, of course," she faltered, glancing at Fairfax.

"No," he said, wondering just how intense had been the hatred this girl took to the Mortlock house yesterday . . . "It was perhaps a satisfaction, then, to know of his death."

Sophie Vertue folded her hands quite calmly. "I would rather have Richard back," she said. "I grieve for Charlotte: but as for him—"

Sir Anthony gave a sudden groan. "No more, my dear. Do not speak of that man anymore—not in that way. I can't bear it. I understand too well. I have heaped blame upon his head and damned him to the lowest hell with curses, and yet it is all nonsense. All nonsense! If you would lay the blame upon anyone for Richard's death, my dear, then it should be me." He went to the trunk containing the dead man's effects, and took out a letter. "This is from me to Richard. It lay open on his bureau when I went to collect his things. It arrived on Monday, and now I do not doubt that he read it when he came home to his lodgings on Monday night, having been abroad all day; and that after he had read it, he went out and shot himself." Sir Anthony pushed the letter into Sophie's hands. "You may read it if you like, my dear, but I can tell you the pith of it, quite simply. I had long been angry with the demands Richard made on my purse, and the way he abused, as I saw it, his expectations as my heir. I had tried time and again to bring him to heel, if you like. And at last, after what I saw as a particularly arrogant request for money, I took it into my head to thoroughly frighten him with a simple ruse. I am a widower without issue, which is why Richard was my heir. But if I were to marry again, and have a child of my own, then he would be my heir no longer; his expectations would be gone. It was not something I had ever thought of— there was no replacing the late Lady Spicer—but seeing an acquaintance of mine who had remarried in middle age and begun a new family gave me an idea."

Sir Anthony sighed deeply. "I wish to God I had never thought of it—but I did. I wrote Richard that I had come to an understanding with a lady in my district, a lady faintly known to him, who is in truth no more than a friend to me. But in that letter I told him that we meant to marry at once, and intended children. I am pretty hale, and the lady is not yet thirty . . . I don't know truly why I did it, except that I was angry with him, and my anger never seemed to have any effect. *This,* I thought, would surely make him sit up. My intention was, I suppose, to give him such a bad fright with this lie that he would set about changing his ways, and then I would tell him the truth . . . but was it really so? I believe I simply wanted to hurt and distress him. I should have known that no good would ever come of a barefaced lie—I who had always been stern in my regard for truth—but I did not know, I did not dream that it would have such a dreadful result.

"Richard was deep in debt, with no prospects but those he anticipated from me. He came home and found a letter telling him he was, in effect, disinherited." Sir Anthony held up his hand and shook it fiercely in front of his face. "It was this hand—this was the hand that did for him! And now, my dear, you know—you know where to lay the blame. Oh, when I heard of Richard's death and came to London, I was wild for Mortlock's blood too: I had little doubt that it was he who had led Richard into the life that had been the ruining of him. And in my grief and anguish I told myself that it was all Mortlock's fault. I greatly needed somewhere to put the blame, to spare me the terror of looking into myself and knowing that I was the one . . . And so, in a haze of rage and sorrow, I even confronted him and challenged him to fight me, half-hoping, I now believe, that he would put an end to me, and everything would be cleanly blasted away. Well, it was not to be. I am sorry, my dear. You loved him and he is gone, and it is very much my fault. I can say nothing to you that will make it better."

The gloves, Fairfax thought: Richard Spicer had told his landlady, the last time he was seen, that he was going out to buy gloves. An ironic reference to the wedding of his uncle, the wedding that was never really to be. A sad story! It explained much, though not, he thought, everything. And though Sophie had plainly loved Richard Spicer, he had his doubts about just how worthy of love the young man had been . . . He was curious, anyway, to see her reaction.

"I know you loved him too, sir," she said after a moment, taking the baronet's hand. "It is plain in your face. And I — I am glad we met at last."

The same impressionable feeling that had made her devote herself to a careless and self-centered young man had opened her heart to his uncle. All very well, thought Fairfax, but he suspected the whole story had yet to be told.

"Your nephew was, as you said, deep in debt," he said to Sir Anthony, "and we know he had not a penny in his pocket when he returned to find your letter. Yet it was not so earlier that night. When Richard met Lord Mortlock at the Cyder Cellar, after leaving the gaming house at King Street, he had plenty of money: enough to pay off a debt to Mortlock and to clear his score at the Cellar. In fact, I think he had come away from the gaming table with a full purse, probably having stripped the bank. It *does* happen, though rarely enough. I doubt, judging by what I have heard of his debts, that the faro bank would have been enough to make him solvent, but perhaps, if he had been allowed to keep his winnings . . ." He remembered Lord Mortlock's dark hints at the faro table; yes, Mortlock had clearly suspected it too. "If Richard had been allowed to keep his winnings, then he might have seen things a little differently, a little less desperately, when he read your letter, Sir Anthony."

"What do you mean? You—you think he was robbed that night?"

"It appears mighty probable. The coat you showed me was muddied—from where he lay in St. James's Park, it was presumed—but there was a tear in the sleeve also, was there not? At some point before he reached home that night he lost a fair amount of money. Or it was taken from him."

"Good God . . . But who? Not that thieves are far to seek in this vile city," Sir Anthony said shaking his head. "And there's no help for it now. D'you think to cheer me with such speculations, sir? That my nephew suffered even further on that dreadful night—?"

"It would be impudent to offer cheer. But you bear a burden of guilt that need not be so heavy, if what I suspect is true. The person who robbed him must surely share it. It is because of that person that Richard came home penniless, and so a likelier prey to despair." Yes: there were thieves aplenty in the nocturnal city, as Sir Anthony said, but Spicer would have been most vulnerable to someone who knew he was leaving the faro table with winnings in his pockets, and who had the wit and cunning to follow him . . .

"Have you knowledge of this person?" Sir Anthony said. "If so, then there must be justice."

"I have a suspicion," Fairfax said, "and trust me, when it becomes knowledge I shall be sure to let you know. In the meantime, Miss Vertue, I must press you on something you have mentioned—the masquerade at Ranelagh. I understand you saw Lady Mortlock there. At least, so I have been told by Mr. Pennant."

"Oh yes, him," she said dully, and that told him all he needed to know about her feelings for Pennant, or rather their absence. So the proposal which had so upset her, renewing the painful memories of her dead lover, was a mere piece of flummery on Pennant's part. A whim, he was tempted to say, but more likely a cool and adroit tactic. Pennant was distancing himself from Lady Mortlock; he could count on rumor and gossip quickly to couple his name with Miss Vertue's.

"So it was definitely Lady Mortlock you saw at the masquerade?"

"Oh, it was Charlotte without doubt. With no sign of Richard I was somewhat at a loss, and could only wander about the Rotunda, hoping . . . It was her voice I heard at first; I knew it very well, and she was not speaking in that absurd disguised squeak some people affect at the masquerade. I would have approached her, once I was sure it was Charlotte, but she was deep in talk with a man, and presently they withdrew together into one of the boxes and remained there."

"What was the man's costume?"

"A monk's habit," she said promptly. "They were so thick together that I did not want to trespass . . . Oh, do not misunderstand me. I did not fear being de trop in that way—they weren't loverlike, not really."

"How so?"

"Well, if I had to describe Charlotte's voice, I would say grave, even tearful. I remember thinking that at least I was not the only one who was unhappy that night . . ." Tears filled her own eyes again, and she rose. "I think I should go home. Perhaps, Sir Anthony, I may see you again."

He pressed her hand. "I should like that. Take care of yourself, my dear . . . Ah, don't fear for me—my madness is over now, trust me. You are not going home alone, I hope?"

"I shall escort you, Miss Vertue," Fairfax said. She nodded, her heart apparently too full to speak; taking leave of Sir Anthony, Fairfax accompanied her downstairs, where he had a few words with the innkeeper to assure him that all was well. In the coffee room an old gentleman was shortsightedly reading a newspaper; a second glance showed Fairfax that it was Wednesday's *Daily Post*.

A polite request to look at the paper fell on stony ground.

After a good deal of haggling, the old gentleman agreed to sell it to him for the sum of two shillings. And only as he was carrying it away did Fairfax realize the newspaper had probably belonged to the inn anyway.

"You are an extraordinary creature!" Miss Vertue said. "To pay two shillings for a newspaper that is two days old! That old man must think he is asleep and dreaming!"

"Well, I have made someone happy today, at any rate," he said, glad to see some of her vivacity returning. All the same, he studied her in a new light as he handed her into a hackney and asked for Hanover Square. This slight girl was someone who had gone to the levee with a very definite grudge against Lord Mortlock: indeed, a motive far more compelling than the notional jealousy he had imagined for her at first.

"You're sure the old gentleman will be all right now, Mr. Fairfax?"

"He should be, he's got my two shillings."

"Not that one, you provoking man. Poor Sir Anthony. I could not find it in my heart to blame him. He wasn't to know that his deception would have such a tragical result . . ."

"And Lord Mortlock? What are your feelings towards him now?"

She stared out of the window. "Can one ever describe deep feelings, Mr. Fairfax? Do they not by their very nature elude words? I pity Sir Anthony: he meant only his nephew's good at heart. But as for Lord Mortlock . . . he seems to have touched Richard's life only to corrupt." She gave him a twisted smile. "A terrible epitaph, is it not?"

Outside Mrs. Stoddart's house another carriage drew up behind their hackney; as they mounted the steps Fairfax looked back to see the opera singer, Mrs. Benaglio, sailing vastly towards them. Her husband followed meekly in her wake, carrying her pet monkey, which was dressed in a miniature three-cornered hat and frock coat. There is a good joke there somewhere, Fairfax thought, but I can't think of it.

Mrs. Stoddart was in the hall to greet them all.

"Mr. Fairfax, you have returned the wanderer to me! My child, how are you? Still hippish? I see a tear but I won't speak of it — not a word. And my sweet Teresa! How ravishing you look! When are you going to sing at one of my parties, my dear?"

"Soon, soon," trilled Mrs. Benaglio. "You must be patient, Louisa, I am demanded on all sides. Everyone, my dear, wants a little piece of me."

Well, there was plenty to go round, thought Fairfax.

"But what is this of tears?" Mrs. Benaglio said, rounding on Sophie, while the monkey made a grab for Mrs. Stoddart's feathered headdress. "So young and so pretty, *cara mia,* how can you be sad to tears?"

"I think I will go and change, Aunt," Sophie said, heading for the stairs.

"The young. Always *temperamentale,*" Mrs. Benaglio said, shrugging, and adding to her husband: "Fool! My cloak, cloak, cloak, take it!"

"Well, my dear, 'tis a little family imbroglio that we have lately had, and not to be spoken of," Mrs. Stoddart said. "At least — I can tell you as an old and discreet friend — Sophie has made a conquest of Mr. Pennant, the musician. He has been here, and he has been ardent, I can say no more —"

"Mr. Pennant? Why, this is curious. I have just lately seen him on my way here, and meant to bring you the news. His beautiful oratorio, his *Ruth,* it seems it will be performed; he was full of it, and asked me, naturally, if I will sing the first soprano. Of course I shall be delighted, if he is backed, and so it seems he is — a benefactor has appeared and offered to put up the money and everything —"

"Who is this benefactor?" Fairfax found himself asking.

Mrs. Benaglio snapped her beringed fingers at him. "Pa, I

know not, sir, I do not concern myself with such vulgarities. Well, *cara mia,* the young man has quite a genius, and now that his star rises, you know, your niece could do much worse. It was natural that he should think of me for Ruth, of course. When I sang in *Jephtha* for Mr. Handel he told me that he could now die happy . . ."

Almost unnoticed, Fairfax paid his respects and took his leave. Looking back at the house, he wondered whether Sophie needed a shoulder to cry on, and whether she was likely to get it.

Coming into Swallow Street, he stopped at the first coffeehouse and pored over his expensive newspaper. The missing advertisement was soon found and, to a practiced eye, soon understood.

LOST: in the neighborhood of Clare Market, Covent Garden: one shagreen leather pocketbook, folding type, tooled with the owner's name, &c. Any person with knowledge of the said article, be pleased to ask for Mr. L. G—, next to the sign of the Blue Posts at Charles Street, Covent Garden.

Fairfax smiled wryly. For "lost," one should read "found." No one who really lost a pocketbook in such a rookery of vice as the Garden would expect to have it innocently returned. What this advertisement referred to was stolen goods—and the kind of stolen goods that the owner would be desperate to get back. He had little doubt that "Mr. L. G—" was none other than Luke Griffey, and the address one of his various properties. He had little doubt, either, that this was the link between Griffey and Lawrence Appleton. Griffey had something that Lawrence would pay large sums of money to get back, hence the young man's frantic pleadings for funds. Just why it was such a matter of desperation Fairfax wasn't sure yet, but he had a grim and sinister suspicion . . .

Whatever was behind it, they were playing a dangerous game, Griffey as much as Lawrence. Of course, what a man

like Griffey counted on in making such an advertisement was
the very fact that his prey didn't want to involve the law. But
still he was sailing close to the wind. If someone else, someone who had nothing to fear from him, should step in . . .
Fairfax looked forwards to talking to Mr. Luke Griffey.

He paid for his dish of coffee and took a chair for Covent
Garden, deep in thought. As well as the matter of Lawrence
and Griffey, he had Mrs. Benaglio's revelation in mind. Who,
he thought, could Stephen Pennant's sudden benefactor be, if
not Mr. Samuel Appleton? Someone with money and influence—and a reason to use them. He remembered Mr. Appleton asking him about Pennant's position and prospects . . .
Was he not determining Pennant's price?

The suspicion grew on Fairfax that in using him to inves-
tigate this matter, Mr. Appleton had a strictly limited agenda
of his own. What mattered to him above all was the reputation of his daughter—the grand lady whom he was so proud
to call Lady Mortlock. Perhaps from the very start he had
known more than he admitted; perhaps from the start he had
seen the hand of a lover behind this, and all he wanted to
know was that lover's identity. Then the man could be paid
off, warned off, taken care of, at any rate: justice would matter less than the avoidance of scandal. To have his daughter's
lover up in court accused of murdering her husband, with all
the sordid details of the affair made public, not to mention
the dark suggestions of complicity it would stir up . . . that
name of which he was so proud would be mud. No wonder
that from Mr. Appleton's point of view almost anything was
preferable, even wholesale bribery.

Well, it made Fairfax's task harder, if his employer was
playing a double game with him. Still, by now he was used
to that, because everyone in this case, he thought, had lied, or
was still lying, or at least concealing the truth. Oddly enough,
Lord Mortlock, for all his vices, had been the most honest of
all.

He rapped on the chair roof; they had come to the swirl of wheeled traffic at the corner of Piccadilly and the Haymarket, and now another thought had come to him—he wanted to speak to Kate Little. As it happened he did not have to turn into noisome Bellman's Court to find her. At the turning before it there was a tavern, with benches outside the door. A small crowd had gathered here to gape and laugh at a figure who was standing on one of the benches, and whom Fairfax recognized as Jack Little, the milk seller's father. Generally unlovable, old Little had surely never appeared to worse advantage. Drunk as the devil, the front-fall of his breeches unfastened and various nameless stains on his waistcoat, he was capering about and bellowing at the top of his crowlike voice. Poor Kate, Fairfax saw, was there to witness it. She was trying to push her way through the mocking crowd, and weakly calling on her delightful parent to come down.

"I say to you, friends, you won't see the like of these for a hatful of guineas! The sss—celebrated fantoccini of Jack Little have performed before the crowned heads of Europe, and their heaps have been praised—praised upon heaps—damn your eyes, you may laugh, you may fleer, but you'll never see the like . . . I am only a little rusty, my friends, a little rusty on account of choosing to retire from the public view . . ."

In each hand Little was pathetically wagging a broken-down jointed figure, unrecognizable as a puppet save for a few frayed strings and tatters and flakes of paint. Some drunken impulse had made him try to relive the days of glory represented by that remnant of a show booth in his cellar, but he and his puppets were alike in their decrepitude. One could only wince—or heartlessly laugh, as the crowd were doing. Someone threw an apple core, and it hit Little in the face. He was so absorbed in crooning a tuneless song for his puppets to dance to that he staggered back in astonishment, nearly falling off his perch; the spectators roared again.

"Who threw that? Show me — show me the shit-gotten bastard who threw that, and I'll have his liver. I'll have you know I was a terror with the singlestick in my younger days, and I'll trounce any bastard now who wants to taste it . . ." Little shook his palsied fist, belching vilely. "Show him, show him to me —!"

"Why, it was me, old shamble-shanks, old crackbrain," said a young costermonger, drunk himself, with his arm round the waist of a young doxy who squealed with laughter. "And here's something else for you." He hawked and spat: the missile caught Little on the neck.

"I think we should get your father down from there," Fairfax said, squeezing himself next to Kate, "else things are likely to turn unpleasant."

"Oh! Oh, sir — will you help? Someone's been treating him, and he's took more than he ought, so he's not himself."

Fairfax feared that Jack Little was very much himself, but he kept that quiet; to the jeers and boos of the crowd he and Kate got the old man down from the bench pretty much by main force, and bore him away. Little was not a person you would care to get too close to in any event, and to have him arm in arm with you, thrusting his boozy face into yours and spitting curses in between belches and stomach-deep groans, was something of a trial. Fairfax was relieved when, turning into Bellman's Court, Little indignantly said, "I can walk, thank ye, damn it, I'm as able as a so'jer," and shook them off, though he proceeded to demonstrate his capability by staggering in a figure eight, and at last almost falling headlong down the steps to the milk cellar.

Once inside he turned to them with a parade of gravity, and held up a finger. "You did well. 'Twas a lucky chance for that bastard, for I would have had to teach him a lesson, and — and there would have been blood. Aye, blood . . ."

He lurched behind the curtain of his booth, and there was the sound of his body collapsing on the bed.

"He'll have such a head," Kate said mournfully. "He don't take so much as a rule, and he's not accustomed. Someone's been treating him, and I wish they wouldn't. It makes him not himself, you see."

Already a rasping, gurgling snore was coming from the booth.

"You have much to endure," Fairfax said.

Her look was faintly surprised, as if the thought had never occurred to her. She averted her eyes.

"We do very well, sir, really. But thank you for helping me with him. It's only when he's not himself."

"But you have a great burden nonetheless. Forgive me, but I imagine all the work is done by you, Kate."

She shrugged. "Sometimes Father fetches the milk from the cow keepers of a morning."

"You are very loyal . . . And now there is Abraham gone missing, which must be a grief to you. As he was your— your friend."

Her dark eyes regarded him expressionlessly. "Yes, it's a great pity."

"And no message to you. No word of how he is or where he is. That is a pity too."

She shrugged again. "It can't be helped."

Yes, she was loyal indeed. If she knew where Abraham was—and he still suspected that she did—then nothing short of wild horses was going to drag the secret from her. Years of coping with that old horror in the booth must have given her this nerveless fortitude. At that moment the snores rose to a pitch and stopped in a choking gasp; but the old man recommenced breathing after a few seconds, unfortunately.

"Kate, I know you may be chary of speaking to me, lest what you say might injure someone you care for. But there is one other small matter that I hope you can tell me about. On the doorpost at the Mortlock house I noticed your tally mark—you chalk it up at all the houses on your milk walk, I daresay."

"Yes, sir. I've always done it. And I make my own tally on these sticks. 'Tis quite usual, I think."

"And it is one stroke for a pint of milk, yes? I ask because yesterday there were three strokes, yet only two pints delivered to the kitchen."

A mild flicker of alarm crossed her face. "Yes, sir, that's so, only I was told 'twould be settled for, sir, right and proper. I hope there's no question of cheating about it, for I only scored it up because I was told, and I'd never dream—"

"No, no, I am suggesting nothing of the kind, believe me. I am only curious as to how it came about."

"Well, sir, I was at the door, and Abraham was there as, as usual, to take the milk in, you know. I was ladling the two pints that was wanted into the jug, when all of a sudden the young gentleman came hurrying downstairs and across the hall, like he had the devil at his heels, and barged straight past Abraham and into me. He was a mite clumsy and off his balance, like, because he had his hands dug in his coat pockets, and so he knocked into me, and half the jug was spilt on the steps—a good pint of milk gone. He said he was sorry, very hastylike, and told me to ladle out another pint, and charge the spilt pint to the house. And so I did, him being the lady's brother, and often about. I thought nothing of it."

"The lady's brother . . ."

"Yes, sir—tall and thin and quite the dandy. He was polite and sorry, but hasty like I said, and he went clipping off down the steps and away, and so I filled the jug again and gave it to Abraham, and chalked up a score of three on the doorpost. I hope I haven't made trouble . . ."

"No, no." Fairfax blinked and shook his head, tried to give her a reassuring smile. "His hands deep in his pockets, you say?"

"Aye, sir. He didn't take them out even when he might

have gone headfirst down the steps. But then he is quite the dandy, and I suppose 'tis the way they carry theirselves."

The last mumblings of old Little came back to him, aptly: *there would have been blood.*

He thanked Kate and left the cellar, breathing deeply the fresher air above. He was a little dizzy with it, and with his thoughts.

There would have been blood . . . and so there probably would have been, indeed, on the hands or gloves of whoever had cut Lord Mortlock's throat. Once Abraham had deserted his station at the street door there would have been no one to see the culprit's bloody hands, of course, as he or she left . . . but Lawrence Appleton had been the first to leave the levee, *before* Abraham had been reported absent. He had had to pass Abraham and the milk seller. He had had his hands in his pockets, and had purposefully not withdrawn them.

It was damning. It was not proven, but it was extremely damning. Indeed everything seemed to be converging on the figure of Lawrence Appleton just now — though not Lawrence alone. The young man was involved in some intrigue with Luke Griffey, and Fairfax would not be surprised to find Griffey, the venomous spider, at the center of the whole web.

It was time to find out.

Chapter Nine

He chose to seek out Griffey first at Lady Harriet Froome's house in King Street, as it was on his way, and, moreover, he had a suspicion that Lady Harriet might also be involved; but he got no joy. One of the thuggish manservants would allow him no further than the hall, and insisted that neither Griffey nor Lady Harriet was there. Fairfax flourished the newspaper, and said he had come in response to a certain advertisement. He thought he heard a light footstep on the stair, and was almost certain that someone was poised above, listening, but the manservant was emphatic, and also large. Fairfax gave it up, and crossed the piazza to find the address in the advertisement.

The house next to the sign of the Blue Posts in Charles Street was no more nor less innocent-looking than any other in this infamous district. The windows were heavily curtained, and the door was stouter than was usually necessary for a private dwelling, with a peephole set into it above the knocker. He rapped several times. Getting no answer, he made his way down a narrow and ill-smelling brick passage at the side of the house, and came to a back door that stood open. A young woman in an apron, slippers, and unlaced stays was leaning there, a cup of gin in her hand, talking to a young man whose exquisitely curled hair contrasted with

the patched shabbiness of his velvet coat and crimson stockings. Both fell silent as Fairfax appeared, and stared levelly
at him.

"I'm looking for Luke Griffey. Is he here?"

After a moment, the young woman, who was pale, pretty,
and patched, shook her head. "He ain't here. You might try
later. He might be here then. I shall be here later, sir, if you'd
care to call."

Above her head, on the lintel of the door, he now saw a
small signboard on which was painted, in black italics, the
words KIND AND TENDER USAGE WITHIN. He lowered his eyes
to hers; she gazed at him, unmoved.

"I really need to see Griffey urgently," he said.

The woman exchanged a glance with the young man, who
said: "It depends what it's about, sir."

"A private matter."

"He don't *look* like a beak's man," the young man said to
the woman; and then appraising Fairfax with his head on one
side, "You don't *look* like a beak's man, sir. If you are, you
know, we can't be as obliging as we'd like."

"I do not come from the magistrates," Fairfax said, and
then, taking a chance, "Indeed they are the last people I wish
to know of my errand. It is in regard to this—this advertisement." He unfolded the newspaper.

The woman glanced down with the blind indifference of
illiteracy, but the young man peered at the newspaper and his
eyebrows went up.

"Oho. That's the game, is it? Well, that's curious . . ."
Again he assessed Fairfax with bright, hollow eyes.

"You know something about this?"

"Well, not direct, as you might say. But 'tis curious, when
I've just come from visiting him . . ."

"Griffey?" Fairfax said.

Ignoring him, the woman said, "Have a care, Jerry. He

may not be a beak's man, but you don't want to get at cross with Griffey, now; *you* know."

"Oh, I know all right," the young man said with a frown. "He's been coming down heavy enough on us lately—which is how poor Patrick ended up where he is—so I know right enough, Poll. You want to mind he's not down on you next, he's that rampaging, damn his splatty old pig's face! No, no, Poll, I'm not sure as I do care." He turned to Fairfax. "I don't know about your pocketbook, but I know someone who does. I can take you to him, if you like. Only he's taken for debt, just this morning, so it ain't a very nice place we'll be going to, and he won't be able to come out of it, not unless you can do something for him."

"Have a care, Jerry," the woman said again. "If Griffey finds out—"

"Oh, cess on him. Like I told you, Poll, I shall leave off this trade soon enough—I'll enlist again, or I'll turn sailor. I shan't be beholden to an old shit-hawk like him anymore. Well, sir, will you come?"

"Your friend definitely knows about this—this matter?"

"Oh, trust me for that, sir. He ought to. But just remember this, sir—we're made to do it. I'll not say any more yet, but bear it in mind, sir."

"Very well. Where is this place we're going?"

"The Fleet. Old shit-hawk threw him in there this morning. Damn him. I'll not fear him anymore, not I. I wasn't afeared when I faced the Frenchie guns at Quebec—why should I fear him?"

"You have been a soldier," Fairfax said as they went along.

"And I shall be again. I'll confess, the floggings and the lice and the flies in your provender turned my stomach for soldiering, and I thought I'd do better out of a red coat. Which I haven't, I'll confess again; but there, we all fall by the wayside now and then, and needs must when the devil drives and all the rest of it. I doubt *you're* shocked, sir, as you're after your pocketbook and all; and as for that side of things, why, Griffey makes us do it."

Jerry marched like a foot soldier, and they went along the Strand swiftly, but it was noticeable that he had a way of looking into the faces of some gentlemen he passed, as if he thought he knew them, and sometimes stared fixedly after them as they went by.

"You work for Griffey, I take it, and so does this man Patrick we are going to see. Does Poll . . . ?"

"You've got it. Poll's in the flogging and birching line, you may as well know. That house has been raided more than once by the constables lately, which is why she's so careful."

"And Griffey owns the house."

"That's it; and the house where I live, and where poor Patrick lived till this morning. I'll tell you how it works: when Griffey sets you up in the house, he makes you sign a note of hand as a deposit on your rent, and for the price of the furniture, not that there's much of that beyond a few sticks and rags. But he makes you sign all the same, a promissory note for fifty pounds; then, if he ain't pleased with you, he goes to the court and swears your debt against you. And of course, as you can't pay such a sum, not in *our* way of living, he has you thrown in the Fleet or the King's Bench, and won't compound for your release till you promise to behave. What Patrick did to cross the old whoreson, I don't know, but then it don't need much."

Fairfax had a fair idea, now, of what he was dealing with. It was a dark, perilous, and largely hidden layer of the criminal world; he felt no surprise at finding Griffey mixed up in it.

The Fleet prison, looming in the cold gray of a late afternoon which was beginning to turn foggy, looked indeed as if it were spectrally conjured out of blighted hopes and miserable fortune rather than built of brick and stone. Having been in a debtors' prison himself many years ago, Fairfax could not suppress a reminiscent shudder as he and Jerry were admitted at the lodge gate. The darkness that no amount of candles could make less gloomy, the oppressive smell of crowded poverty, and the horrible echoes that resounded down from the galleries, all called to him across the years with dreadful familiarity.

"A ghastly place," he murmured.

"Well, there are some who take to it," Jerry said, leading him up flights of narrow stairs; and it was true that some of the people lounging about the landings, or gathering in noisy parties in the rooms that opened off them, were smoking and laughing, playing cards and dice and laying bets, and gossiping as unconcernedly as if they were on a street corner. There were gin shops within the Fleet, Fairfax knew, and some inmates held regular clubs for drinking and singing; there was even an open racket court in the middle of the building. But to him these things were only the grin on the face of the devil, for the one thing he was sure about hell was that there was irony there. Worst of all, he thought, was the presence of children, some of whom had even been born here, and who scuttled about with an elfin, knowing look, more terrible than that of the most hopeless and corrupted street Arab.

"Well, here he is. Rouse up, Patrick!" Jerry said, entering a room on the "common side" of the prison, where half a dozen mattresses were crowded into a space scarcely large enough for two. Three of them were occupied: on one an old man with a wild growth of matted hair slept beneath a pile of rags, on another a man in a back-to-front wig and lace ruffles that were falling apart with dirt and age sat cross-legged, poring over some papers and repeating aloud, in a tone of suppressed excitement, a stream of incomprehensible figures. "Six and two, two and six, makes nine and three over, add the five hundred and a dozen and a half and a quarter . . ." The papers, Fairfax saw, were blank. The third occupant was a shabby youth of no more than eighteen, very slender and fair, who was sitting hunched and nursing his knees, and whose startlingly blue eyes flashed with alarm when he saw Jerry's companion.

"Never fear, Patrick. He's not a blower. He was at Poll's place, looking for Griffey," Jerry said, sitting down easily by him.

"Take him to Griffey, then," the youth said, with a faint brogue, turning his face away.

"Still mopish, eh? Why, cheer up, heart. I tell you he's no blower, I've a nose for it. What he's after is something you know about. Didn't you tell me the other day about a pocketbook?"

Patrick wrapped his arms around his thin body, staring from one to the other. "I don't know," he said. "It would depend."

Fairfax took out the newspaper. "This advertisement," he said, reading it out. "I am anxious to trace this item, and your friend said you knew something of it."

Patrick stared into his eyes for several seconds; it was like the searching looks that Jerry had given the men in the street.

"*You're* not the one," he said at last, turning away again and shrugging his blanket round his shoulders with a petulant cry of "I'm *cold*."

"I'm seeking to recover this thing on behalf of a friend." After a glance at Jerry, Fairfax took a shilling from his purse and laid it on the mattress.

"How did your *friend* come to lose it, I wonder?" Patrick said, picking up the shilling and biting it.

"Fifteen and three quarters at five percent, multiply ten plus nought, add one, take away one, and three is three," muttered the man with the papers.

"Come, Patrick, speak plain," Jerry said. "Don't be afraid of Griffey. I'm not going to be, not anymore. And if we can disoblige the old shit-hawk, then what could be better?"

"Easy to say don't be afraid of him. 'Twas him who had me put in here. I swear I did nothing to displease him—"

"Pah, you don't have to. He grows more vicious every day, just for the joy of it," Jerry said. "Poll was saying he's come down hard on the girls at her place. It's his nature."

"I've heard how you came to be in here," Fairfax said. "And I may as well say that I don't have fifty pounds to secure your release. But if a little money can help you get a better lodging in this place . . ." He glanced over at the muttering man. "Also, I may be able to get my employer to aid you, if all turns out well. I have a suspicion of worse crimes on the part of Luke Griffey, and let us just say that I am not friendly to him."

"Well, look here, *I* haven't got that pocketbook," Patrick said, pouting, "and I hope you don't think I have. *He's* got it, of course. Griffey."

"I was telling the gentleman he makes us do it," Jerry said.

"Of course he does. You know what the buttock-and-file trick is, don't you?"

Fairfax did. It was the term for the picking of her client's pockets by a prostitute. Well, well. If he had had any doubt of what he was dealing with before, there was none now. Curious; he was looking at two men whose activities would cause outraged horror in the minds of polite society, yet they seemed pretty much like any you would meet in a tavern or skittle ground.

"Well then. That's how I know about your friend's pocketbook," Patrick said. "Griffey makes us do it, it's true. He takes half of what we earn to begin with, but we have to look out for extras as well, and we don't see a penny from them."

"''Tis more than your life's worth to do a little dipping on your own account," Jerry said. "Young Ned, d'you remember him, Patrick? He buzzed a stock from a mark one night and kept it for himself, and Griffey smoked him. Poor Ned, he never did that again."

"So you must know," Patrick said, hugging himself, "that I can't get it back for you. Your friend will have to pay, that's the way of it. And I hope for his sake he's rich—from what I remember of him, he seemed well-placed enough—because it won't come cheap."

"Just a pocketbook," Fairfax said, half to himself.

"Oh, there was nothing in it to speak of, I daresay," Patrick said, "not that I *know,* you understand: that's Griffey's business. But that ain't the point, is it? It's the fact of where he was when it was took—when he lost it, I mean. That's why he'll pay, any amount I should think, to get it back."

Jerry was nodding. "Now take you, sir. Have you family— a wife, friends, position, reputation?"

With a low thump of his heart Fairfax said, "In truth I have none of those things."

"Well, that's plain, in a way," Jerry said laughing, "else you wouldn't be sitting here with us. You see it, of course, sir? If a man has any of those things, think how he stands to lose them if a man like Griffey's got certain evidence against him. He can even stand to lose more if the law should be roused," he added, lowering his voice.

Fairfax remembered his night of gaming with Lord Mortlock, remembered Mortlock's grim account of the man who had been placed in the Hart Street pillory, his face like raw mutton when the crowd had finished with him. A dreadful understanding was on him now.

"I must find Griffey," he said. "He is not at the address printed here, nor at the gaming house in King Street. Will you tell me where I can find him?"

The two young men exchanged a glance.

"He has one or two other places," Patrick said. "There's no telling . . ."

"Ah, you know, Patrick, he'll still be at our house," Jerry said. "It's his day for coming down on us. Reckoning up accounts, charging us double for coals and candles." He laughed bitterly and spat into the cold fireplace, then got to his feet. "You do as you like, Patrick. I'm finished with him. I'll show you the place, sir. But perhaps you'll be so good as to forget it was me who showed you — and that you talked to Patrick here."

"You can trust my discretion, I swear," Fairfax said. He placed such money as he could spare on the mattress. "I hope I may be able to help you, Patrick. As for the man — the man you took the pocketbook from. You recall him?"

The lost blue eyes met his. "Hardly at all," he said. "I don't take note. I'm no saint, maybe, but I don't peach on 'em, sir. Leave that to Griffey."

The house to which Jerry led him was at the back of the seedy row of tenements and flophouses formerly dignified with the name of Clare Market, hard by Drury Lane. It had a name for being the resort of coiners and money clippers, as well as for the more shadowy vice in which Jerry and Patrick were entangled.

"A double knock, three times, and a whistle. That should get you in," Jerry instructed him. "I'd come in, only I'm finished with it. There's naught in there I want."

"What will you do?"

"Mebbe go back and see Patrick. After that I'll find a berth, never fear. 'Tis a big city." And with that the foggy dusk of the city swallowed him up.

The knock and whistle brought another young man to the door. This one had a cringing look and a black eye. He hesitated when Fairfax said Griffey's name, but Fairfax elbowed him aside.

Downstairs was drab, with an unlit hall giving on to a room in which a shabby pretense of a chocolate house had been set up—a few bentwood chairs and a counter dusty with disuse—no doubt as a blind against the raids of the law. From above came voices, and going upstairs Fairfax found quite a different world. Following the voices he came into a sort of parlor decorated with faded damask and ornamented with statuettes and pictures of a vaguely Grecian sort, though Attic chasteness was not much in evidence. There was also an overturned chair and some smashed crockery, and sitting on a sofa and clasping his gawky knees as he stared up at Fairfax in utter terror was Lawrence Appleton.

"G-good God . . . w-what a strange meeting, eh, Fairfax? Curious place, ain't it—I had no idea, I—I just happened—"

He flinched as there came a violent shout from behind a closed door at the other end of the room.

"Griffey?" Fairfax said.

"Yes. I'm waiting to see him, you know. He's—he's just dealing with some business in there, and I'm waiting to . . . waiting . . . God damn, Fairfax, what in the devil's name are you doing here?"

"What am I doing here? I've come seeking Griffey, like you, Lawrence. And I can perhaps help you, though I'm not sure whether your folly deserves it, and I don't know yet whether you are guilty of worse than folly. But of course, I shouldn't be here, and neither should you, because this is a mollie-house, isn't it?"

Utterly pale, Lawrence hid his face in his hands.

"A mollie-house," Fairfax repeated, "and it is the most monstrous unthinkable risk for a man to be here. But you have been here more than once, Lawrence. You were here before, and you unwittingly left something behind you: something lifted from your pocket by the boy you were with." He took out the folded newspaper. "Look up, Lawrence. Yes, I know it now."

"Don't tell," Lawrence said in an anguished whisper. "I beg you, Fairfax, don't tell . . ."

"Oh, don't look at me like that. D'you think I'm another Griffey, out to betray you unless I get my price? No, though I might well curse you for your folly—perhaps more. Again, it depends, Lawrence, whether your folly has led you to a far greater crime."

He held the young man's frightened eyes. Could it be . . . ? Just then there was another shout and a crash from behind the connecting door. It burst open and a youth bearing a red mark on his rouged cheek came hurrying out, head down. Looking neither right nor left he ran past them to the stairs. Lawrence began to tremble.

Fairfax stepped behind the door, holding up a warning finger to Lawrence. After a moment Griffey appeared, breathing hard and rubbing his great hands together in that circular motion as if rolling something into a tiny ball.

"You're here, are you, sir?" Griffey said to Lawrence, his choked voice full of danger. "And what do you have for me? Shillings and pence won't do, you know, sir. If it's a matter of shillings and pence again, I fear I shall get angry, and you don't want that, I think, sir. Well? No tongue in your head, sir?"

He was thrusting his great scarred face into Lawrence's when Fairfax stepped out.

"Demanding money with menaces, Griffey? Not wise. I'd have thought you were in trouble enough."

Griffey whipped round, then froze into stillness except for his right hand, which crept stealthily to his pocket.

"Receiving stolen goods and restoring them for a fee, you know, is quite sufficient," Fairfax said. "It was enough to hang old Jonathan Wild, wasn't it? Is that how you fancy yourself, Griffey—a latter-day Wild? Well, you're certainly on your way to it. You have a set of abused wretches in your power, and you seek to enrich yourself from the distress of those you entrap. And rather than stand up as the thief and whoremaster you are, like more honest rogues, you try to hide behind a mask of respectability. Yes, you have all the makings of a Wild: I congratulate you. Of course, you know that Wild tried to kill himself with laudanum the night before they hanged him, so if you are going to emulate your hero to the end, you had better cultivate a little white-livered cowardice, but I'm sure that will come easy to you."

Griffey's small eyes darted to the landing, checking Fairfax was alone. "How did you come here?"

"I don't have to answer any questions from you. I gather you have a piece of property belonging to this gentleman, and have not returned it. Do it now." As Griffey remained silently blinking, Fairfax stepped towards the connecting door. "Where is it? In there—?"

He had the wit to duck as Griffey came at him, and jabbing his elbow back he caught the big man a blow in the face, but still Griffey's great arms came round him. Fairfax put up a protective hand to his neck in the nick of time, realizing what it was that Griffey had whipped from his pocket: the cord tightened agonizingly across the back of his hand, biting into the flesh. A garroter as well, he thought randomly, as he struggled for air, no surprise really . . . Griffey's breath was hot in his ear as the cord tightened and tightened; blood welled from his knuckles and spots danced before his eyes. Strangled by his own hand . . . Fairfax lifted his knee high and stamped his foot down on Griffey's, then kicked backwards, feeling the big man's shin shiver. Griffey yelped with pain and his grip slackened enough for Fairfax to wriggle out of it, falling on his knees, twisting, and scooting away. He glimpsed Lawrence's openmouthed face before Griffey's bearlike shape blotted it out, advancing. I am a dead man, thought Fairfax lucidly, and then as he backed against the fireplace he heard a clatter. With a second to spare he reached blindly behind him. His fingers found the iron poker as if it had offered itself to him.

Griffey put up an arm to ward off the blow, but Fairfax feinted, just as if he were in the fencing court with his old teacher in France, then lunged and caught his opponent square in the midriff. Wheezing, Griffey staggered back, then charged, roaring, with such startling swiftness that Fairfax was nearly knocked over. Stumbling, he just managed to snatch his sword arm away from Griffey's grip, but Griffey's other hand came flailing up and caught him a thunderous open-palmed blow on the side of the head. He reeled away, but his sword arm automatically put a guard up, and then, as used to happen occasionally in the fencing court, time seemed to slow down and he could see his opponent's movements in superb deliberate detail, could pinpoint the moment when the raising of the right arm and the turn of the body created an opening . . . He lunged and thrust, catching Griffey a sharp blow in the chest, and as the big man hunched round in a reflex of pain and protection, Fairfax brought the poker down in an arc on the back of his neck.

Griffey sagged to his knees, moaning, stunned, and blind with pain. It was at that moment that Lawrence darted forwards and fetched Griffey a crack across the back with his own malacca cane.

"There's for you," he cried exultantly, "you damned swindling brute!"

"Well," Fairfax said, as Griffey sank into a sitting position on the floor, cradling his head, "now I'll ask again. You are keeping this man's property as a ransom against his reputation, are you not? And I'll wager you've already received a good deal of money from him."

"I've given him everything I can!" Lawrence cried. "I've brought him every penny I can lay my hands on. Damn it, Griffey, I risked my neck getting that infernal bill back for you—wasn't that enough? You spoke as if that was enough, but now you want more and more, and it's more than a man can stand . . ."

Of course, Fairfax thought, of course Griffey would always want more. It was not the money but the power that really gratified him.

"I know I was a fool," Lawrence said. "Not just in coming to a place like this—for there's something that drives me to it, Fairfax, I swear I can't help it—but in not noticing when my pocket was picked. When I realized, when I knew that he had it in his power to prove I'd been in a place like this, oh, God, Fairfax, you know the penalties; I was so afraid. Even if my father found out, my sister, anyone, I'd be ruined. It is no overstatement: I would be a ruined man forever."

Fairfax nodded grimly. He was remembering a tale from his youth at Oxford. An undergraduate's brother, a clergyman, had had his pocket picked of some personal articles at a brothel; he was on the threshold of a good marriage, and had near bankrupted himself paying the brothel madam exorbitant blackmail to get his property back. It was the stuff of bawdy alehouse anecdote, indeed . . . but that had been a brothel of the ordinary kind. When the establishment was a mollie-house—a male brothel—the risks, and the rewards for the blackmailer, were far greater.

"Foolish, indeed," Fairfax said. "Though I've no doubt the theft was done expertly. Not that those poor wretches see the profit, of course. He makes them do it, and reaps the harvest." He noticed the garrote lying on the floor and picked it up. "An ugly weapon, though beautifully simple. Did you use this, Griffey, to attack Richard Spicer on Monday night, and rob him of the winnings he had taken away from your

faro table? Or was it just a smart cosh in the dark?" Griffey
jerked his head up. "Well, we'll come to that. By the by,
when was it you were here, Lawrence, and lost your pocketbook? Was that Monday night also? The night of the musical
party at your sister's, when she gave you money to go away
and leave her with Pennant?"

Lawrence nodded. "She gave me quite a bit. So I was at a
loose end, and had money in my pocket, and . . . and so I
came here. I can't help it," he concluded, hanging his head.
"I can't help myself."

"That's what the likes of Griffey count on. And so they
play at skittles with men's ruin. But what of your own ruin,
Griffey? Laws were passed expressly to stop what you are
doing, and you have flouted them."

Griffey put up a hand to the back of his scalp where there
was blood. His grimace turned to a sneer as he looked at Fairfax. "Why, you make me laugh, man. Who will stand up and
accuse me, hey? This young coxcomb here? Will he go to the
magistrate and admit that he lost his pocketbook in a mollie-
house? Will you tell the tale? How will you pin me down,
hey? I think, my friend, that I really have nothing to fear.
Who will stand against me?"

"I will."

The voice was that of Lady Harriet Froome, who stood in
the doorway, looking down at Griffey with a faint, weary
contempt.

"I will, if need be, Luke." She came in, taking off her
hooded cloak and tossing it onto a chair with a waft of her
characteristic perfume. "I don't want to, Luke, but I am so
tired. You look as if you have taken a drubbing. Dear, dear.
Well, he who draws the sword . . . This, I take it"—from her
powdered bosom she withdrew a green pocketbook—"is
what all the fuss is about."

Griffey glared at her. "What the devil? How did you come
by that? Damn you, Harriet, I thought—"

"You mustn't be surprised if people learn your tricks, Luke. I took it from your coat pocket this morning, when you were dressing."

"Good God," Lawrence said with a look of distaste.

"Oh, fie, sir," Lady Harriet said with a wave of her hand, "*you* I'm sure know the charm that a pair of strong arms bears for the lonely heart. Yes, Luke, I took it from your pocket—I daresay you thought it was there still, eh?—and kept it by me, because I have simply had enough of this. I won't see you tormenting this poor wretch anymore. We have got what we wanted, and to go on turning the screw for money, over and over, is sheer excess, my dear. You know he's not a man of independent means; and really, Luke, seeing you do this is uncomfortably reminiscent of watching a small boy pull the wings off flies." She held the pocketbook out to Lawrence, who took it wonderingly. "There, sir—'twas dearly bought, I daresay you're thinking, but perhaps it will teach you to be careful; for my part I am sick of it."

"God damn me, Harriet, 'tis late in the day for you to turn moral," Luke scowled.

"Not a bit of it. I am such as I am. No saint but no demon either. Men may throw away their fortunes at my faro table, but that's their choice; and the same with men who come to my bed. I have to live, but I have my limits. My name may be spotted, but I would not have it black, that's all. Mr. Fairfax, you are the one for quoting—what is that line? 'I am Duchess of Malfi still.' Shakespeare, no doubt."

"Not Shakespeare, but very apt," he said. "I thank you for your honesty, Lady Harriet. And in that spirit, perhaps we may talk of the thing Lawrence procured for yourself and Griffey. It was, I think, a bill of forty pounds, drawn by Richard Spicer on Martin's of Throgmorton Street—the bill that ended up in Lord Mortlock's purse, where it might have incriminated you."

Griffey began to bluster, but Lady Harriet held up her hand. "Hush, Luke, and don't be a fool. You have hit it, I see, Mr. Fairfax. A pity, this matter need never have gone awry, but there, 'tis an unpredictable world." She knelt down beside Griffey, taking out her handkerchief. "Let me see your hurt, Luke. Dear, dear—well, it could be worse. It would take more to dent a skull like yours. Now, dear, be still!" With surprising tenderness she ministered to the big man, talking the while. "You are quite a tireless inquisitor, Mr. Fairfax, but I had thought you a man of the world, and to pursue so fiercely after the tricks of the gambling fraternity, you know, smacks a little of the Puritan."

"I am not much troubled about those. Crimes, though, are a different matter. The crime of Lord Mortlock's murder; and the crime that was committed against Richard Spicer. It was Lord Mortlock himself who gave me the first hints of it, when I was with him at your faro table. Spicer won, did he not, on Monday night? Stripped the bank?"

Lady Harriet nodded. "It's odd how sometimes a man will *know* his luck is in, and stay at the table long after everyone else has left off, waiting for his moment to come . . . It happened at a poor time for me, sir, that is all I have to say in extenuation. I could ill afford such a loss."

"And so when he left, well after midnight, you sent Griffey after him. To follow him discreetly, come upon him in a suitably dark spot, and rob him of his winnings." Fairfax frowned. "I have heard of high odds, Lady Harriet, but really that is a little steep."

"What would you have me say?" she said sharply. "I am sorry for it, but gamesters, you know, eat and drink swindling anyhow. There is no such thing as fairness in their world."

"Obviously . . . I'm not sure where you did the deed, Griffey, or whether, indeed, you used your little device, or just knocked Spicer down from behind plain and simple. I would guess it was somewhere about the courts west of the Garden, as when he left the Cyder Cellar some time after one, his purse was full, and when he got to his lodging at Dean Street he was disheveled and penniless. The win was unexpected, no doubt, but so was the loss, and coming upon other misfortunes must have been intolerable."

"And so he did for himself," Griffey growled. "Like the inquest said—like I said from the beginning, Harriet. God rot it, I didn't kill him—you'll not paint me *that* black."

"Fair enough," Fairfax said. "But Spicer's death was closely looked into, naturally, and that made you nervous. There was no one to tell the tale, of course, only you and Lady Harriet knew of it. And yet, and yet . . . there was something that could tell the tale after all. You must have observed that something was missing from what you stole from Spicer: a very identifiable bill for forty pounds, endorsed by Spicer. I would guess he staked it at the faro table, and got it back when he broke the bank. Unknown to you, Spicer had met up again with Lord Mortlock after he left your house on Monday night; they ran into each other in Bob Derry's Cyder Cellar, and there Spicer gave the bill to Lord Mortlock, probably in repayment for a loan his gambling crony had made to him. And when Lord Mortlock came to your house with me on Wednesday night, when the news of Spicer's penniless end was spreading, he must have put two and two together himself, and so he made a great show of producing that bill, and deliberately keeping it to himself. I think he was taunting you both. Plainly he had no love for you, Griffey, and Lord Mortlock and yourself, Lady Harriet, had just as plainly been quarreling. He was a whimsical man, and I daresay it pleased him to show you that he had penetrated your secret."

Lady Harriet was still, her face bleak. "I did not deserve that of him," she said in a small voice. "No matter what . . . he need not have been so."

"That I can't say," Fairfax said. "But what is plain to me is that between you, you decided you must get that bill back. No doubt, Griffey, you took care that Spicer got no glimpse of you when you attacked him. It would have been just another case of an unwary young rake robbed in the dark streets. But Spicer's suicide made his case a very public one. There was talk; and there was a very astute man, Lord Mortlock, in possession of a telling piece of evidence. He had seen your reaction when he showed it to you, and might well be disposed to use it against you. He knew that Spicer had broken your bank and yet arrived home without a farthing— very odd, very damning. You didn't kill Spicer, but assault and robbery are capital crimes too."

"I would have paid its face value," Lady Harriet said mournfully. "But Hugh—Hugh was a stubborn man."

"Yet an opportunity did present itself to recover the bill from Lord Mortlock's dangerous keeping. Neither of you were exactly on visiting terms with the Mortlocks, but his brother-in-law Lawrence was, of course, and that same night of Spicer's death Lawrence had foolishly placed himself in your power by the loss of his pocketbook. You threatened him, I suppose, with exposure—discreetly, via that advertisement—and when he came to you, you named your price: the bill in Mortlock's possession. Get it back, and you would return his pocketbook. And so you did, didn't you, Lawrence? But it wasn't enough. Griffey became greedy and wanted money on top of that, money you have been desperately trying to raise these last two days."

"I'd nothing against Hugh, you know," Lawrence said. "Nothing in the world. In truth, I'd as soon go naked in the street as turn thief, in the usual run of things. But I had to do it, you see. I simply had to."

"Yes," Fairfax said. "You had to get that bill. And so, once you left your sister's levee yesterday morning, you crossed the passage into Lord Mortlock's bedchamber, and there . . . And there, what, Lawrence?"

The young man stared at him, then tore his gaze away, putting his hands to his head. "Dear God, no! Upon my honor, Fairfax, don't accuse me of that! I swear to you, on my poor mother's grave, I didn't kill Hugh! Good God . . ."

"Well, tell me what did happen, then."

"There's little enough to tell," Lawrence said unhappily. "I listened at the bedchamber door a moment, I could hear Hugh snoring, so I slipped in and crept over to his bedside table. It was dim in there with the curtains and all, but I spotted his purse and got hold of it. That's when I had a—a difficult moment and nearly lost my nerve, because there was a box of pills there, and grabbing the purse I knocked it over—deuced things went rattling and rolling all about the place and I had the devil's own job scrambling them up and getting them back into the box. Don't think I missed any . . ."

You did, Fairfax thought, remembering the one he had picked up from the floor. So, credible thus far, at any rate.

"All the time I was sweating, frightened that Hugh might wake up . . . But, bless his five wits, he was snoring deep, and so I managed to open his purse and found that damnation bill folded up in there. And then I, well, I jammed it down into my coat pocket, and hurried out of there. I remember the wretched bill didn't go in my pocket very snugly—they're cut close, you know, as 'tis monstrously unfashionable to have 'em cut deep now—and so I had to keep my hand jammed in with it. And that I thought might look a touch peculiar, so I put both my hands in my pockets, and arranged my face as it were, and got downstairs as quick as I could, and out."

"I see . . . And did anyone see you?"

"Well, only Abraham. And the doxy who was at the door with him—the milk woman, you know. They were deep in talk, and I sailed through 'em and, well, I do believe I fetched the girl a bump, all in a hurry as I was, and she spilt some of her milk, but I just said to charge it to the house and went on my way. Monstrous unpalatable stuff, milk, by the by, never touch it myself . . . And so I brought the bill to Griffey, who did not make the return I expected, damn him. And that, I swear to you, Fairfax, is the whole of it."

Fairfax studied the young man, conscious of three pairs of eyes on him. Well, it chimed with what he had learned; it had a fair ring of truth. And if it were taken as truth, then it told him at least that Hugh Mortlock had been alive at the time Lawrence left. Not that that took him very far—it still remained possible for any of the others to have gone into the bedchamber afterwards and killed him. Even, he thought, Abraham; it was not very long after Lawrence's departure that Mr. Appleton arrived and reported Abraham's absence, but long enough for Abraham to have come upstairs after saying good-bye to Kate and done the deed. All very frustrating . . . And the fact remained that he had only Lawrence's word that he had not killed Mortlock. After all, Lawrence had been a desperate man, trying to prevent a catastrophic exposure by the ruthless Griffey, and surely prepared to do anything to prevent it. Perhaps Lord Mortlock had stirred, begun to wake, and Lawrence had silenced him in the most direct way? But no; the razor had been on the table in the passage, and so, if he had done it, Lawrence must have gone in there with the razor in his hand—in other words, with the settled intent to murder. Could it be that Lady Harriet and Griffey had sent him to do just that—eradicate the danger from Mortlock altogether? It was still possible, possible that this cooperativeness of Lady Harriet's was yet another mask . . .

"Lady Harriet, what was the substance of the quarrel between you and Lord Mortlock?"

She made a haughty face, and he thought for a moment

she was not going to answer. Then she smiled at him with great brilliance.

"Come, Mr. Fairfax, you have been shrewd enough thus far. Don't begin playing the country innocent now, I beg you. What do you suppose the relation between me and Hugh to have been? Honestly, now."

"You were lovers."

"Precisely. The past tense, by the way, is significant. There, can you rise, Luke?" She helped the groaning Griffey onto a chair. "You may have gathered that there is presently a tendresse between me and this dear booby here. And one thing I can say for myself is that I only take one lover at a time. My association with Hugh began some few years ago, and continued, a thing of sunshine and showers, till quite lately. I was never a prospective bride for him, that I well knew: when the time came it would be some chit with money, that I knew also. But I had something of his, and have it still, which pleases me."

"Your son."

"A sweet creature, is he not? Even leaving aside a mother's partiality, he is very dear. Of course, being a growing child, he is also dear in the other sense, and so I came to expect, if not to rely on, a certain supply of funds from Hugh to help with his raising. Not regular, necessarily, and if he could ensure me a steady stream of silly young men for my faro table, then I also took that as payment in lieu, as it were. But ever since he did finally marry his little fudgey-faced chit, he had tended to consider those responsibilities behind him, and we had one or two words on the subject."

"I see."

"You do not see," Lady Harriet said, and there were tears in her eyes, though her face was drawn and aloof. "You *see* a strictly mercenary attitude on my part, and it was not so. I remained fond of Hugh—as fond as I could be of any man, I think. As it was plain that the marriage was no love match, and that he did not consider himself constrained to change his ways on account of it, I thought—well, I thought that like many men in his position, he might continue to take a few pleasures away from home. There's no harm in it, as long as it's kept separate. And I let him know this. But there was a distance, a coldness toward me that was—that was hurtful, and unaccountable, for he was hardly a man to trouble about fidelity to his little bride. The cause of our quarreling was my upbraiding him for it. I was perhaps a little . . . indelicate in my language." She gave a bitter laugh. "But I could not help observing that though my charms failed to rouse him now, it had been quite otherwise before, as the existence of our little child demonstrated. And I said perhaps I should be thankful for that living memento of powers that had apparently waned, as it was unlikely, judging by him now, that I would get another from the same source."

"Damn me," murmured Lawrence.

"And thus we were rather at daggers drawn," she went on, "for I know well that there is nothing men hate more than to be taunted about such things, just as they love to be congratulated on them, though in faith 'tis rare enough to find a performance that merits applause. Well, Hugh took it very much amiss, and hence the clouds between us. I did tell him a while ago, by the by, that there was help to be had. Doctors who make the more—intimate conditions their especial study. I went to one such, when first my babe was coming, and I—I may as well say, God forgive me, that I thought to get rid of it. The fellow claimed to be able to oblige in all such matters."

"Was his name Nimier?"

"That's the man. A great charlatan, no doubt, but some speak highly of him. Thankfully, I thought better of that plan."

Fairfax was surprised to see Griffey gently patting Lady

Harriet's hand. Or at least he would have been surprised, if anything could have surprised him any more.

"And so, missing Hugh's financial aid, you connived at robbery—robbery of a man you had probably already fleeced a hundred times?"

"The air must be mighty thin up there where you stand, Mr. Fairfax," Lady Harriet said sardonically. "When you descend to join the rest of us, you might find things rather different, and rather more complicated. What more would you have? 'Tis told. I may as well add that I missed Hugh's affection more than his money, though I don't expect you to believe me. But then perhaps it was not personal to me. I had often felt of late that Hugh had simply sickened of life altogether, that nothing in it stirred his blood anymore. Perhaps he simply had too much, too early. The great rake, heir to Black Peter—folk saw Hugh as forever burning with an unholy flame. But suppose he found there was no flame left? What was there for him to be? Perhaps it was as well he died when he did." She shrugged. "Well, sir, go on—hurl down your tablets of stone."

"You mistake me," he said—her remark about him standing on some lofty moral plane had needled him. Dear God, he thought, is that what I have become? "My concern is with Hugh's murder. It may have been as well that he died when he did, I can't say; but I believe that no one has the right to choose when another should die. To do so is a—well, there's no other word but sin. That's all. As for Richard Spicer . . . I suppose he is beyond hurt now. And you, Lawrence, have your property back."

"And for that I thank you, Lady Harriet, a thousand times," Lawrence said earnestly; but she only closed her eyes and shrugged again.

"Of course I have still learned much that would be of interest to the magistrate," Fairfax said. Griffey glowered at him. "I'm not sure what to do; finding Hugh's killer is my

charge, and as I am assured I do not see him in this room . . .
Perhaps, Mr. Griffey, if a certain person were to be released
at once from the Fleet prison, with no questions asked, I
might take that as a sign of your goodwill. And of course it
goes without saying that young Mr. Appleton's business with
you is wholly concluded, and any attempt to say otherwise—
to say that he was ever here, in short—will be taken severely
amiss. You understand?"

Griffey blinked his deceptively sleepy eyelids, then nodded.

"Lady Harriet." Fairfax bowed. "I thank you for your candor."

Lawrence followed him out.

"Phew! That was a sight to see, Fairfax—you and Griffey going at it, mad as weavers! I declare when you floored
him, I was never more pleased at anything in my life. I've
hardly slept for nightmares of that brute . . ." Lawrence
sniffed the foggy air appreciatively. "But I say, Fairfax, you
won't—you won't say anything of this to Pa, will you? Not
a word, will you?"

"I see no need, as things stand . . . And if you have been
completely honest with me."

"Oh, I have, I have! Come, have a drink and a bite with
me. For once I have a little money left in my pocket."

They went into the Bedford Head, next to the theatre,
and took a curtained booth. It was not much past six, and
the place was still quiet, though later it would be full to
bursting with the varied clientele of wits, actors, artists,
politicians, fops and demireps who met there, already one
group of men were loudly swapping scandal about one of
the King's ministers and a courtesan revealingly named
Posture Nan.

"Ah, that's the stuff!" Lawrence said, blissfully downing
his brandy and water, and then, very seriously, "You know, I
am an honest fellow, Fairfax. A good deal of an ass some-

times, I'm aware, but not bad-hearted. I wish . . . I only wish I did not have to live as I do. But I shan't go back to—you know, that place. I swear it."

Fairfax's hand was still bleeding from where the cord of the garrotte had cut into it, and throbbing like the very devil. He bound it up with his handkerchief, feeling a little faint, not so much from the wound as from the thought of what would have happened if he hadn't managed to even up the odds with the fire poker. He had an unpleasant vision of his sackcloth-bound body being tossed into the Thames by cover of darkness . . . Well, he had certainly spent his thirty-second birthday in rum fashion, he thought: snuffing up the feverish humors of a debtors' prison, visiting a male brothel, and having a fight with a vicious procurer. Oh, and throw in a brief call at a flogging house as well. He could see the chapter heading in his memoirs: *I enjoy an unusual birthday . . .*

"Certainly, never go back there. And be careful, Lawrence, be wary. I don't know what else I can say. You know that the most liberal of men will recoil from such predilections . . . You are about to cite the practices of the classical Greeks, no doubt, and the easiness of pagan antiquity, but we no longer live in the pagan world, my friend. We live in the Christian one, in which certain vices are forbidden—though you may, in this Christian era of ours, do much as you like with the opposite sex: abuse or neglect them, deal in them like cattle, marry them off against their will, load them with childbearing, cast them off to their own devices while denying them the means of respectable independence, and generally make manifest your contempt for them, all without the slightest hindrance, civil or religious. An odd state of affairs, perhaps, but there it is."

"Damn me," Lawrence said, looking at him with mingled respect and dismay, "I do believe you're a freethinker."

Fairfax shrugged. "*Gedanken sind zollfrei.* Something a friend of mine used to say. 'Thoughts pay no duty.' Never

mind," he said as Lawrence looked blank. "Just be wary, for
God's sake, for there are Griffeys all over this city, and many
are even more inhuman than he."

"Oh, I will, I will," Lawrence said, attacking his slice of
pie. "The thought of Pa coming to know . . . well, it don't
bear thinking on."

"Speaking of your father, Lawrence, how does he stand in
the world now? You said something about his accounts making interesting reading."

"Eh? Oh, well, I was just trying to nettle him a little, you
know. But he ain't as comfortable as he was, that I can tell.
Laying out money to hitch Charlotte to Hugh was the start of
it, and then always having to stump up for Hugh's debts. That's
what put him in low water, if you ask me. But of course, he
goes and finds the wherewithal to slip a hundred pounds to
Nimier, whereas when it's me doing the asking—"

"A hundred pounds? Is that what he gave him?"

"Shocking, ain't it? It was there in his account book. Paying for his time, he calls it. I call it a scandal when he's so
damned parsimonious to his own flesh and blood. His son,
that is, not his precious daughter, of course."

"I'm afraid you are jealous of your sister."

"Well, I've nothing against her, for she's always dealt
fair enough with me; fond of me in her way, I think. But
damn it, yes, I'm jealous of—of what she's always had
and I haven't. At least since Ma died. With Ma I could be
confidential—open my heart, you know what I mean? Not
with Pa. But Charlotte's always had that: she's always
been able to tell Pa anything and be sure of a sympathetic
ear. You've no idea how—how one misses that."
Lawrence sighed and called for another brandy. "You'll
take another, won't you?"

"Thank you, I should be going. I mean to call on your sister before I close the day, and find if there's any news."

"Well, if it's all the same to you, I think I shall stay here and get rather drunk." Lawrence raised his glass. "So, you're to be tutor to the young 'uns when they come back, eh, Fairfax? Good luck to you. I must say . . . I wish you had been my tutor." He laughed awkwardly. "Still, I was a damned dull unteachable dog. Lucky you were spared really."

Wrapped in thought Fairfax walked across the Piazza, where the carriages of wealthy theatregoers were already jostling for space. How vigorously life went on! He was thinking of young Richard Spicer, who had passed his last days among such scenes as this—the Town, with its gossiping and dancing, its drinking and dicing and wenching, its primped and powdered formality and its earthy abandon. Well, though Spicer's hand had pulled the trigger, in a way Sir Anthony and Griffey had killed the young man between them—and Lord Mortlock had contributed too. What a mess! And the killing of Lord Mortlock seemed no clearer.

Yet it was certain that one hand, and one hand alone, had extinguished Lord Mortlock's life, and though Fairfax was no nearer to naming whose that hand was, many lights were twinkling in his mind, where before there had been only doubtful shadow.

Mr. Appleton was certainly up to something. If his suspicion about Stephen Pennant's sudden good fortune was right, then Samuel Appleton was trying to buy off both candidates for the role of Lady Mortlock's secret beau. To avoid scandal, of course, though what Lady Mortlock herself thought about it was a different matter. And he could not eliminate the possibility that there was something darker behind Mr. Appleton's machinations.

And again that name had cropped up—Nimier. The intimate doctor, the dabbler in society's secrets . . . What Lady Harriet had told him had triggered a new speculation. Had the pills by Lord Mortlock's bed come from Nimier;

had Lord Mortlock in fact been a patient of Nimier's? Suddenly he saw that diary entry — *L. Mort., 8:00* — in a different light. It could just as well have referred to *Lord* Mortlock. He could not imagine Lord Mortlock visiting the doctor — or indeed anybody else — at eight in the morning, and in the evening Nimier was, he knew, at the masquerade; but perhaps the figure referred to a receipt. Eight shillings, for example, received from Lord Mortlock — for a box of pills?

But what were they for? At the back of his mind Fairfax had still kept the notion of the "blue pill" for the pox, and had even toyed with the idea of someone killing Lord Mortlock because he was infected — had even, perhaps, polluted his innocent bride . . . And yet a course of the blue pill, and careful treatment, could often clear the disease, and a man of the world would surely make certain of that before he married. Besides, Lady Harriet had mentioned no infection, and she was not mealymouthed. Could the pills, then, be some quack remedy for the other thing she had hinted at — a flagging potency? Ironic for a man of Mortlock's reputation . . . Or had that simply been the bitterness of a rejected woman?

Well, even if Lord Mortlock had consulted the doctor for some reason, there was no doubt that Lady Mortlock *had* made a tryst with Nimier at the Ranelagh masquerade. Which meant that something was going on; something with a conspiratorial flavor.

And still there remained a nagging suspicion of Lawrence. After what Kate Little had told him, he had gone to the mollie-house tonight half-convinced that he would find Lawrence at the root of it all — a desperate and manipulated figure, perhaps, but guilty nonetheless. Now all had been explained away satisfactorily, even down to the matter of his hands being hidden in his pockets. Perhaps it was just too satisfactory; or perhaps, Fairfax thought, I simply can't see the wood for the trees . . .

Suddenly he felt a blow against his legs. He looked down to find that a little Negro page boy, scurrying ahead of his mistress who had just stepped down from her carriage, had run full pelt into him. The little boy begged his pardon and straightened the feathered turban such pages often wore, and then grinned back at his mistress, a lady in brilliant satin who laughed and wagged a jeweled finger at him. "Have a care, Solomon," she said.

An indulgent mistress. There were such, of course; not all black servants were as unhappy as Abraham. But the fact remained that the Negro page boy was looked on as a fashionable accessory, like Lady Harriet's macaw and Mrs. Benaglio's monkey. And that ridiculous costume of turban and trousers emphasized the artifice, the sheer untruth behind it. Fairfax thought about the black population of the city. You saw them mostly in costume—in servants' livery, or in the slops of sailors and watermen, though there were others, marginal and despised figures, scratching a living in their own little colonies in the seedy warrens of the riverside districts. If you were such a person, Fairfax thought, what would you want out of life? The same, surely, as anyone else: the basics of warmth, love, security. He saw that he had fallen into the trap of thinking about the missing Abraham in terms of demonic mystery. Whatever Abraham had done or not done, the same all-too-human motives animated him as everyone else. If only, Fairfax thought, I had talked to him that morning at the Mortlock house . . . But of course, who thought to talk to servants, let alone slaves?

He was weary, and took a hackney to Hill Street, though it meant the money in his pockets was nearly gone; he would have to play Lawrence's part soon, and beg for funds from Mr. Appleton. He saw his employer, in fact, sooner than he expected. Meggy opened the door to him, and almost at once

Mr. Appleton, red-faced and excited, came hurrying from the dining room.

"Is that Fairfax there? Good, good. Fairfax, you must come and see. The most shocking discovery—and yet it settles things, I think. Dear me, yes."

Fairfax followed him into the dining room, where he found two constables, gravely examining a garment that lay on some sheets of newspaper on the great dining table. It was a blue coat with yellow facings—a livery coat, exactly like the one Abraham Drake had been wearing. Beside it, a pair of white footman's gloves—white, except for the reddish-brown bloodstains that spattered them up to the knuckle.

Chapter Ten

"It was brought here but half an hour since," Mr. Appleton said. "A maid servant at the house two doors down was sweeping the area steps and clearing some rubbish there. This coat was among it. It must have been thrown over the railing, and lain there . . ."

"Thrown by Abraham, when he ran away," Fairfax said. "It is Abraham's?"

"No doubt of it," Mr. Appleton said, nodding his head.

"These were in the coat pockets," one of the constables said, lifting up the bloodstained gloves with a certain gloomy drama. "Precious rogue! Fine kid too. Dress 'em in kid, and this is how they pay you back!"

"Nothing else was found?"

The other constable shook his head. "We've searched the area pretty thoroughly. It looks to me as if he cut his lordship's throat, then slipped the gloves in his pockets, bolted downstairs and out, and then once he was outside stripped off the coat and pitched it over the railing before hooking it."

"I would not have believed it," Mr. Appleton said somberly. "Still I would not have believed it of that boy . . ."

Fairfax fingered the coat. There were small spots of what looked like blood near the pocket flaps. A strange and grisly exhibit to be laid out on this gleaming table, and he could not repress a shudder, though the coat was otherwise unmarked and innocent-looking enough, and even had a faint lavender scent about it.

"One of you, I suggest, had better go and report this to the magistrate," Mr. Appleton said. "No matter that the hour is late; you have only to say that you come from Lady Mortlock's father." Even now he spoke those words with a throb of conscious pride. "This is surely the most vital, the most terrible of evidences, and I think the search for Abraham must be made more urgent. What say you, Fairfax?"

Before Fairfax could answer he saw that Lady Mortlock, statuesque and dreadfully pale, had appeared in the doorway.

"My dear," Mr. Appleton said, "I told you, it's best if you don't look upon this thing. There is no need, and you will disquiet yourself—"

"Why, what can it matter?" Lady Mortlock said, sharply and even fiercely. "What can anything matter anymore?" She came forward, and looked at the coat and the gloves, her hands crossed at her stomach. "Not so terrible, Father, after all. Not so . . . It is surprising, you know, what we can bear . . ."

She broke down utterly then, shaking her head and wailing, and running blindly out of the room. Mr. Appleton, with an agonized look, went after her.

"You'd better do as he says," Fairfax said to the constables. "I take it there has been no word of Abraham's whereabouts?"

"Not a squeak," the first constable said, putting on his hat and buttoning his greatcoat. "We've had a dozen men combing the Negroes' haunts downriver, and no go; ah, but you know what those vicious black devils are like—they look after their own. We'll have him, though. If he don't care for the fine clothes his masters put him in, then we'll give him a hemp necklace instead." He left, tossing his head righteously.

"I suppose," Fairfax said, "what we see here is enough to hang Abraham Drake."

" 'Tis a mighty likely piece of evidence," said the second constable, older and more temperate. "That is, if it's surely the coat he was wearing."

"It is the Mortlock livery, without a doubt, and Abraham was the only footman. The coachman has a livery coat, I daresay, but he's a small man, whereas this is very much Abraham's size . . ."

With a thought in mind, he went to look for Lady Mortlock. Voices came from the small parlor on the right.

"There, my dear, all will be well now. You must believe me, Charlotte: look up, my dear. It all seems very intolerable, I know. But it will be well now . . ."

Mr. Appleton was sitting by his daughter and nervously patting her hand. Her face was a stormy mask of tears, and she even looked, Fairfax thought as he coughed and approached, a little wild. Perhaps the sight of the gloves had brought back that more explicitly horrifying sight of Hugh Mortlock lying among his blood-drenched pillows; and perhaps he was surprised to see her like this because she had shown such strength before.

"Lady Mortlock — again my apologies for intruding, but might I just ask one question? It concerns the coat."

She looked at him as if he were mad.

"I merely wondered if Abraham had only the one. If we are to be absolutely sure that this is the coat he was wearing . . ."

"I don't know." She disengaged herself from her father, who watched her walk to the window with anxious eyes. "I can't think. He may have had a second. I don't see that it matters. I don't see, truly, that anything matters." She said this with a dull defiance which seemed, Fairfax thought, to be directed at her father, who looked uncomfortable. "Meggy has the charge of the servants' clothes; she would know, I daresay. You can ask her if you like."

Receiving a nod from Mr. Appleton, Fairfax bowed and withdrew.

He took the stairway at the rear of the hall to the servants' quarters below, where Meggy, occupied along with the other maids by the vast laundry of the household, was very flustered to see him. The great kitchen, filling almost the whole basement level of the house, was starkly unadorned compared with the grandiose upper rooms, though noticeably warmer from the open range. Linen was hanging from drying racks brought down on pulleys; a maid was heating a flat-iron on the range while another plied the goffering iron that was used for crimping cuffs and flounces, and Meggy had the charge of the great box mangle. Easy to forget the heroic labor that went on in these subterranean places, Fairfax thought.

"Why, if that ain't Abraham's coat up there, and his gloves, then I'm a blue-faced devil," Meggy said emphatically in answer to his question. "As for another coat, he never had no such thing. What would such as him be wanting with two coats, I ask you? One blue coat with yellow facings, one pair of white kid gloves, one white waistcoat, two pairs of buff breeches, three shirts, two sets of linen bands, six pairs of stockings—that was his list. I should know, sir, I'm very particular."

He saw no reason to doubt that: there was even, he noticed, a laundry tally board on the wall, and underneath each copperplate heading—SHIRTS, HOSE, SHEETS, and many others—a brass disk that was turned to record the number of items in the wash. Military precision, he thought, and no reason to doubt that the coat and the bloodied gloves were Abraham's indeed, and the ones he had been wearing on the morning of Lord Mortlock's murder. He found his heart sinking horribly as he contemplated the idea he had resisted all along—that Abraham was guilty after all.

"Nell, have a care you don't scorch that," Meggy was saying. "Mary, you go fetch the second-best tablecloth from the linen chest—'twill want a little pressing before it's laid . . . No, sir, you mean well, I daresay, and have to be sure of everything when it's a matter of law, but when I saw that horrid bundle I only nodded my head, for it was just as I'd known all along, 'twas that dirty blackamoor who killed the master and none other. And now I must be getting on, sir, if you'll pardon me, as we're all behindhand with the wash on account of things being so topsy-turvy . . ."

She went to the copper steaming on the range and with a dolly stick stirred a bedsheet that was boiling and billowing within, lifting it from the water with a grunt to inspect it. About to turn and go, Fairfax stopped: there was a pinkish stain on the sheet.

He was surprised.

"The sheets from Lord Mortlock's bed have been kept? I thought they had been burned—"

"Good heavens, sir, what manner of creature do you think I am? Of course they were—I had 'em disposed of directly this morning." She dropped the sheet back into the copper and seemed about to brandish the dolly stick at him like a cudgel. "Now, *if* there's no other way I can oblige, sir, I'd like to see all this mangled afore I go to bed, and I can't be getting on when I'm having to talk a lot of fallalery."

With a murmured apology he left the kitchen and went upstairs deep in thought, almost colliding with the maid who was coming down, her arms heaped with sweetly fragrant linen. In the hall he found Mr. Appleton, buttoning his coat and looking grave.

"How is Lady Mortlock? She seems much distressed."

"The continued pressure on her nerves is too great," his employer said. "The sight of that coat, and those—those ghastly gloves, I think. I wish she had not looked . . . She has recovered her spirits a little, but I believe she cannot begin to have any peace until this matter is settled, and I hope it may soon be. I am going to see the magistrate myself, and press him to the utmost diligence in finding Abraham. If it is a question of recruiting more men to search, then I shall offer to defray the expense. For my daughter's sake alone this cannot go on . . . What is amiss with your hand, Fairfax?"

"Oh, nothing. A small accident. I think, sir, I shall try Kate Little again. She was the one who was closest to Abraham. It may be that with time she will reconsider her silence."

"As you wish," Mr. Appleton said with a shrug. "I doubt there is anything to be got there; if she knows where Abraham is, she will only deny it the more as we close in on him, it appears to me. But as you will. Oh, you have seen nothing of that boy of mine, by any chance?"

"No, not since I left your house this afternoon."

"Hm. A pity he is not here to be with his sister in her extremity, but no doubt he prefers to amuse himself rather than play the part that any good brother would consider his duty." Mr. Appleton put on his hat and stalked out.

About to follow, Fairfax found that Lady Mortlock had appeared noiselessly in the parlor doorway. She had put up her disheveled hair, and she stood as tall, striking, and dignified as ever, though her eyes were red; a full glass of wine was in her hands.

"Hugh's remedy for everything," she said with a tremulous smile. "I have resisted the temptation to tope thus far, but fresh ills have made me give in."

"Fresh ills?"

"Why," she said, bringing the glass unsteadily to her lips, "I did not want it to be Abraham, Mr. Fairfax, truly, any more than you did. Absurd, isn't it?" She held up the glass to him in valediction, then turned and went back into the parlor.

*　　　*　　　*

Outside, the evening air had turned much colder, and the fog, thickened with coal smuts, was as palpable as a damp net. Fairfax made his way to the Haymarket on foot as briskly as he could, but he was aching from his contest with Griffey, his hand throbbed, and he soon felt chilled to the marrow.

There was a vague unfocused anger about him too: anger that Abraham should confirm ignorant prejudices, perhaps. And as he thought about that coat, he grew angry with Kate Little for lying to him. He knew now that the milk seller had seen Abraham after his flight, at least once: the matter of the coat settled it for him.

Coming into Bellman's Court, he was all prepared to confront her about it. What made his anger evaporate, and filled him instead with a dizzy rush of new speculations, was the sight of Kate at the top of the steps leading to the milk cellar. She was passing the time of the day with an old market woman, and as she talked she stood leaning a little backwards on one sturdy foot, one hand on her hip, her midriff thrust forwards. Kate was a large woman but not fleshy; the lamp burning in the doorway of the shop above the cellar picked out the points of her wrist and anklebones, and made a telling contrast with the low roundness of her belly.

And the old market woman had noticed it too, he thought. As they said good-bye, and Kate went down the steps, he saw the market woman give her a long, assessing, slightly spiteful look.

He followed down the steps, slipping in before Kate could close the door.

"Oh! sir, you gave me a fright." She was carrying a loaf of bread and oysters wrapped up in a handkerchief, and nearly dropped them. There was no sign of old Little; still sleeping it off in his booth, he supposed.

"Why, Kate, who did you think it was?"

She recovered herself. "I'm sure I don't know, sir." She took a spill and lit a candle from the embers of the fire. As she walked across the room, shielding the candle with one hand before setting it on a shelf, he saw her shape again. "Sir, I'm not sure as I can help you anymore, and I must be getting Father's tea ready—"

"In a minute. I was just wondering how I could help you, or your father, perhaps. I noticed today he still lacked his coat. Someone had been treating him, you said; a pity he didn't use the money to redeem his coat from the pawnbroker's. But I suppose once he gets the thirst on him . . . It would probably be better if I gave the money to you. How much do you suppose he would need, to get his coat back?"

"I'm afraid he's lost the pawn ticket," she said, turning away from him to stir the embers.

"There was no pawn ticket. He has no coat because his coat is on Abraham Drake's back. No more lies, Kate. I don't blame you in the least for giving your father's coat to your lover. He came here without a coat—or did you meet him somewhere else, and take the coat to him there? Well, no matter. The fact is, Abraham's own coat has been discovered now, and it tells its own tale—a very terrible one. This is serious, Kate. You must tell me your own tale now; you know you must."

She straightened up and turned at last, and he saw her face like wax in the glimmering light. "I—I don't understand . . ."

"Oh, come, enough. You're with child, aren't you? I know you're no light o' love, Kate, and so the child must be Abraham's. It's no wonder, then, that you want to protect him. But in doing so now you face trouble and danger yourself—you and your child. I repeat, it is a deadly serious matter, Kate. They have found Abraham's own coat, with his gloves in the pocket—covered in blood."

She stared at him. "No," she said, shaking her head. "No, it can't be. No, sir, I'm sorry, I have to say that you're lying to me. I don't know you, not really, but Abraham I do know, and he would never tell me anything but the truth."

"You have seen him, then."

"Perhaps I have." She went to the table and began hastily hacking at the loaf of bread, then put her hand to her eyes and sat down. "It don't seem fair . . . We've done nothing more nor less than a thousand other young folks do every day. And it wasn't as if Abraham didn't want to know me. Why, he was pleased and proud when I told him, even though he was troubled about what we were going to do; what mattered to me was that he was proud, and I was too, not ashamed, because we were true to one another . . ." She wiped her eyes. "And he said that I wasn't to fret, that he would make it all right . . ."

"How? What was he going to do?"

"He was going to tell his master about us, and ask if we could get married. It was—I knew it was difficult. He was even less free than most servants, and if his master wouldn't agree to it, then . . . But Abraham said 'twould all be righted; he said his master's bark was worse than his bite. Lots of black men were allowed to get married, he said, and sometimes their masters gave them their freedom that way. He said that when he told his master how things stood, then he would surely give in . . . I had my doubts, I admit it. But Abraham so wanted to marry me, and so I went along with it. I trusted him."

The lights of understanding were blazing in Fairfax's mind now; indeed, for the moment they almost dazzled him.

"It was the morning Lord Mortlock was killed," he said. "That's when Abraham told him about you being with child, and asked his permission to marry you. I was there: Abraham asked to speak to him, and Lord Mortlock took him aside, and then . . . then Lord Mortlock turned furious."

Kate nodded. "He said no. He was angry—wild, Abraham said. Reckoned he'd send him back to the plantations

before he'd allow it. He used—horrible words about us.
Abraham didn't tell me what they were, but I can guess. His
master wasn't going to change his mind, that was certain.
And so . . . and so Abraham decided he would run away."

"That very morning."

"Yes . . . I came to the house to bring the milk about
eleven, and Abraham answered the door and told me what
had happened, and how his master had turned him down flat.
I can't say I was very surprised, but still I was grieved, and I
mebbe shed a tear. Abraham just looked at me and said he
was leaving. He told me to go on to the end of my milk walk,
and then go home, and he would meet me there. As soon as
he could slip away, he said, he would go—just like that—
and never come back. Well, I didn't know what to say. I was
afraid for him. His master owned him, and if he walked out
on his place they could fetch him back, I knew that; and
where could he go, what could he do? But when I started to
say something about that, he just hushed me and said he
would manage it. He would keep out of the way, and find a
new place, and we'd be together in the end. Of course I still
had my doubts. But what else was left to us? He was being
brave for me, and so I was brave for him . . . And that's all
I've got to say, sir. You're thinking perhaps I'll tell you where
he is, but if you've listened to anything I've said, you know
I won't do that."

"Even after what I've told you? About the coat and
gloves . . . ?"

"I'm sorry, sir. I think you're just trying to trick me, and I
ain't stupid. Aye, I gave Abraham my father's coat because
he came away without his—only because he always hated it
so and was glad to be rid of it when he left. He laid that hateful coat and gloves out on the hall table before he ran out—
at least they won't be able to accuse me of stealing 'em as
well, he said; and that's why I know you're trying to trick

me, sir, because I can't believe they've only just been found, when he left 'em as clear as day."

Fairfax stared at her so long and hard that she began to look alarmed.

"Sir, if you're going to get angry, I shall wake my father. 'Tisn't fair you should act so, truly, sir, when I—"

"Wait. Kate, I'm not angry, believe me. I . . ." He was dazzled again by the terrifying new light breaking in on his mind. "That day—when Abraham ran away. You heard about Lord Mortlock's death when you were finishing your milk walk, did you not? And so when you came home, and met Abraham here, you told him the news—and he was frightened."

"He had no reason to be," she said with a mistrustful look.

"Yes, yes, he did. Because having fled from the house that morning he would surely be under suspicion for Lord Mortlock's murder. It looked bad for him—very bad, poor fellow. You must both have realized that, even though Abraham was completely innocent." Lavender, he thought: the coat smelled of lavender. "And so Abraham had to get away from here and hide. Hide from the law that was seeking him, and hope the real culprit would be discovered."

"You—you believe he is innocent, sir?"

"I know it," he said excitedly. "But, of course, few people would believe it when he had the ill luck to make his escape on the very day that his master was murdered. A most unfortunate coincidence, except that it was not a coincidence. As soon as someone saw that Abraham was a runaway, they saw also an opportunity: an opportunity to kill Lord Mortlock. Blame was sure to fasten on the runaway slave. An unmissable opportunity for someone who wanted Lord Mortlock dead."

"Who, sir . . . ?"

He did not answer. Lavender; bloodstains; a box of pills; a meeting in masks; Kate's rounded belly. And a piece of

Shakespeare that had been quoted at the levee: "a consummation devoutly to be wished."

He had it. And for some moments he could only stand in wonder, pierced by the tragedy of it. For if he was right, then Lord Mortlock need never have been killed at all, even from the murderer's point of view. And the murderer probably knew it now: how did that feel? But then, a conscience that could accommodate murder could surely make room for it . . .

"Wherever Abraham is hiding," he said, "you've surely been to see him, Kate. Taken him food, and so on. Isn't that so?"

She was still mistrustful. "Sir, you say you know he's innocent. But from what I hear, the constables are still searching for him. Mebbe if you think you can prove he's innocent . . . but what if you can't? The law's after him, and I'm afraid the law ain't going to think twice once it lays hold on him. He's so dear to me, sir, dearer than anything. Even . . ."

She flushed, her eyes straying to the ridiculous booth. Dearer even than her father, Fairfax thought, and that was hardly to be wondered at. He recalled the old man's drunken antics that afternoon. And then a coldness went through him.

"Kate," he said, "who had been treating your father today? Think, now. He was in his cups, and you said someone must have been treating him."

"Well, I thought that was how it must be. I don't know how else he got the money to be toping so; we surely haven't got it."

"Unless someone paid him," Fairfax said. "Paid him for what he could tell them . . . You haven't told your father where Abraham is?"

"Of course not," she said. "I—I know he's my father, but I fear I couldn't trust him with that."

"No," Fairfax agreed, "very wise. But what if he followed

you to where Abraham is? Think of it, Kate. the two of you. Though I fancy he is often drunk and he must have had his suspicions about the disappearance of his own coat. When did you last see Abraham? This morning?"

She nodded. "I told Father I was going marketing. He— he didn't say anything, though 'tis not my usual day. Oh, but he wouldn't . . ."

Oh yes, he would, Fairfax thought. The old man was surely devious enough to follow his daughter and spy on Abraham's hiding place; surely devious enough to sell the information to the person who had "treated" him today. Well, he would find out.

He took up the candle and thrust back the curtain of the booth, prepared to shake the old man out of his drunken slumber.

The frowsy bed was empty.

"He's not here," he said dully.

"What? Why, where can he be? 'Tis seldom he goes abroad at this time, unless—"

"Unless he has a new thirst."

"Well . . . But his money was all gone."

"He may have bethought him of a way to get more," Fairfax murmured. He turned and held the candle up to Kate's face, fixing her eyes with his. "Kate. I beg you now to trust me. Believe me, I know Abraham is innocent. But if, as I suspect, your father has gone to turn him over to the law, then the constables are going to be mighty fierce about taking him. And your father has already told someone else besides, I believe, and Abraham may be in even more danger from that person . . . It is a desperate hour, Kate. You must tell me where Abraham is hiding. For his sake."

With what seemed like her old unreachable placidity, Kate wrapped the bread in muslin and laid it aside, then took up her shawl. This time, Fairfax saw with relief, it was with decision.

"I will take you there," she said, and blew out the candle.

...very long journey by ferry-... to St. Katherine's Stairs in the ...n making it one entered another ...wer, a marine city came into being as ...reat ships lay at anchor, their tall masts ...dle of waterside dwellings and warehouses: ships ...y nations, Dutch and Swedish and Portuguese, East I...men and, of course, ships of the West Indies trade, for here were the sugar quays and depots and the counting-houses of the sugar factors; ships of every design, sloops and brigs and schooners and cutters, with lights winking on their decks and here and there a bell ringing through the fog, and over all a slow, creaking, groaning murmur from the fantastic cat's cradle of rigging above, as if the vessels were communing in their own language.

They disembarked at St. Katherine's Stairs, and Kate led him swiftly into the narrow streets of the waterside district. There was a tangy smell of river silt and pitch and oakum and whale oil mixed in with the universal reek of poverty. They passed several slop shops, still open, where smoking lamps made sinister their hanging stock of sailors' clothes and glazed hats, and low pawnbrokers' conveniently adjoining gin shops, and ships chandlers and sawyers' sheds and penny lodging houses, all in a tumbledown confusion of decayed courts and alleys that led off an unpaved thoroughfare where a common sewer ran, meandering and bubbling like a ghastly brook. The whole maze hugged close to the river, and one crazy row of tenements revealed, beneath its shoring timbers, a ragged trio of mudlarks still poking about for valuables by lamplight in the silt below. There were plenty of people about, from sailors on a drunken spree to bumboat women toting their great baskets, to solemn gaberdined Jews, but the absence of lighting, the dirt and decay, the shrieks and snatches of song and sharp barks of half-feral curs that came intermittently in the foggy air, g... threatening atmosphere.

"This place we are going to—what ... it?" Fairfax asked.

"'Tis a sort of lodging house," Kate sa... shawl close about her. "They look after black pe... fancy he met a man once in the street, a sailor, who ... about it, and he kept it in mind . . . What's going to happen to him, sir? If the constables have taken him, will you be able to help him?"

"I hope so, Kate. You must trust me."

Suddenly she turned into a dark slit that led to a cluster of peeling tenements. The cobbles were slimy underfoot. She hesitated a moment, then ducked into a brick passage. There was a recessed door that Fairfax would never have guessed at. Kate lifted her hand to knock, then sucked in a sharp breath. The door stood ajar, and there was light within.

Fairfax went first. A damp stone-floored passage led to a large room, overlooking the river, that had been roughly partitioned with sheets of sacking. There were a couple of straw mattresses and lamps and a few cooking utensils strung over a sooty grate. A stout, grizzled old black man with a silver earring stood with arms folded, a clay pipe clenched between his lips, calmly regarding the three constables gathered there with staves and storm lanterns.

"Now 'tis quite a party," the black man said, glancing at the newcomers. "Well, I'll say it again, so you're all sure: I don't know any Abraham Drake, nor nobody like him, and he ain't here."

"Damn it," one of the constables said, spitting on the floor. "The old sot's spun us a tale, and brought us on a wild-goose chase. I've a mind to break his head for him."

Lurking behind the constables was the familiar, unlovable figure of Jack Little. His daughter saw him, and gave a gasp which had no real surprise in it, only aching disappointment.

, Father," she said. "Oh, you did, Father. How could you?"

Old Little grimaced uneasily at her, wiping his mouth with his sleeve, and then turned in appeal to the constables. "I tell you, this was his den. If it ain't now, it was. I should know—I came after *her* this morning, and watched her come in here, with a pie. A pie, I ask you! When does she ever give *me* pie, me what's her father and done right by her all her life, and me with my malady and all—?"

"Well, I don't see him," the first constable said, spitting again. "And laying false information for a reward, you know, is a matter the law don't look kindly on. I've a mind to shake those shillings out of you, blast your eyes—"

"'Tis true, I'm telling you!" Little quavered. "Ask her, she'll know; and as for this damned black-faced devil here, why of course he's lying, they all do, 'tis their nature—"

"I fear the old man is right, though I deplore his language," came a new voice. Mr. Appleton stepped forwards from the shadows made by one of the partitions. "I too sought Abraham here, but I fear we are all too late. Our bird has flown, unless I am much mistaken. By your leave, sir?" He took one of the lanterns and held it up to the window. Directly below the tenement was a timber wharf, and just beyond it a small brig was under sail, tacking across the river. It was a collier brig, its very timbers black from its trade. Several figures were visible on the lamplit deck. Mr. Appleton pointed a steady finger. "Unless I am much mistaken, Abraham is there: he has taken ship, and she is underway and meaning to slip out of the Pool tonight." His eyes met Fairfax's briefly. "We are all too late."

It was Kate who cried out first, and ran from the room; the constables, cursing, clattered after her. Old Little wiped his nose and nodded in self-congratulation, then laid a hand on Mr. Appleton's sleeve.

"'Twas right, after all, wasn't it, sir? I told them right, like

I told you. Perhaps, sir, I might ask a little more, in consideration, on account of the raw night, sir, and my malady being what it is—"

Mr. Appleton looked down in disgust at the old man's outstretched hand, then stalked after the others.

Fairfax, his heart beating loudly, followed. Another passage led down to the wharf itself, a creaking construction of half-rotted timbers. The constables stood at the end, waving their staves and hallooing to the brig, which was wearing steadily away.

"Come in! You've a wanted man aboard! Come in, in the King's name!"

"What about this?" the youngest of the constables said, producing a pistol from his pocket. "'Tis primed and loaded. I could try a shot at him—"

"Good God, what are you thinking, man?" Fairfax interposed. "Did the magistrate send you to kill an unarmed man?"

"Any reasonable means to bring him in," the constable said sulkily.

"We are too late," Mr. Appleton said again. "Well, well. His guilt is sealed, God forgive him, but we are too late. The brig is bound for Flushing, I think—he won't see these shores again."

Kate had pushed the constables aside. She was weeping, and waving her shawl at the ship.

"Abraham!" she cried, her voice carrying shrill across the water; and then she wrapped her arms about herself and fell to a kind of desperate keening. "Oh, my dear, oh my dear one, you're leaving me . . ."

On the deck of the brig one of the lamplit figures could be seen standing very still. And then, all at once, the figure mounted the rail and went over the side.

"He's jumped!" one of the constables cried. "There he is, see? Damn me, he's coming in to us!"

Fairfax, standing close to Mr. Appleton, felt his employer give a tremendous start.

On board the brig the other figures had run to the rail and were looking down into the water, black as oil and drizzled with lamplight. A bell rang, but it was not from the brig. Turning, Fairfax saw a pilot boat leading a schooner upstream.

"Abraham! Oh, my dear . . . !"

A dark head and a glimmer of shoulders could be seen steadily plowing towards the wharf. Fairfax, pressed against Mr. Appleton at the end of the wharf, could feel him shivering, though it was not very cold.

"Constable," Mr. Appleton said in a low gritty voice, "shoot now. Perhaps you had better shoot now . . ."

"Nay, we'll take our man with no trouble," said the first constable, already kneeling down at the wharf's edge. The man swimming strongly towards him was recognizable now as Abraham Drake; his eyes, Fairfax saw, were fixed on Kate.

"Yes, we will take our man with no trouble," Fairfax echoed, and he took hold of Mr. Appleton's sleeve with a firm grip.

Mr. Appleton turned his head and looked into Fairfax's face, his eyes widening, his lips trembling.

"Come up, you . . ." The constables were pulling a gasping, dripping Abraham onto the wharf. Kate knelt and flung her arms around him, pushing the constables away.

"I couldn't go," Abraham said breathlessly, clutching her. "Couldn't—not away from you, Kate. When I saw you, I just . . . I'll stay, my dear, face it out, for I've done naught wrong, and I must trust . . . I'm sorry, sir!" he cried, struggling to his feet, and extending his hands beseechingly to Mr. Appleton. "'Twas good of you to try and help me—I'm not ungrateful—but 'tis best I stay, and face it—"

"You have nothing to face, Abraham," Fairfax said, keeping his grip on Mr. Appleton's sleeve. "Only the fact that the man who procured you the passage on that ship, and tried to get you away, is rather curiously also the man who committed the crime of which you are accused. Yes, sir," Fairfax said in Mr. Appleton's ear, tightening his grip, while the constables stared dumbstruck. "I know how you did it, and how you took the opportunity to throw the blame on Abraham—but only so that it would not fall on you. You much preferred *not* to see Abraham hang for your son-in-law's murder, though his supposed guilt was useful, and that's why you tracked him down today, using that wretched old man, and told him that the net was closing in, or something like, and that he had better fly. That you were not convinced of his guilt yourself, having always liked him—something like that, wasn't it, Abraham? And so, sir, having much influence in the shipping trade, you had got him a working place on a ship going out of the country—one of your own ships, perhaps, or one in which you own a share? At least, Abraham, you would be free, though you would be presumed guilty of the murder here, and so that would be the end of it . . . It was kindness, sir"—he returned his gaze to Mr. Appleton as the man moaned and tried to wriggle free—"kindness and pride, a peculiar mixture, have characterized you all along. Kindness to your daughter, and pride in her station, were what led you to cut Lord Mortlock's throat—"

"No, no!" Mr. Appleton cried, with a wild glance at the constables. "Damn it, don't—"

"It's all right, I shan't speak of that secret matter before strangers, sir; I know how important it was to you, important enough to warrant murder. I am only curious as to know precisely when you retrieved Abraham's coat from where you had hidden it in the linen chest in the hall, with the bloodied gloves you wore in the pockets, and threw it down the basement area steps to be found. Today, perhaps, after you were certain of finding Abraham and getting him away? Well, no matter. But what an irony, that you need never have killed Hugh at all! Isn't that what Charlotte revealed to you today, sir, that the terrible thing had not happened after all? I wonder if she suspected, by the by, that it was you who had done the deed; I reckon she must have, but love and loyalty won out in her heart, and shouted suspicion down. Kindness, sir, the tender feelings of the heart, never underestimate them; they were enough to make Abraham jump ship when he saw Kate, and throw your plans awry. Kindness ran out, I think, then, as you suddenly preferred to have him shot . . . Ah!"

Mr. Appleton had seized his hand and dug his nails into the still-bandaged flesh, and with surprisingly agility writhed away from him, and away from the flailing arms of the constables. With a moment's hesitation, and a deep breath, he plunged into the river.

The constables shouted after his laboriously swimming figure, and Abraham seemed about to plunge in after him, but Fairfax stopped him with a warning hand.

Mr. Appleton was heading, as best he could, towards the brig which lay to on the other bank, but he lacked Abraham's strength, and his flared coat, spreading in the water, was encumbering him. A bell rang again, urgently. The pilot boat arrowed through the dark water a dozen yards away from him, and voices shouted to him from on board. Someone extended an oar in his direction. Treading water, gaping like a fish, Mr. Appleton seemed to shake his head and turned about. The voices shouted louder, and on the wharf Kate let out a scream. Mr. Appleton had only swum a few weak strokes when the shadow of the schooner's great prow fell over him, obliterating him.

The tall ship plowed its stately way past the wharf. Its foaming wake danced and twinkled in the light of the lanterns aft, but no figure appeared in the swirl, and none broke the inky surface after its passage.

"He's gone," one of the constables grunted. "Rest his

soul . . . We'd better speak to the master of that ship when she heaves to. What's that name on her? Art—something."

"*Artemis.*" The old black man had come out to the wharf, and stood puffing on his clay pipe and regarding the ship with narrowed eyes. "She's a slaver."

Chapter Eleven

"I still cannot comprehend him," said Mr. Saunders Welch, the magistrate, pouring a glass of port and passing Fairfax the bottle. "A man of wealth and influence, not lacking in education or understanding, and seemingly of the most phlegmatic temper, yet capable of such a monstrous crime."

"The key to his character lies, I think, in his private capacity as a proud and loving father," Fairfax said. "That was what drove him to such ends."

"Hm. Proud and loving fatherhood I can readily comprehend, but it has naught to do with murder."

"Well, in Mr. Appleton the pride and the loving were peculiarly mixed. His wife died early, and he was long accustomed, as poor Lawrence Appleton pointed out to me, to enjoying the warmest confidentiality with his daughter, whose brilliance and beauty he was so proud of. In a way I think he was both mother and father to her. He was the one person to whom she turned in times of trouble, in whom she reposed the utmost confidence and trust. And he in turn valued her above everything — valued her, most especially, when she realized the dreams of his industry and ambition, and linked him with the aristocracy. She was not only the dear child of his love; she had also made him the father of Lady Mortlock. His pride in that shone out in every word he spoke.

"And so when all seemed far from well with the marriage he had been so eager to promote, his businesslike brain set out to find out why. One course was to send me as a kind of spy to accompany Lord Mortlock in his nocturnal revels, and find out why he was so disaffected from his bride. Chiefly, was there another woman? He charged me also with discovering how much Lord Mortlock was gambling, for he did not greatly like funding such activities, but that was really a side issue. The matter of the marriage was what concerned him."

"He must have known that Lord Mortlock had a rakish reputation."

"Indeed he did, and did not mind it, I think, as he would not have minded anything so long as the proper forms were observed. He knew that the — well, the aristocratic standards of the world he had joined were rather different from the ones he had been brought up with. And when it came to his ears that his daughter too was rumored to be straying, I think his main concern was to contain the scandal and make sure the boat was not rocked too recklessly.

"But events had taken a turn he could never have guessed. And it was revealed to him, I believe, that very evening that I was roaming the gaming dens with Lord Mortlock. He went to see his daughter that evening — a thing he at first denied, and then shrugged off as a mere social call; in fact it was a mightily urgent tête-à-tête. Her father had always been the person she turned to, and she turned to him now, in her desperation, to confess her great dilemma. She had indeed taken a lover, though she refused to say who he was. That did not matter so greatly, just then; what mattered was that Lady Mortlock was pregnant, and the child was not her husband's. And *could not be* her husband's. Because the marriage was unconsummated."

"A fearful confidence for a daughter to make to a father!" Mr. Welch said, with a dismayed look into his port.

"So it was. Unconsummated—the word has a very cool, neutral, legal sound. But not to her, I daresay, and I noticed at her levee that she was strangely put out when someone quoted Shakespeare—'a consummation devoutly to be wished'—though I did not understand it at the time. Yes, the marriage was a sham, in that sense. Lord Mortlock was impotent, and could not consummate it; a great irony, considering his reputation! Of course he had not always been so. He had an illegitimate child by Lady Harriet Froome, and they had been lovers until quite recently. What the cause was, who can say: he may have contracted a malady in his earlier debaucheries which caught up with him; some might say a life of dissipation itself had left him in that case. It may well have been a matter of the mind, which you'll agree, sir, is a great ruler of the flesh; Lord Mortlock was a prey to black moods, a pessimistic emptiness which seemed at times to border on the pathological. But certainly he was not equipped in temper to bear such an affliction easily—it drove him more bitterly in on himself, I think. And hence his excessive reaction when his slave, Abraham Drake, approached him to ask permission to marry, as his sweetheart was pregnant. It must almost have seemed he was being mocked with his impotency on all sides.

"But he did not know, at any rate, that his wife was pregnant, as she revealed to Mr. Appleton that evening. And the dread of his knowing—which he was bound to do quite soon—was what made her turn to her father in despair, and what made Mr. Appleton come to his terrible, private decision. For Lord Mortlock had made it plain to his bride—baffled, hurt, and resentful as she must have been by her strange nonmarriage—that her bargain was struck and there was no going back on it. There was no pretense that it had been a love match: Charlotte Appleton had walked to the altar with him simply in order to become Lady Mortlock, the fifth baroness, with all the attendant honor and privilege. She had got what she and her father wanted, and Hugh made it clear to her that she should expect nothing more. In fact, he explicitly told her that he would claim no bastards under his roof. This Lady Mortlock told me today, having agreed to speak privily with me once only; and so she must have told her father, that evening when they were alone.

"And Mr. Appleton must have known, of course, that Hugh, as a born peer and a man, had might on his side. He had the stature and means to divorce her as an adulteress, if she should shame him, and he made it plain he would not hesitate to do it. The question of nonconsummation, of course, raised the possibility of a petition for annulment of the marriage on her side, though the law is notoriously partial to the man in these matters. But her adulterous pregnancy would remain a fact, nonetheless. Indeed, as soon as Lord Mortlock found out about it, Lady Mortlock would be pretty well ruined. All the grandeur of her title and her manner of living—which despite the unhappy state of affairs between her and Hugh, she liked very much—would be thrown in the dust. A divorced woman, of course, is a social outcast, and as for a woman bearing an illegitimate child . . . She could not even hope to retain the dubious degree of eminence of Lady Harriet Froome, who was born to a title, and who could live no better than as mistress of a gaming house, consorting with panders and thieves. Ruin, and nothing less, awaited Lady Mortlock because of that pregnancy.

"And the prospect was so fearful that she had already made inquiries about that most dangerous of undertakings—aborting the child. The night before her confession to her father, she had made a rendezvous at the Ranelagh masquerade with a man called John Nimier, a doctor who has a name for dealing with the intimate medical problems of the great. Little did she know that her husband had been to see Nimier earlier that day, in search of a solution to his own difficulty. It must have gone hard with him to ask the doctor for a remedy for impotency; but some self-despising, half-rueful impulse must have made him give it a try, and Nimier's reputation was built on his strict confidentiality. Nimier gave him some pills—a quack remedy, perhaps, who knows? Anyway, Lord Mortlock paid eight shillings for them, and took them home. And that evening, Dr. Nimier kept the assignation that an anonymous lady had made with him at the masquerade. And there she haltingly asked him about the possibility of ending her pregnancy. I believe, to do Nimier credit, that he was frank with her about the terrible risks involved in a procedure that takes so many women's lives; and Lady Mortlock, having learned this information, knew that she simply did not have the courage. And that, she thought, would be the last she would see of Nimier. She had given no name, and counted on the protection of the mask to preserve her anonymity. But Nimier is a very clever and sophisticated man, and he knows society. Some clues in what she said, the way she spoke, led him to hazard a guess at her identity. And given that Lord Mortlock had consulted him on impotency that morning, he felt he had hit upon something very interesting, and resolved to attend one of Lady Mortlock's levees, and see if his guess was correct.

"But in the meantime there was Lady Mortlock's dilemma, which she poured out to her father. What did she expect from him? I suppose in the first place there was the relief of talking, of sharing her dreadful secret with the person who had always been her ally and protector. And perhaps she hoped, somehow, that her father would get her out of her predicament. Again I wonder how much she knew or guessed, when she saw her husband's body the next day . . . Well, it is certain at any rate that Mr. Appleton was a tower of strength, and consoled her, and told her that all would be

well. But of course, how could all be well? What way out
was there?

"Well, Mr. Appleton thought of one. Whether he hatched
the plan full-fledged in his mind that night, or only dared to
toy with the idea and then seized his chance when he arrived at the house the next morning, I cannot determine.
Certainly the unexpected absence of Abraham, coupled
with what he knew of the troubles Abraham had been having with his master, furnished him with an opportunity that
he grasped with great decision. But I would hazard that
overnight, as he thought over the matter in his logical way,
he came to the conclusion that only Lord Mortlock's death
would solve the problem.

"And it would solve it so beautifully. If he were to die,
then Lady Mortlock might reveal her pregnancy to the world
after a while, and it would merely appear to be that tragic yet
in a way hopeful thing—a posthumous child. The first and
only child of Lord and Lady Mortlock, sadly coming into
the world after its father's decease. No one would be any
the wiser, for only Mr. Appleton and Charlotte knew that the
child could not be Hugh's. At least, so he thought. There
was the matter of the lover, whom Charlotte still refused to
name: how much did he know? Well, that could be dealt
with. Money could achieve a great deal. The important
thing was that to the world at large, Lady Mortlock would
simply bear the child of her tragically short marriage. She
would be Lady Mortlock still, a peeress, with not a jot of
her consequence diminished—and that meant, of course,
that not a jot of Mr. Appleton's consequence would be diminished either. He could still say, with bursting pride, that
he was Lady Mortlock's father; and indeed, he would be
grandfather to the child, which would be titled—the next
Baron Mortlock, indeed, if it were a boy. Grandfather to the
sixth Baron Mortlock! And in the absence of the father, probably he would have much to do with the child's upbringing!

All that he had wanted from that marriage, indeed, would continue and even increase. Whereas if Hugh Mortlock lived, it would all be lost, spoiled, blighted in disgrace.

"And so the next morning he went to call on his daughter, and saw his chance. Abraham, the footman, did not answer to his knock, for shortly before that, having been angrily refused permission to marry by his master, Abraham had decided to run away, and had told his sweetheart so. He had stripped off the hated livery coat and gloves, laid them on the table, and made his escape. When there was no response to his knocking, Mr. Appleton opened the street door and walked in, which he was pretty easy about, as he was often there. And then he saw Abraham's discarded livery and guessed at once that the unhappy slave had finally absconded. There was no one in the hall: the maids were down in the kitchen toiling over the laundry, and it wasn't their job to answer the door, though old Meggy had heard the repeated knocks and was making her slow way up, as she confirmed to me today. There was ample time for Mr. Appleton to take the white gloves and put them in his pockets, and to lay the coat in the linen chest that stood in the hall. And so when old Meggy came up at last, and apologized to Mr. Appleton for no one being there to answer the door to him, there was nothing out of the ordinary to be seen.

"And so Mr. Appleton went upstairs to the levee, where he learned that Hugh, as he expected, was sleeping it off in his bedchamber. He did not need to cast about for a weapon to use: the razor, with the shaving tackle on the landing, was perfect, though no doubt he would have found something else if need had arisen. He stayed a while at the levee, studying the men there—Mr. Pennant, and Dr. Nimier—and wondered, no doubt, if either were his daughter's lover. And then he took his leave, went across the landing, and picked up the razor, and went into his son-in-law's bedchamber. He put on the white gloves and cut Hugh's throat. All very quick.

"He must have taken off the bloodied gloves then, stowed them away in his pockets, and gone quickly downstairs. The hall was empty again. It was the work of a moment to lift the lid of the linen chest, put the bloodied gloves into the pockets of the livery coat, and then stow it away again. I wonder whether he thought, for a moment, about taking the coat with him and disposing of it somewhere outside there and then, but I would guess he feared it might be too conspicuous if he went into the street carrying it. He just had to trust that no one would have occasion to use the linen chest, and the coat would not be found just yet.

"For though he wanted the murder to appear to be the work of a resentful slave, he did not want Abraham Drake actually to suffer arrest and punishment. This is the curious part: he liked Abraham, and wanted him both to be accused and to escape. His plan was to find the slave himself and secure a means for him to flee on board a ship, and only then to allow the incriminating coat and gloves to be found. And that was the plan he carried out, at last taking the coat out of the chest when he was sure he would not be seen—naturally he was at his bereaved daughter's house a good deal in the days following the murder, and could pick his time—and throwing it into the basement area of a neighboring house, where it was sure to be found. And then, once it *had* been found, he hurried off to Abraham's hideout by the riverside, to which Jack Little had led him for a handsome bribe earlier that day, and oversaw his escape. That, of course, is where things went unexpectedly wrong.

"And he had left clues. When I first saw the recovered coat, I detected a sweet scent about it that I could not understand—not until I went down to the kitchens, and a maid passed me bearing fresh linen from the chest. It smelled of lavender . . . like the coat. But how could a coat that had lain for two days among basement rubbish smell of lavender? From a residence in the linen chest, of course; and that, together with Kate's account of how Abraham had left his livery in the hall *before* he ran away from the house, alerted me to how Mr. Appleton had done the deed.

"There was a clue of another sort in that kitchen: a bloodstained bedsheet. It was not the one in which Lord Mortlock had died so horribly. What then? Alas, as I began to speculate, the whole thing became clear to me. The sheet was from Lady Mortlock's bed, and the blood was menstrual blood. She had seemed almost hysterical that day, in a way I couldn't account for. Now I could. I remembered what Lady Harriet had told me: that early in her own pregnancy she had considered being rid of it, and had mentioned Dr. Nimier's name. I put together what she had hinted about Hugh Mortlock's curious coldness, with the pills that I was now certain he had bought from Dr. Nimier; and the sight of Kate Little, obviously pregnant, set light to the whole chain of ideas like gunpowder. All along the question of motive had perplexed me, and now I saw someone who had had the most pressing motive for terminating Lord Mortlock's existence. And with a tragic end-piece: for the sheet revealed that Lady Mortlock was not pregnant after all. It need never have happened—not that murder should ever happen, of course, but you take my meaning."

"Good God—could she not be sure that she was with child?" Mr. Welch said. "I know women have these false alarms, but . . ."

"I have spoken to her of it, as gently as possible, and she was as certain as it was possible to be, without having been examined by a physician. I fear . . . I fear that, rather than a late menses, the blood was indicative of an early miscarrying. Small wonder, perhaps, given her late distress and trouble. Well. She must have told her father, that day, that all was over, and he . . . Well, we can never know how appallingly it struck him that he had killed his son-in-law for no reason after all; but he seems to have resolved to make the best of things — for she was Lady Mortlock still — and to carry through his plan."

"Dear, dear. It is a wry, grim world sometimes . . . But what of the man who put her in that condition? What part does he play? I take it Nimier wasn't the man."

"No, though Mr. Appleton had some initial suspicions on that head, as so did I. But Lady Mortlock's only connection with him was a professional one: she went to the masquerade to seek his advice. Not that that prevented her real lover from going into a jealous pet when he heard about the two of them being together. But Dr. Nimier did have a role to play, and not an honorable one. As I've said, he suspected that the anonymous lady was Lady Mortlock, and had it confirmed when he attended her levee and recognized her as she did him. It must have been a torment to her, to have to entertain him in a whole group of company, knowing that he knew her secret — or part of it. And in fact he knew the whole, more or less, for Lord Mortlock had consulted him on impotency, and here was his wife who had privily asked him how one went about aborting a child. He is no fool, and soon must have put two and two together, and I daresay relished his knowledge and the power it gave him. Certainly he wasted no time in trying to turn it to his account. He called late to see her that evening, alone, a circumstance which made me suspect some intrigue between them. In fact, what he was doing was blackmailing her. She had to see her banker and give him a large sum of money. As did Mr. Appleton the next day, but Mr. Appleton was still unsure whether Nimier was her lover, and he was simply offering money for the doctor to keep away; as he did to the other suspect, Pennant — or, at least, he offered Pennant what he wanted even more, which was influence on behalf of his career. The last thing Mr. Appleton wanted, you see, was for Charlotte's lover to rear his head and set scandalous tongues wagging. He was prepared to lay out any sum to make sure that this lover faded into the background, and left the widow and the coming heir in peace. If he had only known that Dr. Nimier was in on the whole secret things might have been different, and perhaps worse: Nimier might have found himself in danger, for a man who has killed once to achieve his aims is never very far away from killing twice."

"This fellow Pennant, then, was the lover?"

"He was, of that I'm sure, as Lady Mortlock has said so — though Pennant still denies it. He is a charming young man in some ways, and no doubt in the lonely bewilderment of her marriage Lady Mortlock found much attraction in him. But he has a very strongly developed sense of self-love. She tried to speak to him of her condition on the Monday evening, when they had their music lesson, but he would have none of it; all but stopped his ears, said she was mistaken and so on. And from that moment, I think, decided it was time to disentangle himself, though he was puppy enough still to be piqued at the thought of her keeping a tryst with another man, and to behave very petulantly at the levee on account of it. Perhaps, indeed, he thought to use that rumor as an excuse to separate himself from her. Certainly I think he scarcely needed any encouragement from Mr. Appleton to keep away. He all but threw himself at another girl so as to make it crystal clear he had no interest in Lady Mortlock, past, present or future."

Mr. Welch frowned. "Worthless hound . . . and I cannot think of Lord Mortlock in much friendlier terms. Yet Lady Mortlock seems the most delightful and sensible of women — how came she to be tied to such contemptible creatures?"

"You echo my own thought; but then perhaps when a beautiful woman likes a man other than ourselves, we always tend to call him contemptible . . . Well, if there is any consolation, it is that she will be tied thus no longer — nor, I would add, tied to the worldliness and ambition of a father who seems to have given her everything but the means to value her own worth, and the judgment to discern what is right from what is expedient." Fairfax thought of Lady Mortlock as he had seen her today, a week after her father's death: tremendously, desperately alone in the world now, and registering it in every pale, proud quiver of feature. And yet not diminished by her solitude, he thought: if anything she seemed fully herself for the first time. It was never, Fairfax knew, too late to grow.

"So, what of your own future, Mr. Fairfax?" Mr. Welch said, passing the bottle again. "You were to tutor Mr. Appleton's younger sons, I understand."

"That I don't know. Mr. Lawrence Appleton inherits half his father's estate — the other half, of course, goes to his daughter — and is in a manner the head of the family now, though the boys' aunt at Weymouth means to take a hand in their bringing up, as no doubt will their sister. Lawrence is very eager to retain my services, he says, and won't hear otherwise, so it may be that I shall have the charge of them yet. We must see."

"Their father's acts leave them with a good deal to live down, I fear."

"So they do. But they may find better models, perhaps, in their brother and sister. Lady Mortlock has already made a generous reparation to Abraham. She has given him his freedom, and a present of money to begin life with Kate. Their first banns were called, I think, this morning . . . Well, sir, it's been an honor to dine with you. If you will excuse me, I promised to call in at Mrs. Stoddart's this evening. She has a metaphysical German in residence, who is going to read us his paper on moral philosophy and deism, and that of course I must not miss."

"Why, I'll wager what really draws you there is that niece

of hers," Mr. Welch laughed, rising and shaking his hand. "Miss Vertue—an uncommonly pretty and spirited creature by all accounts."

"So she is. But my heart does not incline that way, which is just as well; for though she is an orphan, she is a lady of good family, elevated in society, and I—well, I cannot aim so high." Fairfax thought a moment, and then smiled. "Thank God."

About the Author

Hannah March was born and brought up in Peterborough on the edge of the Fens and was a student in the University of East Anglia MA course in Creative Writing under Malcolm Bradbury and Angela Carter. She is now married and lives in Peterborough.

A Mystery of Georgian England
by
Hannah March

The Devil's Highway

Travelling to his new employer's country home,
private tutor Robert Fairfax discovers a tipped
stagecoach—and the dead bodies within it.
But this is more than a robbery.
And the victims are not who they appear to be.

"SETTING A DETECTIVE NOVEL IN THE
[GEORGIAN] AGE IS A MASTERSTROKE."
—THE TIMES (LONDON)

0-451-21071-9

Hazel Holt

"Sheila Malory is a most appealing heroine."
—Booklist

MRS. MALORY AND THE SILENT KILLER
0-451-21165-0

The entire village of Taviscombe is left reeling when popular Sidney Middleton dies in a tragic accident. However, it soon becomes apparent that his death is a most deliberate act.

MRS. MALORY AND DEATH IN PRACTICE
0-451-20920-6

No one in town is warming up to the new veterinarian. So when he turns up dead, Mrs. Malory is faced with a whole roster of townspeople as suspects.

MRS. MALORY AND DEATH BY WATER
0-451-20809-9

When Mrs. Malory is given the unenviable task of sorting through her dear departed friend Leonora's voluminous estate, she begins to doubt whether the cause of death was due to polluted water—or natural causes.

MRS. MALORY AND THE DELAY OF EXECUTION
0-451-20627-4

A schoolteacher at a prestigious English prep school dies suddenly, and Mrs. Malory gets shanghaied into being a substitute—with a little detecting on the side.

Available wherever books are sold, or
to order call: 1-800-788-6262

www.penguin.com

S447/Holt